The Wind in the Willows
Short Stories

To Helen,

Much Love,

Lucy

Christmas 2010.

KENNETH GRAHAME SOCIETY

The Wind in the Willows Short Stories

Edited by
Nigel McMorris

First Published in 2009
(on the 150th anniversary of the
birth of Kenneth Grahame)

All rights reserved.
No part of this book may be reproduced or transmitted in any form or by any means, electronically or mechanically, including photocopying, fax, data transmittal, internet site, recording of any information storage or retrieval system, without prior permission from the copyright holder(s) and editor.

© Copyright remains with the individual authors
and the Kenneth Grahame Society
- applies to all texts in this book except the original writings of Kenneth Grahame which are now in the public domain.

ISBN 978-1-4452-2872-3

Printed and published by Lulu Inc
(www.lulu.com) and the
Kenneth Grahame Society,
37 Ashtree Hill, Tandragee, Co Armagh,
Northern Ireland. BT62 2HP.

To
*everyone who assisted with the
publication of this book.*

Contents

Introduction	ix
Acknowledgements	xvii
1. Moonglade *by Robin Bailes.*	1
2. Turnip Soup *by Wendy Bradley.*	11
3. The Water Rat *by Janet Lesley Smith.*	25
4. The Calling Of The Piper *by Dr. E. J. Yeaman.*	37
5. At The House Called Beautiful *by Elizabeth Parkhurst.*	49
6. Ma Weasel *by Ruth Sheppard.*	61
7. Encore *by Jennifer Moore.*	71
8. Mr Toad's Wedding *by Martin J. Smith.*	85
9. The Toad Rush *by Margaret Bulleyment.*	101
10. An Unexpected Uncle For Toad *by Jessie Anderson.*	115
11. Below The Waves *by Belinda Beasley.*	127
12. The Naiads In Arcadia *by Professor Peter Hunt.*	141
13. Welcome To Toad Hall *by Marilyn Fountain.*	155
Afterword	169
The Authors	187

Introduction

It is usual that the writer of an introduction has some role, or specific area of interest, that constitutes a relationship with the subject matter in the book, and that role, often referred to metaphorically as wearing a hat, generally has a bearing on the nature and content of the introduction. Occasionally, the writer may have multiple roles and, hence, multiple relationships with the subject matter. I have a small collection of Willows-style hats: short-story competition organiser, editor and publisher, Kenneth Grahame Society founding member, enthusiastic reader of Grahame's works, lay student of literary criticism of Grahame's works, and a few others besides. They make for enjoyable wearing, although none of them is very grand. But there lay the problem that puzzled me: which should I wear, in order to write this introduction from the most appropriate perspective? The short-story competition organiser's hat seemed to be the main one to wear, but an unusual one I'd like to don too, at least initially, is that of the rereader.

The term rereader, although coined, is probably self-explanatory; it is that enthusiastic reader who returns periodically to a book, *The Wind in the Willows* in this case, and reads it many times. Grahame's classic provides great enjoyment on the first reading, but it also rewards the rereader with fresh details and perspectives on the plot and characters, revived impressions of the style, wit and charm of the writing, and uplifting revisits to the nostalgia-steeped world of the River Bank. Many readers, and especially rereaders, of *The Wind in the Willows* must sometimes wish that Grahame had written more of the same. It can be enjoyed many times – reading it ten times is not unheard of – but more of the same would be very welcome, even in the form of sequels written by someone else.

While I'm not in total disagreement with the views of others, who feel that a book like *The Wind in the Willows* cannot be emulated, and that many attempts at sequels have been so flawed that the books should not have been published, I have been so impressed by a few sequels that I maintain the view that good sequels are worth encouraging and supporting. That impression grew and, at some point nearly two years ago, the idea of the Kenneth Grahame Society hosting a competition for short-story sequels to *The Wind in the Willows* was born.

The years 2008 and 2009 are of considerable significance to Kenneth Grahame enthusiasts, October 2008 being the 100th anniversary of the first publication of *The Wind in the Willows* and

Introduction

March 2009 being the 150th anniversary of Kenneth Grahame's birth. The Kenneth Grahame Society planned to commemorate these years, and it seemed like an ideal opportunity to hold a short-story competition and publish a collection of the best twelve entries in a single volume. The proposal was readily approved by other Society members and, in March 2008, the details of the competition were announced on the Society's website and on the websites of numerous writers' groups. (A copy of the announcement can be found at the end of this introduction.)

We received almost one hundred entries. Each one was read in its entirety, and a shortlist of twenty was produced for the panel of three judges to assess. The panel read each entry and returned their individual results, which were subsequently combined to derive the following lists of winning entries and stories for publication:

1st. "Mr Toad's Wedding" by Martin J. Smith.
2nd. "Turnip Soup" by Wendy Bradley.
3rd. "The Toad Rush" by Margaret Bulleyment.

4th equal, in alphabetical order by author surname:
"An Unexpected Uncle For Toad" by Jessie Anderson.
"Moonglade" by Robin Bailes.
"Below The Waves" by Belinda Beasley.
"Welcome To Toad Hall" by Marilyn Fountain.
"The Naiads In Arcadia" by Professor Peter Hunt.
"Encore" by Jennifer Moore.
"At The House Called Beautiful" by Elizabeth Parkhurst.
"Ma Weasel" by Ruth Sheppard.
"The Water Rat" by Janet Lesley Smith.
"The Calling Of The Piper" by Dr. E. J. Yeaman.

I heartily enjoyed reading all the stories. The collection represented an enormous variety of themes and characters and, consisting of three prequels, two counter texts and eight sequels (thirteen stories in total, rather than the twelve which had been the initial target), the authors' handling of prequels and counter texts, as opposed to sequels, also made an interesting study in itself.

The first of the prequels, "Moonglade" by Robin Bailes, is a charming bit of storytelling about the Water Rat and some irrepressible young rabbits, who are learning to swim. It has a story within a story, and there's a delightful twist at the end that I did not foresee at all.

"Turnip Soup" by Wendy Bradley is set about six months

Introduction

before *The Wind in the Willows* begins. Mole meets a group of musical, party-going pack rats one evening – the Rat Pack? – and he gets carried along by their influence. The story is full of layers and nuances, and the irony of the reader knowing exactly where Mole is, but Mole himself not knowing it, is wonderfully played out.

"The Water Rat" by Janet Lesley Smith is an immediate prequel to *The Wind in the Willows*. The Water Rat reflects on his friendships with Toad and Badger, feeling that, good as they are, he'd like to have a friend who is more available for sharing his interests and activities. I loved the rich style of this story, feeling at times I was reading sentences that Grahame himself might indeed have written.

Of the two counter texts (or parallels) in the collection, the first in chronological order is "The Calling Of The Piper" by Dr E J Yeaman, a retelling of chapter seven of *The Wind in the Willows*, "The Piper at the Gates of Dawn". It tells of the Greek gods Pan and Artemis. I had originally associated Eos (or Aurora) with "The Piper at the Gates of Dawn" as she is associated with the gates of dawn, but most of the chapter's events take place in moonlight, making Artemis an appropriate alternative. The story is mythology layered on top of animal fantasy, but it is so well conceived that, surprisingly for such a combination, it is perhaps one of the more plausible stories in the book, in terms of meriting a place in the Willows canon. It subliminally convinces the reader of the involvement of the gods in "The Piper at the Gates of Dawn", to an extent that bears comparison with the way that Jan Needle's *Wild Wood* convinces the reader of the class-conflict theme in *The Wind in the Willows*. A scholar's favourite.

Counter texts will probably always evoke comparisons with Jan Needle's *Wild Wood,* as well as with *The Wind in the Willows,* and "At The House Called Beautiful" by Elizabeth Parkhurst is teeming with contrasts and similarities. Whereas Needle's *Wild Wood* takes the perspective of the male stoats, weasels and ferrets, this story presents the perspective of the female stoats, weasels and ferrets. In the limited confines of a short story, there are some wonderfully colourful characters and sensitive insights into the womenfolk's life during those few months at Toad Hall.

"Ma Weasel" by Ruth Sheppard is an immediate sequel to *The Wind in the Willows*, the events narrated in it taking place within days of the end of Grahame's original. Part of the nostalgic charm of *The Wind in the Willows* is its peripheral references to Victorian trades, crafts and working-class life. The charm is continued here with numerous references to Ma Weasel's work as a needlewoman, interwoven into an interesting character study.

Introduction

"Encore" by Jennifer Moore tells of another of Toad's schemes: the stage. The story reassuringly portrays Toad, one year after *The Wind in the Willows* ends, as being the same pompous, foolish, unchanged creature, whose antics provide lots of humorous entertainment – often to the dismay and exasperation of his friends.

"Mr Toad's Wedding" by Martin J. Smith was the winning entry in the competition. Few critics dwell much on the humour in *The Wind in the Willows*, although its humour is one of its greatest attributes. The wedding antics of Toad are told in this sequel with a measure of humour, particularly wit and farce, strongly reminiscent of Grahame's balance of humour in the original.

"The Toad Rush" by Margaret Bulleyment and "An Unexpected Uncle For Toad" by Jessie Anderson are excellent examples of the genre of amateur detection. I'll not give too may clues in case I spoil the stories for the reader, but it suffices to say that they have both very entertaining plot lines.

"Below The Waves" by Belinda Beasley has many echoes of chapter two of *The Wind in the Willows*, "The Open Road". It tells of another madcap scheme that Toad tries out, and a highly original one it is too; Toad purchases a new contraption and inveigles poor Mole to join him for an unforgettable trip down the river.

Toad has another attempt at getting married in "The Naiads In Arcadia" by Professor Peter Hunt. If someone had claimed, before the competition, that a successful Willows sequel could be written, that contained matrimonial, feminist and even traces of suffragette themes, I'd have been incredulous. "The Naiads In Arcadia" is surprisingly convincing; it is delightfully told and it embeds a great depth of detail from Grahame's original.

The extra story, "Welcome To Toad Hall" by Marilyn Fountain, is one that, perhaps, falls slightly outside the expected sequel range, since it does not actually feature the Mole, Rat, Badger and Toad we know but, rather, their great-grandchildren. That makes it, chronologically speaking, the last sequel by quite a few years. Toad Hall is opened to the public, somewhat like a National Trust property, and the opening day is rather chaotic. At one point Otter delivers a wonderfully ambiguous statement that is worth keeping an eye open for. It is interesting to note that using a later generation of characters allows a small departure from some of their forefathers' characteristics, without loss of plausibility.

Will readers regard the stories as having levels of continuity and plausibility that could, theoretically, be mistaken for Grahame's work? It depends a lot on the individual reader. Some readers will happily extend their usual "suspension of disbelief" to include

Introduction

aspects of style, plot and actual authorship, but academics and literary detectives will probably find a few telltale clues that identify many of the stories as counterfeits. The collection is, more than anything else, a thoroughly entertaining revisit to the River Bank and the Wild Wood, renewal of acquaintances with Ratty, Mole, Toad and Badger, and fuller introduction to some characters, who were only briefly mentioned in *The Wind in the Willows*. In those respects it succeeds wonderfully.

Nigel McMorris.

Introduction

Kenneth Grahame Society – Short-Story Competition

As part of the Kenneth Grahame Society's celebration of the centenary year of *The Wind in the Willows*, a short-story competition is being held to echo some of the beauty of Kenneth Grahame's classic. This is a unique opportunity for creative writers everywhere to write a short story in the same style as *The Wind in the Willows* and have it published. It is, similarly, a unique opportunity for academic writers to use creative writing as an alternative approach for presenting some new insights into the book. And it is an opportunity for all to pay homage to their favourite book and add to *The Wind in the Willows* canon.

Prizes

1st £500   2nd £150   3rd £100

If there is a good response and sufficient strong entries, a number of further entries, along with the top three, will be published in a collection of short stories at the end of the year. These entries will be awarded a £50 prize and a copy of the book.

There is no entry fee.

Title/Theme

The title is open, but the story is to be written as a sequel, prequel or counter text to *The Wind in the Willows*.

Guidelines and Formats

The length of the short stories should be approximately 5000 words - similar to the average length of the chapters in *The Wind in the Willows*. (Entries of 4500-6000 words will be accepted.)

The cover page should clearly state the title and number of words, and provide essential contact details - name, address, email address and phone number.

Entries should be printed on A4 paper with double line spacing and wide margins. (No handwritten entries, please.) After the judging of the entries, authors of the winning short stories will be asked to submit their story in MS Word format and append a brief biography.

Entries will be judged for their plausibility and continuity as a Willows sequel (or prequel or counter text), as well as for the quality of their storyline and style.

Entry Deadline and Results

Entries must be received by July 31st 2008. The winning entry will be announced and read at the Kenneth Grahame Society's Willows celebrations in

Introduction

Fowey, Cornwall, on September 6th-7th 2008.

Entries should be posted to:
Kenneth Grahame Society
c/o 37 Ashtree Hill
Tandragee
Co Armagh
Northern Ireland. BT62 2HP
E: badger@kennethgrahamesociety.net
W: www.kennethgrahamesociety.net

(Acknowledgement of receipt will be sent out for all entries which are received before the closing deadline.)

ACKNOWLEDGEMENTS

This collection of short stories is the result of the efforts and contributions of many people, and I would like to wholeheartedly thank everyone for all those contributions.

Numerous writers' groups and authors freely hosted the original announcement on their websites and forums, leading to many writers becoming aware of the competition and, ultimately, to the large number of entries which we received. I cannot overstate how much I valued this help, because I feel certain that we would have otherwise received a relatively small number of entries

I would like to thank each author who submitted an entry for the competition. A colossal amount of work went into the short-listing but, in spite of that work, the large number of entries was an encouraging confirmation that there is broad enthusiasm for writing a sequel to *The Wind in the Willows*.

I would like to express my sincere appreciation to the panel of three independent judges, Dr. Kate Macdonald, Annie Gauger and Sandra Cunningham, who did the hard work of deciding the winners and which entries to include in the publication – work which I most gladly left in their hands.

After the judging, it seemed that some edits might be needed in a few of the stories, prior to publication, and I would again like to thank the authors for their patience and cooperation in collaborating with me at this editing stage. I missed more targets than I met, and some of my amendments must have seemed, to the authors, like the cuts and clauses of outrageous editors, but I can say that it was very enjoyable to have that period of one-to-one collaboration, and my main regret is that I was so busy that I could not correspond to the extent I would have liked at that time.

As the book approached completion, I found that I had read everything so many times that I could no longer see even simple syntax errors which needed correction. At that stage I greatly appreciated the proofreaders who corrected various sections. Most of all, I would like to thank David and Barbara Holmes for their highly professional work in doing the final proofreading of the whole book.

Finally, I would like to thank Bonny Kinloch for her enthusiasm and great work in producing the illustration for the front cover.

I feel that the project has been enjoyable and very worthwhile, and I would like to thank everyone again, collectively, for all those contributions which made it possible.

Nigel McMorris

Moonglade
by Robin Bailes

"Moonglade: the reflection of the moon in the surface of the river." The Rat was not sure where and when he had first heard the word, or if he had in fact made it up himself. If so then he had been on rare form that day. The word seemed to describe so perfectly the bright, shimmering image that flickered in the ripples – not a real thing but something ethereal and strange that cast an atmosphere from its shining luminescence and stirred emotions in even the most casual of observers. Now if only he could think of a rhyme for it, preferably one that would fit neatly into the poem on which he had been working all that lazy summer evening.

A splash from the centre of the river broke the Rat's concentration and he sighed. There was no need to ask himself what that was; the chorus of squeaks and squeals that followed it would have told him even if he could not have guessed; it was always the same at this time of year, and this particular year seemed to be worse than usual. The young rabbits were learning to swim, urging each other on into deeper and deeper water until they got out of their depth, which was fairly limited to begin with, and began to flounder.

The Rat got up from his comfortable seat on the bank, got into his boat, untied it, and shoved off in the direction of the urgent splashing. It was not that he had anything against other animals learning to swim, quite the reverse, he was all in favour. But there were ways to go about it; supervision was required from someone who knew what they were doing, and you did not go out at night and in deep water after only a few lessons. It was not that he minded rescuing them either; any excuse for a quiet scull was the Rat's avowed philosophy, but he was aware that the young rabbits now chose this stretch of water specifically because they knew he lived nearby and that they had only to cry out if they got into trouble. They treated him like a safety net, and the Rat did not like to be taken for granted. There were deeper concerns in his mind as well. He enjoyed the summer nights and would often stay up late working on some poem or other, as he had been doing tonight, or just listening to the pleasant sound of the river passing, of which he never tired, but this was not his unchanging pattern and sometimes he was happier to enjoy an early night; if the rabbits were to get into trouble on one of those nights then it did not bear thinking about. They were becoming too used to having him there and it led them to take unnecessary risks. One day they would take one when their safety net was all tucked up in his bed, lost in peaceful slumber.

The Rat thrust a paw into the water and hauled out a dripping and bedraggled rabbit that looked at him with a more or less equal mixture of guilt and mischievousness in his eyes.

"Any more of you?" asked the Rat mildly.

The rabbit shook his head, "They all stayed on the bank. I was the only one brave enough."

"Fool enough is more like it," scolded the Rat, dumping the little fellow unceremoniously in the bow and striking out for land. From the bank up ahead came the sound of rabbits cheering and the Rat followed it. Clearly his sodden passenger, for all his foolhardiness, was a hero to his drier friends.

As soon as the boat's nose hit the bank the rabbit bounded out to enjoy the acclaim of his fellows who rushed around him, clapping him on the back, shaking him by the paw and offering a constant litany of congratulation.

"You really should be more careful," said the Rat, trying to remonstrate above the happy cries and laughter, but he knew that it was falling on deaf ears. "It's not safe for you to be out there all by yourselves – not at this time of night at any rate."

But all the remonstration in the world would not have been enough to pour cold water on the mood of the Rat's current audience. The jollity only increased and the Rat had a sneaking suspicion that he would most likely be out here again tomorrow night. He got back into his boat and struck out for home, where an unfinished poem lay on the bank awaiting his return. As he rowed, the ripples and little waves that pushed out from the boat splintered the reflection of the moon in the river's surface; the shards separated, rejoined, broke again, floated away and back, changed shape and, as the boat moved away from the reflection, seemed to regain their cohesion and flowed into one another to resume their original form. The moonglade.

The Rat's premonition that he would be similarly occupied the following night proved to be all too accurate when the quiet night was interrupted by splashing and squealing. This time there were two rabbits, who had both sought to imitate their hero of the night before and had succeeded in every respect. The night after proved no better, nor the one after that, and the Rat, now operating a nightly rescue service, began to entertain serious concerns about what might happen if he was out of earshot or otherwise occupied when the inevitable call came. It would not be his fault, and yet he would certainly feel guilty. Something had to be done.

Moonglade

But what? This was not the sort of situation which the Rat felt fully equipped to deal with by himself, and at such times there was only one person whom he wanted to talk to, only one person on whom he felt certain that he could rely for sage advice.

So it was that, on the fifth morning, with a few provisions and an appropriate gift stowed in his knapsack, the Rat set out for the Wild Wood. He had at first considered talking to the families of the rabbits themselves; their parents were older and wiser after all and should share his concern for the safety of their increasingly reckless offspring. But the Rat never felt entirely at ease talking to rabbits. He had nothing against them; they were nice enough, decent folk and very polite, but he found them a bit flighty. It was hard to get them to stick to one topic, and after a few minutes conversation he always felt that they were looking over his shoulder or thinking about what they would be doing later in the day.

Although the Rat never much cared for venturing into the Wild Wood, or indeed for straying far from his beloved river, in summer the journey was one which he was willing, if not happy, to make. He did not constantly feel that he was being watched or even stalked, did not feel the necessity to go armed as he sometimes did when walking this track in the darker winter months. It was also much easier for him to find his way through without the blanket of snow cloaking every recognizable feature. When he went to the Wild Wood it was almost always for the same purpose, so this route that he now took was the most familiar to him and, if he could not quite walk it blindfolded, then neither did he have to stop and check his bearings every few minutes. It was not long therefore before he reached the familiar dark green door, well appointed and set into the bank. He tugged at the bell pull.

Although the Badger disliked society, and indeed went out of his way to avoid it, to those who knew him best, and the Rat was one such, he was the most agreeable of hosts. Within minutes of his arrival the Rat found himself seated in the Badger's homely kitchen at his old oak table with a drink between his paws. The Rat was nothing if not polite, and he had come craving a favour, after all, so he had brought a bottle of something himself, even though he knew that the Badger had a well stocked cellar.

"So what do you think?" ventured the Rat, after he had outlined the problem to the Badger, who was preparing a light lunch for them.

"You've spoiled them," came the Badger's typically gruff reply, as he cut a thick slice of bread.

"Spoiled them?"

"Like the boy who cried wolf," the Badger elaborated. "By

always saving them you've led them to believe that you always will save them."

"Well I could hardly let them drown, Badger," the Rat pointed out, not unreasonably.

"If early on you had just been a little less eager to be the hero, let them help themselves and each other every once in a while, then they wouldn't be taking such risks now," the Badger persisted. "They'd have a better understanding of the dangers."

The Rat had to admit that this did have more than a grain of truth in it as many of his earlier rescues had been from the shallows, close enough to the bank that the danger was negligible and, with a little help from their friends on dry land, the rabbits could undoubtedly have dragged themselves out had the need arisen, had he not been there to make matters easier. Since then the intrepid rabbits had ventured deeper. The Rat reckoned that each night they got a little further out; they saw no risk because he was always there to eliminate it and now it was too late to let them learn for themselves.

"So what do you suggest?" asked the Rat, openly acknowledging the mistake that he had made.

"Well," mused the Badger, stroking his chin, "You missed the chance to give them a little scare the first time around, I think you might need to concoct one for them."

"For their own good?"

"Exactly," said the Badger, "There are times when one has to be cruel to be kind. You recall the necessity with Toad last autumn?"

"The ballooning incident," the Rat nodded. That was not something he was likely to forget in a hurry, no matter how hard he tried.

"Where Toad is concerned," the Badger continued, "I would not be surprised if the necessity arose again."

Once more the Rat was forced to agree. Toad was a fine fellow in many ways, but he shared with the young rabbits a complete misunderstanding of the concept of risk, and was all too accustomed to having friends there to bail him out in the nick of time.

"I think the rabbits might learn faster than Toad," commented the Rat.

"I am inclined to agree," said the Badger darkly.

"Any ideas?"

But ideas could wait until after lunch. The friends ate in silence as they both applied their minds to the problem at hand.

Moonglade

Following lunch, as they washed the dishes and stored them away in the capacious cupboards that lined the Badger's kitchen, they discussed possible courses of action, and by the time the Rat set out for home in the late afternoon, he knew what he had to do. Which was just as well.

That night the Rat once again found himself forced to leave his comfortable seat on the river bank, abandon his poetry, interrupt his creative train of thought, and venture out into the river to fish out the soaking rabbits. Perhaps if he had received a 'thank you' for his trouble then the Rat might have felt differently, but none was forthcoming. Which only seemed to underline the Badger's point; this had gone on too long. It was too much to suppose that the rabbits might actually learn to swim well and beat the currents before one of them had a serious accident. The Rat resolved to put the Badger's plan into practice the following afternoon.

It was a glorious summer day; the damsel and dragonflies flitted lazily this way and that across the river's bright shimmering surface, doing whatever it is that damsel and dragonflies do with their time. As was his wont in the summer months, the Rat was up with the lark to enjoy an early morning's row down the river, exchanging hellos with any others who might also be getting the full benefit of the summer morning, and thinking out exactly what he was going to do this afternoon. These thoughts continued as he had a light breakfast and did a few chores about the house; he was a creative soul but this afternoon was still going to require every last drop of his imagination. As he did all this, and indeed as he made and consumed his lunch and dozed through a pleasant early afternoon nap, the Rat was aware, just within earshot, of the sound of young rabbits at play. During the day, despite the heat, the rabbits did not see fit to continue their swimming lessons; those could wait until night when it was at its most dangerous and when there were less animals around who might help them. The Rat's resolve stiffened.

As the afternoon wore on he began to put together a large and impressive picnic. Anyone watching would have assumed that the Rat was expecting a whole host of guests, but mid afternoon became late afternoon and no one arrived. Instead, the Rat packed the food into his neat picnic hamper with a purposeful air and left his waterside home. He plumped the hamper into the bow of his little boat, got in, cast off and struck out for the opposite shore where, in the light of the reddening sun, the young rabbits continued to play before their parents called them in for dinner.

"Good afternoon!" the Rat hailed the rabbits.

A chorus of merry greetings welcomed him as the boat came to rest and the Rat nimbly climbed ashore. The rabbits all knew who this was – it was their personal saviour and unwilling playmate and they were delighted to see him. They were fascinated too by the picnic hamper he produced from the boat.

"I was wondering if you'd care to join me for a spot of dinner?" proposed the Rat, lifting the lid of the hamper with a flourish and displaying the excellent food that nestled appetisingly within. The rabbits' eyes widened at the sight and their tiny tummies rumbled with expectation.

A pair of rabbits, agreed by all their fellows to be the fastest runners, were swiftly dispatched homeward to explain to the youngsters' parents that their offspring would be dining out tonight courtesy of Mr Rat from across the river. It was a situation which found considerable favour with the older rabbits. At this time of year the rambunctious youngsters, so full of energy, became a bit much for even them, so an evening off was quite a treat. And of course they all knew and respected Mr Rat.

"Settle down then," urged the Rat, as he spread out a check blanket onto the grass and tried to command the attention of the excitable young rabbits who were so insistent on continual movement that he was not yet even certain how many of them there were. "Everyone sit down or you won't get anything to eat!" A little discipline was clearly called for. "If Badger was here there wouldn't be this problem," the Rat muttered to himself. But the threat of losing their place in the banquet seemed an adequate one to make his guests at least sit, though they continued to fidget considerably as the Rat unloaded the picnic hamper, and the youngsters were forced to hold their appetites in check in the face of the feast which was to come.

"Now," the Rat continued, "Fetch yourselves a plate... One at a time! One at a time! Point to what you want and I'll serve you. I said I'll serve you! Paws to yourself! Paws to yourself! I saw that! You wait your turn or you can go straight home."

While the serving of the food was something of a stressful affair for the Rat, with the rabbits at their most disobedient and mischievous, the eating was a quite different matter altogether. There are few animals who enjoy their food as much as rabbits do, most particularly the young ones, and they are quite happy to devote their whole attention to it and thus, for the first time since he had arrived, the Rat found himself in near silence, the only sound being the contented munching of his guests.

"Would anyone like to hear a story?" suggested the Rat.

Lost in the pleasure of eating though they were, the rabbits were excited by this new prospect as well. This was shaping up to be a very good day indeed.

The Rat settled back on the blanket, leaning on his elbow, and addressed his little audience, "Once, many years ago, a rabbit, not that much older than yourselves and from this very river bank, yearned to see the world. Most especially he yearned for the sea. A life on the ocean waves, tossed and spun by the currents, washed up on sun burnt beaches of far-off lands, seeing things that no English rabbit had ever seen before. It was all that he dreamed of night and day. He taught himself to swim and to handle a little boat, sailing up and down the river day in day out, sculling until his elbows creaked. He studied maps and learnt to read them. He tracked down what travellers he could find and listened to their stories for hours on end. He saved up his pennies in the hope that one day his chance would come – his chance to be like them, to voyage far from home.

"With time he realised that, in this life, you cannot always wait for chances to come your way; you have to make them for yourself and forge your own destiny. He put those few belongings he could not bear to part with in a little bag, said goodbye to his mother and father, to his brothers and his sisters, to his neighbours and friends, and set off down the river in his little boat, letting the water take him ever onward in the direction of the sea.

"Only a few days later he found himself in a lively port, where he swiftly acquired the position of cabin boy on a trading vessel. For what distant land across the seas the vessel was bound did not really matter to our young rabbit – he just wanted to see all that the world could show him. He could barely contain his excitement. For the first few days he was lost in wonder; it seemed that each passing hour brought some fresh sight the like of which he had never seen before. He saw shoals of flying fish keeping pace with the boat like tiny silver darts, equally at home in air or water. He saw in the distance the massive body of a whale break the surface of the rough sea to let loose a blast from its blowhole, before dipping sedately back beneath the waves. And he saw a storm boiling on the horizon ahead of their slender, fragile craft; a glowering sky that cast its dark shadow across the ocean and made hardened sailors shiver.

"The next twenty four hours of the rabbit's life were more filled with incident than the rest of his life to that point had been. Shame to say that not all of that incident was pleasant and, in fact, little enough of it was. The storm hit the ship with a violence and fury that defied belief and imagination. Rain lashed the deck, the wind grabbed the craft, picked it up and threw it down with a crash and a splash into the tortured waters of the ocean beneath.

The sailors fought to keep the ship afloat, rushing this way and that, hauling in the sails, battening down the hatches and tying down anything that looked like it might get loose. The rabbit, with no experience to call upon, and no idea what he ought to be doing, crouched in a corner clinging to the side as hard as his paws would let him. He had never seen anything like this before, and suddenly wished very much that he could be back safe and warm in his little burrow near the river bank with his family and friends.

"But things were about to get worse for the little rabbit, and he was about to see something even more extraordinary than the waves themselves. The storm had not just tossed about the surface of the ocean; it had burrowed down and stirred up the depths into torrents, disturbing creatures that had lain undisturbed there in the dank blackness. Out of the sea, barely more than a paw's distance from the rabbit, a creature rose, vast and dark, huge suckered tentacles gripping the ship and, most terrifying of all, a single, massive, white eye set into its slippery, black skin, which trained its relentless gaze on the cowering rabbit. As other sailors struck at the creature with whatever they could find and fought to keep the ship afloat in the turbulent waters, all the rabbit could do was stare at the eye which had him completely mesmerised. But he was not the only one whose gaze was so caught; as he stared at the eye, it stared back at him. The creature had never seen a rabbit before – never seen anything so unutterably fascinating and alien to it. Did it think the rabbit looked friendly? Did it think he looked tasty? Or did it think he looked different? Whatever it was the creature could not look away from this tiny animal that had so caught its interest.

"Suddenly, and without a sign of warning, the creature ducked back beneath the waves, letting go of the ship as it went and leaving only the violent seas for the crew to contend with. After the terror of the monster the storm was almost a relief to the sailors; here was a terror they had faced before, one which they knew how to handle. Working with the speed and experience of long years at sea, and pushing the recent attack to the back of their minds, they set themselves to the task of weathering the storm.

"After what seemed like an age the winds began to drop, the rain first slackened and then stopped, and the violent sea calmed. The dark clouds parted to reveal a blue sky and a cautious sun. Only now could the sailors take stock of the damage; it did not look good, in fact it looked like they should consider themselves very lucky to be alive. Certainly there was no possibility of continuing with their journey, and they were glad that they were only a day out of port as it was barely within the beleaguered ship's capability to limp its way home, where it could get the repairs it so desperately needed.

"No news could have pleased the rabbit more. His taste for travel might not have completely abated, but his taste for the sea certainly had. There was plenty to explore in England, plenty of places to go and things he had not seen, and plenty of inland waterways in which he could put his sailing experience, such as it was, to good use. It was a happy rabbit who leaned over the rail of the ship that night and saw the lights of an English Port on the horizon ahead of him.

"But that was not the only light that he saw; as he looked down to the water, he saw beneath him, travelling fast, keeping pace with the ship, a huge white circle, gleaming in the darkness – the eye of the monster. Frantic and frightened, the rabbit ran to find the first mate and dragged the man to the side to show what he had seen, but the massive eye was gone, vanished once more into the depths.

"The next day the ship docked and the crew disembarked, the rabbit feeling that he would be happy never to set foot onboard such a thing ever again. He set out for home with a warm feeling in his heart for the burrow he had left behind. But that night, when he camped by the river bank, he was scared out of his wits once more; there in the river, staring at him with that incessant interest was the creature, its single unblinking eye shining through the waters of the river.

"Something about this rabbit had intrigued the creature of the depths. It wanted to know where this curious beast had come from, and if there were more like it, and it was not about to give up its search now."

The young rabbits had sat, wide eyed and enthralled through the Rat's tale, and only now did one of them dare to voice a question, "What happened to the rabbit?"

"Oh he came back here," the Rat said conversationally, "I think he travelled a bit, around and about the country, but he always came back here. This was his home."

"What about the monster?" that was what they all really wanted to know.

"Well," the Rat continued, "it got a taste for rabbits. Not literally," he added quickly, "At least not as far as I know. Not that anyone's ever found out. Not for certain. But it surely takes an interest in them."

"It's still down there?" the young rabbit's eyes had got even wider, approaching the size of saucers.

"Oh certainly," said the Rat with confidence, "It only comes out at night as it doesn't like the sun. Why do you think none of the animals around here ever swim at night? I mean, we don't know if it ever would eat anyone, but why take the risk? Actually," he glanced over to the water, "You can see it some nights."

He stood up on the blanket and walked towards the side of the river where his boat was moored. A group of stone-silent rabbits followed him, huddled together for the strength that came with numbers.

"Ah, there we are," breathed the Rat, pointing a paw towards the water, and the rabbits clustered around him in a chorus of gasps. There in the water, gleaming at them, was the eye of the monster. For a heartbeat the rabbits stared at this monstrosity and it stared back at them, a white circle, unblinking and relentless, then, as one body, the rabbits took off back to their burrows, running as fast as their little legs would carry them. It would be a long time before any of them would consider swimming by night again.

The Rat went back to the blanket and, whistling a tune to himself, packed the dinner things away into the hamper from whence they had come. This done, he stowed the hamper back in his boat before stepping in himself and casting off. Across the river he sculled with skill and ease, glancing with a smile at the bright circle that stared up at him as he went; the eye of the monster – the moonglade.

Turnip Soup
by Wendy Bradley

On a pale golden evening in early October, the Mole was stumbling along under the hawthorn hedge, tripping over hidden roots, slipping into holes and ditches. Daylight was fading fast and the Mole's eyesight wasn't very good, but still he soldiered on.

"Six fours are twenty four," he muttered, "Put down four and carry two...and nineteen is... No. That's not right... Put down nine and carry one..." The distant clouds were tinged pink with the setting sun, the hills silhouetted in shades of purple, and the fields lay dreaming of long winter days beneath the coming frosts. But the Mole only wanted to get home to his own fireside.

The mist hung low over the valley, swirling across the ploughed earth like gossamer curtains, streaming in ever-thinning ribbons along railway embankments and river backwaters, trapping a layer of wood smoke underneath.

The faintest hint of burning clung to the bramble branches as they arched over ditches. It permeated the spiky hedgerows with memories of smouldering bonfires, but the Mole remained oblivious to it all. On and on he stumbled, his little pink hands firmly clasped around a bulging leather bucket.

A white liquid swirled and slapped against the bucket sides, now and then escaping over the rim with gleeful plops, slurps and splodges as liquids do when they are forcibly shaken, bumped and bounced from side to side and generally agitated. It dribbled down the front of the Mole's immaculate black velvet jacket, dripping onto his toes, oozing and squelching between them as he scrabbled towards home.

Behind him a trail of muddy white footprints led all the way back to the Great Barn. Winter was coming and the Mole was laying in supplies. His hand-to-mouth existence beneath the fields and hedges of The Farm meant he must take his chances when he could. And the Mole had seized his chance.

The farmer had, just that very day, mixed up the whitewash for the next stage of his grand project, 'Doing up the Great Barn', to let it out for next year's farm holiday trade.

The Mole had seen the farmer, leaning up against the old barn door, smoking his pipe and thinking deep thoughts, as one does at the end of a long day when the work is all complete and the prospect of a hearty supper and an evening spent before the fire awaits enticingly. At his feet the newly mixed whitewash was lapping the edge of an old tin container, so tall that it reached

The Wind In The Willows Short Stories

right to the top of his Wellington boots.

And later when the farmer whistled for his old, grey Bess to follow on, and left the barn door only loosely hanging, the Mole had crept forward and stood on tip-toe, peering over the rim of the container.

Oh the smell of it, so rich and fresh. The surface and the depths of it, all frothy white and full of secret promises. A dozen tiny bubbles popping here and there, like pancake mixture lying in the pan, just ready to be flipped.

The Mole smiled a gleeful smile. He was an animal who liked to keep his home all spick and span. A place for everything and everything in place. A time to clean. A time to decorate. A time to sit back and admire one's handiwork.

"Why, just the job," he said. "That'll do very nicely. Now if I just had a little something, a tin, a jar or something, to transport this with..." His head buzzing with plans for newly whitewashed walls in bedroom, hall and pantry, he burrowed through the pile of rubbish on the old barn floor, emerging in triumph with an old-fashioned leather bucket. "Yes," he whispered over and over. "Yes, yes, yes."

The bucket dipped beneath the glorious white and gleaming surface. Again and again he trailed it through, left furrows in the thick and gooey mess, and hauled it, not without some difficulty, to rest, filled to the brim, against the edge of the old tin container.

The Mole set the bucket down very carefully on the earth floor of the barn and scratched his head in thought. Now would this be enough to do the rooms he had in mind...or, worse still, be too much? And, if so, then far too heavy and unwieldy for a mole to carry home?

There was a rustle and a scuttling in the hedgerow. Someone was watching. Tabitha the farmer's cat. Discretion was the better part of valour. Hoisting his new-found prize close to his chest, the Mole stumbled forth, determined to make himself scarce and beat a path for home.

"Here Kitty, Kitty. Come and get your supper." called the farmer's wife. The farmhouse door flew open and a long chink of yellow light spread outwards, wedging into the dusk, but stopping short in front of the frightened Mole. The Mole stood stock still as Tabitha stalked past, her tail held high. Miss High and Mighty. She let him know she'd seen him, but her supper in the cosy farmhouse kitchen meant there were better things on her mind than measly little moles. The farmer's wife scooped up the cat and the kitchen door closed softly behind her, leaving the night to Mole.

Turnip Soup

"Oh my, oh my, but that was close." he thought, not daring to move a muscle until he'd stilled the beating of his heart. Then he set off homewards, following the wood smoke smell, his little sensitive nose twitching in anticipation. He was thinking of winter nights beside the open fire, the chestnuts roasting on the hearth, his slippers warming nicely and his supper on the range. Home. Safe and dry, deep underneath the ground where nobody could find him.

And as he made his way, his mind was busy. Busy with little calculations. His paint brush wide enough to cover half a wall in six long strips. So every wall would take at least a quarter of a pint...and he would need...

"Now. Let me see," he said "Six fours are twenty four. So put down four and carry two..."

On and on he stumbled, tripping over tree roots, dragging the bucket under thick hawthorn hedges, laden with berries, ripe red for picking. He was scratched and scored across with spiky branches, his feet were hurting and the bucket seemed heavier and heavier with every obstacle he encountered.

His way home ran straight across a ploughed field, cutting through the edge of a little copse before descending into the meadow beyond. He stopped for a moment, considering the best way forward.

"Perhaps it would be easier," he thought, "if I take the path along the edge of the field and through the middle of the copse. The ground there will be smoother and I can use the handle of the bucket to pull it along, instead of carrying it."

So the Mole set off again, refreshed in body and spirit, because now he had a plan. It should have been successful. The rabbits that lived in the hedgerow had long ago scampered back to their burrows. They wouldn't bother him that night. The owls were not yet on the wing, and the foxes had their own night plans, way back in the farmyard.

The Mole concentrated more and more on heaving the heavy bucket along the ground. He discovered that, if he stood in front of it, he could pull it towards him, a few feet at a time. Progress was slow but steady. However anything was easier than carrying it in front of his chest, his little, pink paws straining to meet across the wide expanse of the bucket's waist.

He saw the first of the silver birch trees swaying on the edge of the copse, and followed the path between the elder trees. He worked to a steady rhythm. Trudge, trudge, haul. Trudge, trudge, haul. His head was full of thoughts of home and hearth, and supper waiting there.

The moon rose gracefully above the trees. The first stars twinkled in a sky that changed from pink to lilac and to shades of darkening purple. The Mole was tired, finding he had to stop more often than he pulled. Then, with a sudden, terrifying twang, the handle of the bucket snapped and he went rolling backwards, head over heels, until he came to rest against a tree trunk, and knew with awful certainty that he could go no further.

He looked around and found himself in a little clearing between the trees. Moss and lichen covered a scattering of pebbles, and the ground beneath was hard as a rock. The last wild flowers of Autumn grew in between the stones, and a pile of crisp, golden leaves, stirred by a gentle breeze, had collected at the base of the tree trunk where he lay. The Mole dug deep into the pile, showering the leaves in every direction, and found to his surprise a hole beneath the surface roots, big enough to squeeze into. Then, following the passage upwards, he emerged into a vast chamber with moonlight filtering through the roof. A hollow tree trunk. The very place to spend a night in safety and in comfort. Within minutes he was sound asleep.

"It is, I tell you. It is. It is. There's a monster in the tree. Can't you hear him snuffling and growling?" whispered the squirrel, sitting bolt upright, her nose twitching, ready to flee at any moment.

"What you saying, Sister?" Her brother looked at her scathingly.

"A big green monster, with ugly horns and scaly skin and dripping fangs."

"Don't be such a ninny," he sneered. "You know there's no such thing."

"There is. There is," she wailed. "Can't you see him down there in the shadows? He's eating all the nuts. What we goin' to do?"

The squirrel sat with his twin sister on a single branch which jutted out like a signpost from the top of the hollow trunk. He shook his head in disbelief. It was just like his sister to start this kind of scare. He knew the monsters were only in her head. They didn't really exist. Come to that, he wasn't entirely sure that the nuts existed either. (Squirrels are absentminded creatures on the whole. They spend so long stashing food away for the winter, it takes them an age to find it all again. They don't have any counting system and rely on memory alone to recognise their hiding places.)

So the squirrel had a problem. He and his sister ran back and

Turnip Soup

forward along the branch and made such a song and dance about it all, arguing about what was best to do, that they wakened the Mole. Even more confusion followed as he tried to explain to them who he was and why he was there, while the squirrel, who wasn't listening anyway, kept yelling that he could just stay where he was until Father Squirrel came to sort it out. The poor Mole, who only wanted to be friendly, tried to make his way out through the roots, but somehow got disorientated and failed to find the passage. He collapsed in a sorry little heap on the floor, wondering what was to become of him.

Then they all heard the music; coming ever closer, a rapid, jiggly sort of tune, repeated and repeated, the tramp of marching feet and the voices singing, almost all together.

The squirrel and his sister froze, then fled as a dozen young rats emerged into the clearing from beyond the trees. Their skins were shiny brown, their eyes as bright as stars, their tails were smooth and sleek and their paws were squeaky clean. Between them they trailed a handcart, loaded with musical instruments: squeeze-boxes, fiddles and drums, all shapes and sizes. Each rat held a metal tankard in his hand, drinking from it repeatedly, replenishing it from a large black pot in the middle of the handcart.

"Turnip Soup, Turnip Soup...we love Turnip Soup," they chorused.

They were the Pack Rats, 'out on the razzle', on their way back from camping in the old quarry to a 'ding-dong of a party' at a secret location: the underground tunnels of a large country residence somewhere west of the Wild Wood. The Pack Rats stopped in amazement when they spied the old leather bucket, its wooden lid askew and whitewash dripping down the side.

"Hello. Hello. What have we here?" they said. They left the handcart down, drained off their tankards and clustered round the bucket, curiosity getting the better of them all at once. They'd used this woodland trail more times than they could remember, but never before had they seen anything like this.

"Face paint!" cried the youngest one, doing a little jig of sheer excitement. The others took him up immediately,

"Face paint. Face paint.

Spooky white face paint.

We'll paint all our faces.

Yes, that's what we'll do."

And all at once they were dipping their paws deep in the bucket, using the Mole's precious whitewash to adorn, not just their faces but their bodies too. They spread the stuff around the forest floor so that the flowers and leaves and the stones below were liberally splattered with a coating of white.

"Stop. Stop." cried the Mole from deep within the tree "That's mine. I brought it here. You're wasting it!"

The Pack Rats shook their heads and dipped their tankards in the Turnip Soup.

"Ay up." they said, drinking deep and long. Then, turning to their leader, they waited for him to speak.

The Chief Rat crawled forward to the bucket, slid the wooden lid back into place and leapt nimbly on top. Standing on his two hind legs, he could just peer over the rim of the hollow trunk into the darkness beneath.

"Oh please." said a small mole-like voice. "Please. I don't mean any harm. I was trying to get home with my bucket. I only came in here for a bit of a lie down, but now it's all gone wrong and I don't think I can get out again. You see it took me ever so long to get it this far and I'm so tired and cold and damp that..."

"Now, here's a turn-up for the books," said the Chief Rat winking at the others. "A little fellow in trouble. All by himself in the cold, cold night, and he can't find his way home...All together now..."

"Aw..w..w"

"We can't have this my friends. Oh no indeed. We are the Pack Rats. Pack Rats to the rescue. Let's get this fella out of here and then see what is what."

The Mole tried hard to scrabble up the inside of the trunk, but his little feet were made for digging, not climbing, and he couldn't get a purchase on the shiny bark. He just kept slithering down again.

"Stay where you are, mate. We're coming to get you," shouted the Chief Rat. Then, turning to the others he told them quickly and quietly, exactly what they had to do.

The Pack Rats worked as one. With their leader fully in charge of operations, they climbed on top of each other again and again, until the last one reached the rim. Then this last rat turned around, ever so slowly (which isn't easy when you've four feet to manoeuvre and the rim in question is less than one inch wide) and draped his tail down inside the trunk. He curled it securely under the Mole's armpits and heaved him up and over to land on the bed of leaves outside. The Mole was grateful to be free, but thoroughly winded with the excitement of flying through the air and landing with a bump.

Turnip Soup

The animals stared long and hard at one another. Then the Chief Rat said, "Have a drink, old boy. Turnip soup. Do you the world of good."

The Mole drank deeply, all the while protesting that he just needed to get home. His supper was waiting, slow cooking on the range.

"More soup. More soup," cried the Chief Rat, and everyone else agreed.

The Mole was beginning to feel better. The more soup he drank, the better he felt, and the less anxious he was about his strange companions, or about getting home to house and hearth, and the more inclined he was to have another tankard full of soup.

So, in the end, it was a jolly, laughing party of animals who continued on their way to the tunnels of The Hall. Behind them they trailed their handcart with the soup pot, the whitewash bucket and the musical instruments. In their midst, the Mole danced and jigged along, feeling happy and contented. He was altogether a different animal from the one he had been some hours before.

"This is the life," he chorused with the others,

"A life of ease

'Cos life's a breeze.

Think not of tomorrow

Think only today.

Eat, drink and be merry,

is what we all say."

Hours passed in this way, but eventually the animals, trudging along the forest track, fell silent. The night was cold and frosty underfoot. The branches of the trees swayed far above, and a myriad of tiny stars glowed in the ink-blue sky.

"Tell us a story," said one of the younger rats.

The others took up the call. "Tell us about the party...Tell us about the secret place...Tell us where we're going."

The Chief Rat sighed, then said resignedly, "Once, long ago, a family of strangers came down from the hills. The father had made his fortune in the lead mines, and now wanted to live out his days in comfort. He bought an imposing gentleman's residence...We'll call it 'The Hall' for now."

He paused to ensure everyone was listening. Then he continued, "In time the father died, and ownership of The Hall passed to his son, Mr T. Now, Mr T. is a delightful fellow, engaging, ebullient, with a great deal more money than sense. He mounts extravagant banquets for friends and acquaintances, both business and personal. He thinks nothing of abandoning The Hall for long periods, when he gets caught up in one of his schemes. The result is, he's hardly ever there. So that makes it the perfect place for us rats to party, eat, drink, dance until we drop, all courtesy of Mr T. Esquire."

"Are we nearly there yet?" asked a small voice from the back.

"Not far, my friend, not far." The Chief Rat lifted the smallest rat onto the hand cart where he promptly fell asleep. But everyone else kept trudging on, each one turning over the details of the story in his mind, and anticipating with relish all the good times that were to come.

The Mole didn't have any idea how long they had been on the road, but he was convinced it had taken most of the night to reach the boundary of The Hall. By the time the clusters of red brick chimneys and the tiled roof came into view, the sky was lightening and the spider's webs in the gorse bushes were glistening in the morning dew. The Mole stood gazing in wonder at the building high above him.

"I say, I say, what a magnificent place this is," he gasped.

Never in all his life had he seen anything so imposing or extensive. The house seemed to go on forever, sprawling sideways like a silent, basking lizard. Row upon row of windows and balconies looked out over a wide deserted courtyard. Outbuildings of every kind clung to the edges of the yard. Stables and storerooms, laundries and glasshouses, all bolted and barred by stout wooden fixings ...and this was only the back.

"You want to see it round the front, mate," said the Chief Rat, "You wouldn't believe it. But that's not for the likes of us. We've got our own way in, and we won't be pulling the bell on the Great Front Door either."

The Pack Rats sniggered, and gathered round, waiting for instructions. The Chief Rat waved his arm expansively.

"This my friends is The Hall, the pride and joy of the county, the home of Mr T. a true country gentleman. He is NOT in residence at the moment, which suits our purpose very nicely. Mr T. is liable to be absent for some time. I have that on the best authority. He is up and away on one of his madcap schemes."

"He's like that, is Mr T. Always something new on the horizon. Always on the go. Just lurches from one crazy scheme to another.

Turnip Soup

Last month it was the circus. Out looking for clown acts, trapeze artistes and animal trainers. Brought the whole thing together in a huge red and white striped tent back of The Hall. Locals thought it was the eighth wonder of the world, until all the lions and bears escaped and Mr T. was in trouble for not looking after them properly."

"Bears. You mean, real live bears?" asked the Mole peering cautiously under the bushes for fear they were still around.

"Please don't concern yourself my friend," said the Chief Rat, patting him on the shoulder in a friendly fashion, causing the nervous Mole to flinch. "No bears. No lions. Nothing. All locked up safely in the Zoo. Mr T. has now moved on to other things." He nodded and winked, touching the side of his nose knowingly with his finger.

"What other things?" said the Mole, glancing about him as the party moved on, skirting one of the outbuildings, following a sign marked 'Tradesman's Entrance. No Hawkers. No Gypsies. By Order.'

"Ah. That would be telling. But then again, that's why we're here," said the Chief Rat mysteriously. Then seeing the Mole's look of confusion and uncertainty, he softened. "'S all right mate. Mr T.'s latest venture's got no wild animals involved. It's gunpowder. Well, not exactly gunpowder. Fireworks. Hundreds of 'em. Planning the biggest display in the country. Been wining and dining a certain Chinese gentleman, name of Lung Ching. Got long whiskers down to his waist and his hair tied up like a pony's tail behind. Mr T. threw a banquet here at The Hall last night to sign off the arrangement. Then he drove away in a horse and carriage, to inspect his latest acquisition, the biggest fireworks factory in the country."

"Oh my, oh my," said the Mole "I've never even seen a fireworks display."

"You've never what?" said the Chief Rat, looking at him in amazement. "What do you do at Halloween? Don't you go out and party? Don't you make turnip lanterns and dress up and have fun, dunking for apples and the like, even if it's only in your own back garden?"

"Oh no, nothing like that," the Mole assured him earnestly. "I keep myself to myself. I like it that way. It's peaceful and quiet. You know where you are when you've only yourself to please."

"Yes, well. I'm sure," said the Chief Rat. "But today my friend, we're going to introduce you to party time at The Hall. There's going to be food aplenty, music, dancing and a top class luxury version of that Turnip Soup you've been so enjoying."

"I'm not sure I..." began the Mole.

"Of course you will. It'll be a breeze. Last night's banquet means food everywhere, leftovers of every kind. The tables will have been groaning. None of them ever clears their plate. They think it's not polite. The kitchen staff are lazy, probably still sleeping. Easy to get into the tunnels and behind the wooden panelling to the pantry and the banqueting hall. Then it's help ourselves and back to the tunnels, at which point my friend, let the FUN begin!"

As they got closer to the back yard, the Mole could see that The Hall beyond was much less salubrious than he'd first thought. The brickwork was cracked and flaking in places. Rusting black drain pipes criss-crossed between rows of wooden sash windows, leaking damp patches and staining the walls with green. The pipes then ran downwards to end in broken gratings rank with damp leaves and other debris. The Chief Rat took a deep breath and rubbed his nose appreciatively.

"That, my friend, is the smell of decay," he said, "And we rats love decay. Decay and putrifaction, rotten vegetables and rotten meats. The longer they leave 'em, the better it is."

The Mole wasn't quite so sure. He liked things fresh and clean, air you could breath without choking and earth all crumbly and crunchy, the 'get-up-and-go' smell of hay meadows and cornfields, and honeysuckle in full bloom, trailing over hedges. But he was a polite animal and not inclined to argue the point with his newly made friend.

The Chief Rat led the others stealthily along the edge of the yard wall until they came to a heavy iron gate, hanging loosely on rusty hinges. A faded sign read 'TRADE ONLY THIS WAY'.

"Aye. That'll be right," he said slipping through the gate, crossing the cobbled yard, searching for something along the base of the house wall. "Ah, here it is," he murmured, pointing to a small, wooden door set low down almost at ground level. He unlatched it carefully and peered into the dark recesses beyond.

"Is it?" said the Mole, not understanding at all what was going on.

"Why yes, Moly my friend, this is the ash pit below the outside water closet, where the..."

"No Chief Rat. Not that sort of detail. I can do without..."

"Fear not dear Moly. All is not as it seems. This here's a dead ash pit. Dead, deceased, defunct. Ain't been used in years. Not since Mr T. installed the latest flushing system that only his sort of money could buy. No-one's used this place in years.

Turnip Soup

Consequently only us rats know of the secret entrance to the tunnels."

Greatly relieved, the Mole, too, peered inside. As his eyes became accustomed to the gloom, he noticed that the far corner of the pile of ashes had been carved out to form a passage wide enough to climb into. Excited now by the prospect of exploration underground, he offered to go first. After all, 'subterranean' work, as he called it, was something he knew a great deal about.

So the handcart, with the soup pot and the whitewash, having been stowed in the far corner of the yard, behind a convenient water tank, the animals moved in single file into and along the passage. They used their fore limbs to protect their musical instruments, as they crouched low and followed the Mole towards a dim light glimmering far ahead.

The Mole was in his element. Why this was just like home! A long straight tunnel, opening into a larger chamber, but the walls here were not the familiar earth and sand. Instead they were regular lines of bricks and stones, forming great arches overhead. The place was lit with oil lamps burning low, set into little niches in the walls. It smelled of damp. Fungus adorned the ceiling and moss grew in between the cracks.

The Pack Rats busied themselves immediately, scurrying off up side passages, returning with salvers of sandwiches, ham bones with chunks of meat still left to gnaw, roast vegetables, potatoes, onions, carrots. Cold congealed gravy sunk deep into pitchers, custards, puddings, and pies of every sort. And finally, a giant soup tureen filled to the brim with extra rich and creamy Turnip Soup.

The chamber was filling up now as crowds of guests poured in. There were rats of all shapes and sizes, sleek rats and fat rats, black rats and brown rats, stable rats, sewer rats, barn rats ready to party, pushing and jostling, all after the rich, creamy soup.

The Mole could smell it now, the strange, putrid, festering mass in the tureen. The sweet, clingy odour that pulled you towards it, that cried, "Drink. Enjoy. Live for the day. Live for the hour. Enjoy. Enjoy."

And so he did, with all the rest. And the more he drank the easier life became. He began to perceive how lonely his previous existence, how convivial the crowd, how enriching the experience of life in the tunnels. The Pack Rats, suitably fortified with Turnip Soup, took up their instruments and the walls reverberated with music and dancing. Faster and faster they played till the room seemed to spin around the Mole, as he was caught up willy-nilly in the deep, primeval rhythms of the dance. Tossed this way and that, whirled around by dancers with flying limbs, his eyes tight closed, he was away on flights of fancy all his own. The atmosphere was alive with the joy of being...until, as suddenly as it began, the music ceased.

Everyone stopped still, staring at the main passage back into the Hall. A huge black silhouette was standing on its hind legs, feet apart, arms raised in accusation. This was The Guardian, a rat of enormous proportions, his sagging belly folded down across his knees, his white teeth bared in anger, gleaming in the lamplight.

"What in Thunder's name is going on?" he boomed, his voice echoing across the chamber.

Silence. A shuffling of feet. One or two younger rats at the back tried to move stealthily towards the exit.

"No you don't. Don't move a muscle anyone. I've got eyes in the back of my head...and I don't like what I see." The Guardian fixed them with a steely gaze.

The Great Black Rat, caretaker and guardian of The Hall, had been roused from his slumbers in the stable yard, by the din of jollification deep within the tunnels, and had decided to investigate.

"He Who Must be Obeyed" had expressly forbidden all such dawn raids on the kitchens of The Hall. Yet, there before him, were the perpetrators, caught in the act, not only of stealing food, but also of indulging in forbidden Turnip Soup...and then the greatest outrage of all, celebrating the felony with music and dancing.

The Great Black Rat was furious, and even more so when he discovered in the midst of the throng, a stranger, an alien creature who could reveal the secret of the tunnels, and "Rumble Thunder knew what consequences that might have."

"Come here you greasy, little spy. Come here and answer for your temerity in entering our secret world," he said.

The Mole looked round. A space, a widening circle of no-man's-land, was forming all around him as the rats shrank back into the shadows. There could be no doubt. The Guardian was addressing him.

"Please Sir," said the Mole, looking humble and wringing his paws in supplication. "Please, Great Sir, I'd like to say thank you for your generous hospitality. The meal was lovely and the entertainment just first class...and now, with your permission, Sir, I'd like to fetch my jacket and go home."

Turnip Soup

The assembled company stood quite still, each holding his breath. It could go either way. No-one had ever had the courage to answer the Guardian back. No-one knew how he would react. And as for saying "thank you", that was an alien concept. No-one ever said "please" or "thank you" in their world.

The Guardian gnashed his teeth and made a hissing noise somewhere between a grimace and a grin. He wasn't about to let anyone off the hook. Wrongdoing was wrongdoing after all. But at the same time, looking at the Mole, he saw himself, a young rat, long ago, out of his depth, out of his environment, wishing himself somewhere else...and at that moment, anywhere else would do. His heart softened, but only slightly. He barked orders left and right, his words ricocheting off the walls like bullets.

"Clean this place up. Get rid of that food. Put that stuff away, NOW. Coats on and out of here in thirty seconds flat, or else! And you lot, (indicating the Chief Rat and his friends) including you Roly Moly... I'll see you in the cellar pronto!"

In no time at all, the central chamber was cleared of food, debris and visitors. The bandstand where the Pack Rats had set up was polished and shining and the wall lights were trimmed. The Mole trailed after his companions, retreating down a side passage into the cellars of The Hall. He shuffled along, disgraced, remorseful, silent. He was beginning to wish he'd never been born.

The cellar was lined with stout wooden barrels. Wide marble shelves were laden with cheeses, pottery bowls, and slabs of fresh, roasted venison. Poultry and game hung from rusty hooks set into the walls above, and the walls were brilliant white. They were shining with whitewash, clean as a whistle, lovely, pristine whiteness just like home. The Mole could hardly bear it, as he gulped back the tears.

The Guardian squatted atop a pile of barrels in a corner of the room, looking more intimidating than ever. He dealt with the Pack Rats swiftly, confiscating their instruments, confining them to their quarters for a fortnight, and sentencing them to sewer duty until further notice. Then he turned to the Mole.

"You my friend have got in far too deep. Too deep for comfort but I think you know that. Yes?"

"Yes Sir. Yes Great Black Rat, Sir."

"I therefore sentence you to be escorted from this building, to be marched to a point on the road where our ways must part forever...and to swear that, whatever happens, you will never reveal the entrance to the tunnels that lie beneath."

"Yes, Sir. Thank you Sir, Great Black Rat, Sir."

The Mole was spluttering. His eyes had misted up disgracefully and his legs were wobbly. He said his sad goodbyes to every Pack Rat present, and put himself into the hands of the Guardian.

And so it was that the Mole found himself outside his own front door, taking leave of the Great Black Rat.

"Now then, my friend," said the Guardian, "Remember the bucket of whitewash? The one you stowed away behind the water tank? Thought no-one would ever find it, didn't you?" The Mole opened his mouth to protest, but the Great Black Rat continued, "Well, it was found. Found during the big clean-up after the party. Didn't take long to work out who had left it there either."

"The whitewash," said the Mole. "What's happened to it, Sir?"

The Great Black Rat looked at him long and hard. Then he bent down to retrieve from his knapsack, a small, brown paper bag, filled to the brim with soft, white powder.

"Know what this is?" he enquired, raising an eyebrow.

"No, Sir. I've no idea, Sir."

"Just as I thought," sighed the Guardian. "This, my friend, is slaked lime powder. I've brought it along especially for you. Listen carefully and I'll tell you what you'll do...You'll take charge of this. You'll keep it dry. You'll store it 'til the days are lengthening and the nights are growing shorter. Then you'll mix it up with water in a bucket and you'll find you've all the whitewash you could ever need."

The Mole nodded his head slowly, beginning to understand.

The Great Black Rat was smiling now. "No use of trying to drag a bucket of liquid whitewash half way round the country. Just leads to all sorts of complications. Take my advice, there's a good fellow. Wait until Spring before you start to whitewash."

So the Mole accepted the bag of slaked lime powder with good grace, and sighed as he offered the Guardian his paw.

"I see it all so clearly now," he said. "I am an animal built to live alone, going my own way. It's what moles do. I should have been content with what I have. I will be in the future. No more living it up for me. I don't much like adventure after all."

The Guardian turned to go, laying his hand on the Mole's shoulder, ever so briefly, like a blessing. "Wise words, my friend," he said, and added with a rueful smile "And absolutely no more Turnip Soup for you!"

The Water Rat
by Janet Lesley Smith

The Water Rat had been up and about, and exceedingly busy, since a first weak beam of sunlight had made the feeble promise of a glorious, spring dawn.

After an excess of cleaning: dusting, sweeping, mopping and general mayhem, he had put his home into perfect order. A final, critical examination of his recent handiwork had assured him of its readiness to face the comings and goings that traditionally recommenced at this season of the year. Now, as he stood in the doorway of his newly spruced-up dwelling, there was an air of rightful self-satisfaction about his small, neat figure.

Today, you could not have found a smarter animal along the entire length of the river bank. From the end of his black, button nose to the tip of his sleek, ringed tail, his grooming was faultless. The Rat's abundant, brown hair lay smoothly brushed over tidy ears and matched the glossy shine of his splendid whiskers. His kindly, brown face wore an expression of quiet contentment and a pair of bright, intelligent eyes glistened in a fine morning's early sunshine, which flickered into the dusky entrance hall and burnished his oak front door's little brass knocker.

His house, of which he was inordinately proud, was discretely tucked beneath the river bank's grassy overhang of verdant meadowland, its living space safely situated above the otherwise intrusive waters below. Carefully excavated deep into solid, dark earth, it was barely visible to the casual observer.

In the cool silence of his cellar, which had completely dried out after the river's winter incursions, the Rat had ranked stone jars of lemonade and ginger beer in orderly rows, standing them at attention like soldiers awaiting the "At ease" command, for warm summer days' needy refreshment. He had filled his capacious larder to bursting point with a range of tempting foods which intimated their future, generous disposition at many gourmet picnic feasts to come.

His kitchen's freshly whitewashed walls were hung with mirrored, copper pans; each one's crimson reflection blazoned with the glow from the floor's highly polished red tiles. The kitchen table's wooden top had been vigorously scrubbed to pristine, bleached whiteness and at its centre he had placed his finest cake stand, its gilded tiers attracting an additional flicker of light from the row of gleaming utensils.

No other room in his snug home was as welcoming as the

Water Rat's cosy parlour at the front of his house. A sparkling, sunlit window highlighted a comfortable sofa's bright covers. Two armchairs had been drawn up invitingly before a fireplace that had been laid purposefully with paper and sticks, only requiring the application of a match to blaze away the chill of crisp spring evenings.

In a glass-fronted cabinet the Rat had accumulated the treasures of an avid collector. These were his finds from the river, exposed to his keen eye at times of low water; a small, brass cup, gleaming from his assiduous attentions, jewelled hatpins, winking through decorative, leaded panes, a blue glass bottle and a shiny, silver whistle. All these were items, accidentally discarded by careless passengers from passing steamers and inebriated boating parties.

Upstairs, he had made up the best bedroom, as though expecting a well-loved guest. On the bed, fresh, white linen was draped with a flowered coverlet that complemented a patterned china basin and ewer, which he had set handily on the dresser with a folded towel to await the discerning visitor.

Downstairs, mats had been rigorously shaken and rugs strenuously beaten in a frenzy of good housekeeping.

Having done his absolute best by his riverside abode, Rat told himself that he had every reason to be pleased. What, with the onset of spring that marked the demise of winter's late rising and early nights, and the lively stirrings of his near neighbours, the river bank, *his* river bank, was again becoming the industrious, exciting habitat that he relished.

While he contemplated the hustle and bustle of renewed life and the total absorption of the river folk in a number of suddenly important jobs, a small, doubtful cloud of discontent scudded across the placid sky of his complacency.

"Could it be that he was the only indolent fellow in existence?"

As a long term resident of the river bank, knowledgeable in its ways, he had learned to adjust his daily schedule to incorporate the more-or-less pleasurable interruptions by neighbours, intent on enjoying his company (he provided excellent tea and scones) or to seek specific advice on some immediate problem. And, as he modestly admitted to himself, he was a chap who could be depended on to give sound counsel to less resourceful animals.

It dawned upon the Rat, with an unexpected pang of hurt pride, that being completely engrossed in their own affairs, not one of his neighbours had passed him the time of day. There had been no cheerful waves, no merry "Good mornings," not even a polite salutation or a nod of acknowledgement. He began to feel a little down.

The Water Rat

"Once they have all finished their chores," he surmised, "the river bank will return to being its usual interesting place and I don't doubt that I will be bothered again from dawn to dusk. Anyway, until then, I am more than capable of finding a useful activity to keep me enjoyably occupied."

With that verbal expression of good sense, he squared his shoulders which had begun to slump and turned from the continued admiration of his property, having nothing left to do in that respect, and regarded its frontage's extensive river view. This superlative aspect of the river, with the great swathe of meadow that stretched alongside, generally brought him only peace of mind and could be relied upon to provide a gentle relaxation in times of stress.

"On such a day," he thought, "I will compose an ode."

The soothing progress of harmonic waters acted as a source of constant inspiration to his poetic muse in the composition of many amusing ditties, with which he would entertain his friends.

The river however, was about its own business this morning, and in the devil of a hurry. Its waters alternately lapped and splashed, plashed and gurgled in separate channels and conduits, each displaying its own eccentric character.

Here, a translucent rivulet swashed cleanly over pebbled beds. There, a rushing tide enveloped a stony outcrop, only pausing to descend in a foaming flood, before continuing its eager journey downstream.

Upstream, a stronger flow gushed against the river's banks, gathering dead leaves and twigs, flushing out sprigs of trespassing watercress and weed, as it carried its arbitrary harvest triumphantly toward a hungry ocean.

From its rumbustious passage, rainbow drops of spray rose in a glittering arc to fall in a shower back into the river. Their disturbing descent created small eddies, which whirled in wild circles, dispersed, reformed and sank like bath water disappearing down a plug hole only to re-emerge further along the wayward current in a more intricate pattern. The water sang a medley of little songs, with a tinkling trill when it fell over a stone, a mighty chorus when it rushed along a gully and a chuckling comic reprise when it whistled through hollow reeds.

The Rat became quite dizzy watching these erratic convolutions and he closed his eyes, hoping to find divine afflatus in the musical sounds of the river's succession of lively allegrettos. But, so hasty and hurried were the confused rhythms of the water's rapid onward surge that he could not discover the right rhymes. In the excited voices of each wandering wavelet, the river spoke in a thousand tongues and, in this watery Babel, his carefully chosen words all jumbled together and made no sense.

"Bother!" said he, and with a resigned sigh of surrender, he abandoned his versifying and considered taking some exercise.

"I might take a swim," he said to himself, and looked for his friends, the dabbling ducks that he liked to tease as he swam beneath their webbed feet.

As though conjured by his fancy, a flotilla of mallards paddled swiftly by, so intent on some unknown purpose that they passed the Rat without the familiar quack of "Hello Ratty". They were closely followed by a little moorhen family, which similarly sailed speedily and silently past.

A kingfisher too, perched on a convenient branch, gave him no greeting, though this latter lapse of good manners could be explained away by the handsome little bird's beakful of wriggling minnows that rendered him mute.

"Well really!" said Rat. Indeed, he would by now have been most put out by these exclusions but the sight of his freshly painted rowing boat, bobbing and dancing by its landing-stage below, restored his former good spirits.

With expertly applied coats of both blue and white paint, the little craft looked brand, spanking new. A pair of varnished oars lay in the well, and fat plumped-up cushions gave the guarantee of a comfortable ride.

The mooring rope alternately pulled and slackened. One moment the boat lay tamely and obediently alongside the landing-stage, the next saw it tugging wildly at its tether, anxious to be free.

"Let's be off!" it seemed to say. "Today is just the day for an adventure."

The Rat found himself in total agreement with this sentiment, but there was really no fun in going on one's own. Adventures were for sharing, but where might he find a kindred spirit when the whole world was so annoyingly occupied in boring, mundane tasks?

"Otter will come with me," he thought. "He's a good fellow, although he gets easily distracted."

He looked around, as though he might summon up his friend at this time of need, and almost immediately his eyes noticed a v-shaped ripple in the water, a tell-tale sign of Otter's presence. The Otter's flat head surfaced for a second, while he despatched a passing damselfly, then he submerged completely before Rat could call a cheery greeting, and then the only indication of his

The Water Rat

passage was a stream of tiny bubbles moving rapidly away.

"Drat!" said his friend, with a groan of disappointment. "Blow!"

It then occurred to him that the Badger might appreciate a jolly jaunt after his gloomy winter sojourn at home in the Wild Wood. He gave a nervous glance toward the distant edge of the wood, which shadowed darkly where the meadows ended. Things were stirring in the woods as well as on the river bank. In that part of the night when dreams disturb a restful sleep, he had woken to hear the predatory cry of a dog fox and later an answering vixen scream. The Rat gave an involuntary shudder. Life in the Wild Wood or the Wide World beyond it was something he did not wish to investigate. Although he had met various friendly rabbits and squirrels, residents of burrows and drays among the woods' tall trees, there were other less law-abiding animals that he would not wish to encounter. He had no intention of leaving the security of the river bank to look for Badger. Badger would find *him*, if and when that stripey gentleman wished for his company, as he was an animal who did not always appreciate Society.

Sadly, he dismissed the possibility of one old friend's companionship in favour of another.

"I wonder," the Rat paused. His brow wrinkled as he concentrated on the advisability of seeking out his old acquaintance, Toad.

Mr Toad, as he liked to be called, was easily the most affluent of the river-bankers. Passers-by had only to regard the attractive, red-bricked Toad Hall, with its carefully tended lawns and flower-beds, that bordered a picturesque sweep of river, and its many outbuildings, to appreciate that the owner was rich. Had they been invited inside, as the Water Rat had been on many occasions, the magnificence of the internal furnishings of this well-appointed home, notably the splendour of its grand staircase and elegant dining rooms, would have confirmed the opinion that Toad was *very* rich indeed.

The Rat had to admit that Toad was not the brightest of chaps. He was sure that he had several good qualities, though Rat could not recollect immediately what these might be. Certainly, Toad could be a generous host when it suited, but he was also "careful" with his money, except for the regular expenditure afforded by his innumerable hobbies and madcap schemes.

It was the recollection of one of these later "good ideas" of Toad's that had caused the frown of indecision on Rat's normally calm face.

Exercise had long been a desirable element in the Toad's daily routine. Unfortunately, due to his indulgent lifestyle, any serious attempts at physical exertion left him breathless and disenchanted with whatever sport or pastime that he had decided to undertake.

"The main problem with Toad," thought the Water Rat, "is that he goes at everything with such enthusiasm that he's worn out or bored within a few days or, at best, weeks."

He could not remember how many different types of river craft his friend had tried during a prolonged craze for boating. The boat-house must surely be full of rejected vessels. The latest of these, he recalled, had been an expensive sailboat. The last time he had seen it, it had presented a sorry spectacle. Toad had evidently steered into the willows, which had deposited several branches about his portly person and had broken the mast in half. The waterlogged sails, once colourful and gay, were dragging forlornly over the stern, while the captain suffered the indignity of being towed home.

For weeks after this encounter, the distinctively checked pennon that had flown so bravely at the masthead, flapped raggedly in one of the damaged trees, until a mischievous gust of wind sent it flying unkindly onto Toad's front lawn.

This poignant memory of Toad's chagrin only served to remind the Rat of another occasion when he and his exuberant companion had shared that same shameful emotion.

Before his obsession with water sports, the Toad had developed a keenness for cycling, intent on strengthening his leg muscles. The roads in the vicinity of Toad Hall had seen a varied collection of velocipedes, unicycles, bicycles and tricycles. Predictably, their owner had hastily tired of what he described as their "limitations". What he actually meant, was, that the effort of achieving an exhilarating pace far outweighed any enjoyment, and the resultant exhaustion deprived him of any beneficial effect.

The Water Rat had so far resisted the numerous, effusive invitations to join his friend on any one of his many wheeled excursions, until the Toad had discovered a magazine advertisement for the "Scarlet Runner". The makers of this infinitely superior, racing cycle claimed that, due to extensive research by its manufacturers, an advance in engineering science ensured that the rider could achieve a remarkable turn of speed without the intensity of pedal power that other models required. Toad had ordered one immediately and could not wait to show it off.

"Come on Ratty!" Toad had been insistent. The Rat could think of no excuse to justify yet another refusal. He had given the scarlet machine a doubtful look and its rider's togs yet another.

"Outrageous," he had muttered under his breath as Toad fixed

The Water Rat

a pair of cycle clips to the bottom of vivid, predominantly yellow, tartan trousers.

"What next?" he had said, when Toad adjusted shiny goggles beneath a peaked, sporting cap and insisted on wearing it at a ridiculously jaunty angle.

Nevertheless, Toad had fixed a large wicker basket to the handlebars and thoughtfully placed a soft cushion for the use of his intended passenger.

"Hop in, old chap. Time's a wasting!" he said.

And, against his better judgement, the Rat had hopped in.

After the first few tentative wobbles as Toad had pushed off, the motion became smooth and, as the manufacturers had promised, the racing cycle soon reached a smooth and speedy pace. The Rat made himself comfortable on his cushion and began, cautiously, to enjoy this new experience. His delightful, elevated view of hedgerows, overlooking a pleasing patchwork of fields and farms, was made even more engaging by the Toad's unaccustomed silence. Apart from a steady wheezing and an occasional puffing, it seemed that, due to his dynamic pedalling, Toad was incapable of speech.

Their peaceful ride was not of a lengthy duration. Toad, who considered himself the master of a number of subjects, about which he expressed a variety of opinions, began to boast of his expertise on this powerful machine. Rather alarmingly, he accompanied this noisy speechifying with what seemed to the Water Rat to be quite extravagant gesticulations, waving his arms to underline any especially relevant point in his orations. These rash movements caused the cycle to waver and wander from one side of the narrow road to the other.

They were fast approaching the entrance to a small farm. Rat, in his forward position, had just the time to admire its flowered gateway and to notice a colourful display of farm produce on a roadside stall, when the "Scarlet Runner's" front wheel gave a violent wobble.

"Look out," cried the Rat, but Toad, who had raised both arms to the sky to emphasise the significance of his words, was oblivious to the danger ahead.

The cycle's initial collision into a sack of potatoes could have been much worse, but much worse was to follow.

At the moment of impact, Toad gave a loud shout and his rather corpulent form was cascaded onto the farm's produce stall. He was fortunate enough to land on a tastefully arranged selection of green vegetables, which helped to break his fall. Unluckily for Toad, for it incurred the wrath of the farmer's wife, his not inconsiderable weight caused the collapse of the flimsy wooden structure, which supported them. Not only did this disaster send the distraught woman's cabbages, potatoes, turnips and carrots tumbling into the road, but it also overturned her basket of newly laid hen's eggs, whereupon every last one was smashed.

The Water Rat was by now feeling truly mortified as he pictured the embarrassing scenes that followed this debacle. Up to now he had not chosen to be reminded of his own miserable part in the affair.

As the juddering front wheel hit the potato sack, he had been flipped over the top of his travelling basket to land painfully on his nose in a patch of nettles behind the farmyard wall. He rubbed that nose gently, imagining for a moment that he could still feel the large painful blister that had been the result.

When he had pulled himself together, his first thought, for he was a kind creature, was of Toad's welfare.

This notion was immediately dismissed when he stared into the greedy, green eyes of the farm's tabby cat. She had been abruptly woken from her afternoon nap by the Rat's crashing fall. Prey and predator eyed each other. Neither moved.

The Water Rat could hear Toad's booming voice. From its strident tenor, he concluded that its owner had sustained no serious injury.

"Now. Now! My good woman—" The Toad was at his most patronising as he attempted to mollify the farmer's wife, who was screaming angrily and demanding a more-than-generous remuneration for her spoiled produce.

"Who are you calling a good woman? Look at the likes of you! Consider yourselves gentlefolk? You think you own the countryside, riding roughshod over honest, hardworking folk." She ceased this harangue just long enough to demand an exorbitant sum from a spluttering Toad.

"How much?" he gasped.

"Pay up," she yelled, "or else!"

"Or else what?" said the Toad very rudely.

The air became filled with flying vegetables. The cat, having been hit with a stray parsnip, miaowed and abandoned the nettle patch for safer ground. The Rat, too, was stirred into action and clambered over the farmyard wall, peeping from behind the gatepost in order to see what was happening. Perhaps, he thought, no one had noticed that Toad was carrying a passenger.

The Water Rat

The Toad, forgetful of that same passenger, had taken to his heels, the farmer's wife in hot pursuit, armed with her basket of broken eggs. The Rat, who followed gingerly behind, remarked that she had an extremely accurate aim. He dogged the couple's increasingly slow footsteps, keeping well out of sight, until he caught up to the red-faced wife, who had abandoned the chase and had collapsed in a breathless heap under a hedge. He crept past unnoticed and found Toad a little farther on and in a comparable state of distress.

An ignominious lift home in an unpleasantly smelly hay cart brought that day's expedition to an inglorious end. Neither Rat nor Toad had ever mentioned the "Scarlet Runner" again, nor was it ever retrieved from the farm. A rumour circulated along the river bank that the farmer had sold it for a goodly amount, which more than compensated his missus for her losses, and that *she* had been seen at church on Sunday in a new feathered bonnet. Toad had pretended not to hear the local gossip. By then, of course, his badly bruised ego had recovered and he had taken to the water.

The Rat gazed at his own impatient little boat, which was built for two, and tried to imagine the bulky figure of Toad, seated in the prow. The trouble was that Toad was incapable of keeping still and, in such a frail craft, his uncoordinated actions would have them over in a trice. There was no possibility that Rat would knowingly disturb the tranquillity of the river; after all, he had his own well-earned reputation as a skilled oarsman to protect.

Having decided that it would not be to his advantage to call on Toad, and having discounted those among his other friends who might have been persuaded to join him on so adventurous a day, the Rat came to an important conclusion.

"What I really need," he remarked to a pair of preoccupied dabchicks, who happened to be passing by, "is a boon companion, a David to my Jonathan. In a nutshell, the very best of best friends. I need someone I can teach about the ways of the river, someone who has time to listen to all the old stories. Not like Otter, who finds it difficult to concentrate, nor Badger, who is very wise but not always approachable, and definitely not like the egregious Mr Toad, whose company is fine in small doses but who likes to dominate any conversation. In fact he is a bit of a know-it-all."

The Water Rat was now faced with the same problem that he had encountered earlier. Where would he find a new companion, to accompany him on his intended outing?

He cast a wistful look toward his neighbours, half expecting a suitable candidate for best friendship to reveal himself, but they were still actively engaged in the urgent pursuit of some important employment. However, he felt a little better when one doffed his cap and another called cheerfully, "See you later."

Much encouraged by that simple exchange of pleasantries, he reflected at length that perhaps it was the sort of day when one should just stand, listen and look and absorb the beauty of one's surroundings.

Having taken his own good advice, the Rat stood basking in strong mid-morning sun. The river, more babble than Babel now, ambled along at his feet. With its banks spring-cleaned to its satisfaction, its language was less excited than before but still muddled, with no discernible rhymes. The fluid motion of its luminous waters had attracted a hatch of iridescent flies that hovered in a sparkling display and were suddenly surprised by a leaping brown trout. A coot was collecting nesting material from a clump of reeds, and a shoal of silver minnows went flashing by.

Everywhere, the world was in resurgent motion, from a multitude of budding trees to the burgeoning hedgerows, with their infinite variety of flora and remarkable assemblages of small animal life.

Over on the far bank, where the meadows stretched almost out of sight, a lark rose and the loveliness of her melodious singing sent him into a profound reverie.

He could see lush, tufted turf and festoons of young grasses springing from the fertile ground, soft and feathery with new growth. Soon the sleeping flowers would awake and the meadow would be white with daisies and golden with buttercups, celandines and marsh marigolds. The willow-herb would flaunt its rose-pink blossoms and later, scarlet poppies would colour the fields. After that, sturdy bulrushes would dominate the banks. Already the reed-beds were green with fresh leaves, covering last year's woody stalks. So too the branches of the drooping willow trees at the river's edge were heavy with pale, thrusting shoots.

Apart from the lark, in her almost static flight, against a backdrop of cloudless, blue sky, nothing disturbed the serenity of his meadow view, until a slight movement at the limit of his vision brought him out of dreaming into alertness.

Rat gave his head a shake in puzzlement, as if to say, "Wake up."

"What on earth is that?" he said to the lark, but she was too involved in the intricate cadences of her song to reply.

Whatever or whoever he thought he had seen came nearer and nearer. The peculiarity of its circuitous approach was marked by

The Water Rat

the frantic waving of the downtrodden plants in its path.

Above the meadow's rampant greenery he noticed a small black arm, which appeared and disappeared with increasing rapidity. Of course it need not have been the same arm on every occasion. Rat imagined that its owner, whatever creature it might be, probably had two. Eventually a little head popped up over a clump of sorrel. Its pink mouth opened wide and uttered a joyful whooping noise. A determined thrashing in the undergrowth, with occasional glimpses of feet, arms, a backside and then that head again, suggested that here was an animal with a penchant for acrobatics. Somersaults and cartwheels followed one after the other, accompanied by faint cries of delight. At last, the whole animal emerged in its entirety further down the river bank, hopping and skipping like a child let out of school. His antics were still defined by a series of exclamations and agitated hollering. The Rat craned his neck to observe this strange individual and his even stranger behaviour at closer quarters.

He had to admire the creature's black velveteen suit. A better-dressed chap, apart from himself, had not been seen on the river bank before.

The visitor seemed fascinated by the river. He ran up and down the bank, burbling the same sort of nonsense as the chattering waters below, until he came to an exhausted standstill immediately opposite the Rat's partially concealed viewpoint, where he sat himself down and stared, as though transfixed at the water's steady flow. How long he might have remained in this position one could not say, but the gentle sigh of a spring zephyr whispered through the willows, ruffling his black silky fur and, at that, he lifted his eyes, blinking in the sunlight, and steadied his mesmerised gaze to look directly across the river.

The Water Rat, as yet undecided as to the intruder's intention, retreated swiftly and noiselessly into the shadowed security of his home's obscured entrance and stared with his bright eyes at the odd little figure.

"Well, Ratty," said he to himself, "I think that I have discovered my new best friend or, possibly, that *he* has discovered *me*?" Emboldened by such positive thoughts, he stepped out into the sunshine of an optimistic day and called over the water's noisy procession, "Hullo, Mole!"

The Calling Of The Piper
by Dr. E. J. Yeaman

It had been one of those cloudless summer days, when the sun god ruled the heavens and oppressed the earth. For sixteen hours, his rays had blasted the countryside, seeming to scorch the very life out of the air, so that everyone sought the shade, gasping in vain for respite from the all-pervading heat.

Now, as the great silver moon rose to dominate the sky, much of the warmth had drained from the fields and meadows, but the air remained sultry. The creatures of the day tossed and turned, unable to sleep, while the creatures of the night were seized with lethargy, which made them loath to attempt their customary occupations. The nocturnal chirp and bustle was subdued.

Beside the river, it was different. After earlier rain on the hills, the river was higher than its normal level, chuckling in enthusiasm as it bustled along much more purposefully than its usual summer dawdle.

Its animation communicated to the nearby air, cooling and stirring it, making the river and its bank into a band of comfort in the surrounding sultry stillness.

To the bank of this river, there came a woman. She seldom appeared in places frequented by mortals, but the conditions had tempted her to make this visit. She was glad she had done so; this place had a raw wildness that was missing from her own lands. She strolled along the bank, rejoicing in the moonlight gleaming on the water, the casual rustle of the leaves, the lingering scent of the meadowsweet, and the fresh air, stirring her hair.

She was young and beautiful, divinely graceful, with dark eyes, long fair hair, and skin so smooth that it reflected the moonlight. She wore a simple white dress of some light material that floated around her. The skirt seemed too wide for walking among the vegetation of the riverside, but it never snagged on the clutching leaves or twigs; it slipped through them like the moonbeams. In fact, the woman herself might have been a moonbeam, flitting along the bank, sometimes in the open, sometimes among the trees.

Thus she glided along the river bank, until, about to emerge from a band of osiers, she paused. Ahead of her, the river widened to a shallow pool, into which a track shelved from each bank. This had been a ford, although the shadow of a bridge suggested it might be falling into disuse.

The gap in the trees let the moonlight reach the water, which shimmered as the rippling surface shivered the moon's reflection. Silhouetted against that bright patch, an otter stood on a spit of gravel. Despite the late hour, he was alert; his head was up, and he repeatedly darted glances from side to side.

With a mixture of apprehension and curiosity, the woman backed among the trees, but he showed no sign of having seen her; his attention was on the shallows at the sides of the ford.

In the daylight, the woman could imagine him at that place, perhaps sunning himself or fishing, but he was not fishing now. His attention was not on the water; he was scanning the banks.

Occasionally, when a nocturnal creature rustled in the undergrowth, he would stiffen to full attention, jerking round to face it, but, when the creature appeared, or failed to appear, his body seemed to sag, although he remained alert, his head swinging from side to side.

For some time, the woman remained there, watching him. She loved small animals, and this one disturbed her, although she found it difficult to understand why. His strange behaviour, in that place in the middle of the night, was disquieting. She sensed she was in the presence of deep anxiety.

When she finally moved on, much of her carefree spirit had gone. She could not forget that solitary shadow, on its apparent vigil by the ford. Farther upstream, she sat beside a patch of water mint, hardly noticing the sharp, sweet scent, and hardly seeing the silver sheen of the moon on the water.

Her reverie was interrupted by sounds of clunking and splashing, approaching up the river. Subdued voices reached her over the swish and gurgle of the eddies. In front of her, the patch of gleaming water became more agitated, as the shadow of a small boat crossed the edge, with two figures in it. One, in the middle, was sculling steadily while the other sat in the stern, steering. As she watched, the vessel glided towards the bank a little downstream of where she sat.

The voices came clearly to her now. "Can you jump ashore from there?" Thud. "Good. Tie her to that willow."

Thud.

Another voice asked, "Is he likely to be here?"

"I don't know, Mole, I don't know, and that's a fact. It's the kind of place that might attract him, with that overhanging bank for shelter, and the slope giving access to the water." The voice rose a little. "Portly! Portly, are you there?"

A few seconds silence followed, broken only by the hiss and gurgle of the water, and the cry of a distant owl.

The Calling Of The Piper

The second voice said, "He's not here."

"We ought to have a look round. He may not hear us if he's gone to sleep, or... or for some other reason."

"Oh, Rat, I can't bear to think of that. He is such a bright little fellow."

"Cheer up, Mole. Look on the bright side. He's been missing before, but someone always finds him, and brings him home."

"But he's young, and you said yourself, Rat, he's never been away from home for so long. And don't forget that weir. It's not far away from here. He might be attracted to play near that. You know what young ones are like. And...and he's not totally confident in his swimming yet."

"Mole, Mole, don't be such a pessimist. You'll...what's that? Up there, beside the water mint."

The listener stiffened, but relaxed when the other voice answered, "It's nothing. Just the way the moonlight shines through the leaves. I'm sorry, Rat. I don't mean to be miserable. We must go on in hope."

"That's my Mole. You search along the bank there. I'll look in the hollow."

Sounds of movement followed, and occasional subdued calls of, "Portly!"

Rat said, "He's not here. Any luck there, Mole?"

"No. I don't believe... Oh, bother!"

"What's the matter?"

"I put my foot in a hole. It's so difficult to see. The moonlight makes such deceptive shadows."

"You're not hurt?"

"N...no. I was looking for Portly, instead of where I was putting my feet. I don't think he's here."

"Well, that's one more place eliminated. Jump aboard. I'll take a turn with the oars. I assume you want to go on?"

"Yes of course, Rat." Sounds of scraping and splashing came to the listener, as the boat moved away from the bank. "I could not sleep, knowing that poor Portly is missing."

"We'll try that gap in the other bank." The shadow of the boat splashed across the patch of moonlit water. "He may have taken shelter there."

"We must try all we can. Oh, Rat, imagine if your only son was missing. I feel so sorry for Otter. I think of him waiting at that ford. Waiting and hoping."

"That was one of Portly's favourite places. If he happens upon it, he may recognise it. It's a small chance, but it's a chance." After a few moments' silence, the same voice went on, "Can you get ashore there, by that stump?" The voices faded as the boat vanished into the shadows of the opposite bank.

For a short time, the woman sat, unmoving, staring at the gleaming water without seeing it. Then she stood, and moved more purposefully.

Such were her powers that she soon found herself in a magnificent palace. She went outside, to a terrace whose ornate roof was supported by a row of smooth pillars of flawless white marble. Here, it was daytime, warm after the cool breeze of the riverside. The sun shone from a cloudless sky the colour of milkwort, making the pillars appear translucent, almost like crystallised moonbeams.

She hurried down three marble steps and along a straight path between immaculate lawns, surrounded by borders overflowing with bright blooms. This garden seemed meticulously tended, but no gardener was in sight.

The woman sighed gently as she went through a white marble arch, to a meadow of close-cropped grass, dotted with flowers of white, yellow, pink and blue. From a clump of trees, birds chirped their joy at being alive in such a place, and, from the distance came the peaceful baa-ing of sheep.

The woman sighed again, and cocked her head to listen. Yes: the distant sound of pipes floated through the air to her. She had come to the right place. She hurried in the direction of the sound.

As she drew closer, the pure notes became clearer, an exquisite melody. She did not know the tune; indeed it was likely that the invisible piper was improvising. No one was singing, yet the melody inspired emotions that sent accompanying words swirling through her mind.

No matter whither I may roam,
   'Midst lakes and mountains grand,
I still prefer my home, sweet home,
   My own, my favourite land,
In Arcadia.

It's here my heart will ever lie.
   It's here my soul finds ease.
Where toils and troubles never try,
   And prospects ever please.
In Arcadia.

The Calling Of The Piper

Resisting the urge to luxuriate in the song, she moved on. The sound of the pipes was coming from behind a little knoll. Going round it, she discovered the piper, lounging in the grass with his eyes shut, apparently lost in the melody he was playing.

She stood, looking down at him. She considered him coarse, but she had to admire him. The back-curving horns, the face that was youthful yet weather-beaten, the virile body, toned by years as a herdsman, and the powerful, shaggy hips and legs.

She wasn't aware of having made a noise, but the music stopped, one eye opened, and the corners of the mouth curled up in a quizzical smile.

As she sat beside him on the soft grass, he sat up, and he listened attentively while she spoke. When she finished, he nodded seriously, and hurried away. She watched him till he was out of sight, then she remained seated there, staring at the grass between her feet.

Two flowers grew there – a white one, and a pink one. They were the same shape, reminding her of a daisy, but she couldn't identify them.

Meanwhile, the piper was walking by the moonlit river, studying the banks. His shepherd's eyes, trained by looking for lost sheep, probed every shadowy hollow.

Like the woman, he was conscious of the difference between this place and his usual fields. The air here was sharper, the vegetation was wilder. It was like comparing a boy who was washed, polished, and trapped in his Sunday best, with the same boy, dirty and carefree, playing in his ragged weekday clothes. The image made the piper smile.

As he progressed upstream, the water became more agitated, muttering in complaint as it tumbled over the gravel. He was near the weir. He could hear its subdued roar, although he couldn't yet see it in the darkness ahead. Opposite him was an island, with the ragged silhouettes of trees and bushes against the starlit sky. The water lipped among a patch of reeds at the near side. Behind it, the river escaped into a backwater.

He might have to investigate that, but his instinct urged him to check the weir first. As he hurried up the bank, the roaring of the water grew louder, and he discerned the curve of white, gleaming in the moonlight, where the water poured over the edge.

Standing on the grassy bank just above the weir, he studied the river there. It was wider, and dotted with boulders, black shapes, sticking out of the dark grey water that swirled and jostled as it waited its turn for the plunge. The moon was past its zenith now, so everything was less distinct.

He saw nothing alarming. Logic urged him to seek elsewhere, but his instinct, honed by years of seeking animals in distress, insisted that he was in the right place. He was reluctant to leave, continuing to scan the water, checking and rechecking every boulder.

A faint mewling, barely audible over the roar of the water, reached his sensitive ears. He traced it to a piece of log, perhaps the branch of a tree, which had been swept down the river during winter storms, and had lodged at the lip of the weir. Beside it, almost hidden in its shadow, was a dark mound, mostly under water. As he watched the shape, it moved feebly, and the mewl was repeated.

Without hesitation, the piper strode forward into the swiftly flowing water. It soon became deep enough to reach his thighs, but that did not deter him. He did move more carefully, because the river bed was uneven – big boulders with hollows between them, treacherous under his hooves.

He battled on. Now the rushing water had reached his waist, tugging at his legs and roaring over the lip less than a yard to his right. As he drew closer to the log, he saw that the dark hump was a small animal, clinging desperately to it, while the clutching water swirled round him, eager to carry him over the edge.

The piper moved on with greater urgency, groping forward with one hoof then the other, trying to find level, stable footing. He drew nearer and nearer, until he could see the gleam of the frightened eyes of the little animal, sometimes hidden by a foaming crest of water surging past.

Two more steps. One. Then he would reach the little fellow. But, as he moved on, his left knee bumped something, invisible in the dark water. It must have been an underwater part of the branch, because the visible part jerked sideways.

That was enough to dislodge the little otter's feeble grip on the water-slimed wood. With a despairing squeal, which ended in a gurgle, he was swept away.

The piper, seeing the young animal's peril, lunged forward to seize him. As his grasp closed on a tiny foreleg, his footing went, and he overbalanced. They plunged over the weir, a confused tangle of piper, otter and log.

The next few seconds were hectic for the piper. He retained a hazy recollection of tumbling around, but instinct made him hang on tightly to the slim leg he had grasped as he toppled.

When the chaos released him, he was sitting on the gravel in the shallower water of the pool below the weir – but he had not let go of the little otter. He gathered it into his arms, a tiny bundle of wet black fur. The log bumped on, down the river.

The Calling Of The Piper

He staggered to his feet, with the water cascading off him. The current had carried him rather nearer the island than the bank, so he splashed towards it. In his arms, the little otter whimpered. That brought a surge of relief to his heart; his effort had not been in vain. As he walked, he gently rocked it, murmuring soft words of reassurance.

He had to trample through the reeds, and push past a hawthorn bush before he reached a dry footing. He wended round bushes, in the shadow of trees that were bushy but not tall, before he reached the centre of the island. Here was a clearing in the trees, letting in enough light from the sinking moon to reveal a patch of soft grass.

He sat at one end of that, leaning against the trunk of a silver birch, and spoke quiet and comforting words to the little animal in his arms.

As he did so, the whimpering and trembling gradually subsided. The little otter felt the strong arms, bearing him safely. He opened his eyes, seeing the kindly face smiling down on him. He gave a contented murmur, snuggled closer to the powerful chest, wriggled into comfort, gave a long sigh, and drifted into an exhausted sleep.

The piper was wet and slightly cold, but he sat without moving. He was content to relax after his exertions in the water, warmed by the glow of pleasure at having saved an innocent life. Looking down at the trusting little animal, cradled in his arms, he was reluctant to disturb the restoring sleep.

In time, the chill of the pre-dawn air penetrated to him, reminding him that he was becoming cold and stiff. Gently, he laid the otter on the sward between his hooves. The little animal stirred and murmured, but didn't awaken. With his rough shepherd's hand, the piper stroked the soft fur. The murmur settled to peaceful breathing.

The piper lay back against the trunk, a loving smile on his face. Despite the chill, he was loath to leave that place. He loved his own fields; they were delightful, but they lacked the atmosphere of this island.

From somewhere down the river, clunking and splashing and calling voices reached him, intruding on his contentment. He frowned, wondering why anyone would be on the river at that time.

Cautiously, he rose to his feet. Looking across the clearing, and through the trees at the far end of the island, he caught glimpses of a small boat with two figures aboard. They were sculling slowly up the river, scanning both banks.

At the rear, the water-rat, steering, took the little vessel into the bank at the left. They clambered out, and spent some time prowling up and down, peering into hollows in the bank, looking under tree roots, and searching behind bushes. Watching them, the piper understood. His heart went out to them.

As he watched them, the river began to shed the drab grey of its night attire. Above the bank, the meadow turned from dark grey to pale grey. Beyond the trees, the sky grew brighter, crystallising the fuzzy interface between earth and heaven. A new day was near.

The little boat continued its progress up the river. It went out of the piper's sight, behind the thick vegetation that fringed the island, but he heard the voices more clearly, enough to distinguish the occasional word, and to discern the weariness in them.

That gave him an alarming thought. With the coming of the day, their weariness might persuade them to abandon the search. And, even if they continued, they might not visit the island. It had proved a timely and convenient refuge for him, but the searchers were likely to believe that the little otter could not have found his way to it.

They must be drawn to the island, so that they would find what they sought. But he could not have direct communication with mere mortals. He had made an exception for the young otter, because that had been a matter of life and death. In any case, there was little risk: when the child told his story, his parents would dismiss it as fantasy, perhaps inspired by the stories he'd heard.

But the mature animals were different. Certainly they were intended to believe that he existed, but not as a visible, tangible being, on the same plane as themselves. They were expected to regard him as an invisible presence, moulding their destiny. He dare not reveal himself to them, by waving or even calling. How could he draw them to the island?

As the answer came to him, he smiled in triumph. Quickly he threaded through the bushes to the patch of reeds at the side of the island. He broke one cleanly off, and took it back to the birch, where the little otter still slept peacefully.

He tested the reed by blowing gently through it. It gave a note that was clear, but so weak that it failed to penetrate the trees around the clearing. Marvelling at the timbre of the note, he blew again, more strongly. This note was braver, creeping farther through the trees. Convinced that his plan would work, he blew with his usual strength, producing a note which burst exultantly through the trees, and over the river beyond; a note much richer than he could ever produce from the pipes of his homeland.

The Calling Of The Piper

In the backwater to his left, beyond those trees and the thick band of yellow irises that clothed that flank of the island, he heard the splashing of the boat, the mutter of the voices, and the rustling as the searchers pushed past the leaves. Snatches of conversation carried to him. "Don't you hear it, Mole?"

"No, Rat. Are you sure you're not hearing the breeze sighing though the reeds?"

"No, Mole. Listen! Listen hard!"

That gave the piper some satisfaction, but now he had acquired a mission of his own. He did want to attract the searchers to the baby otter, but he also had another purpose. He hurried to the reed-bed, and made a careful selection, breaking off the straightest and sturdiest stalks.

Eagerly, he hurried back to the birch, where he sat, leaning against the trunk, with the sleeping form of the baby otter between his hooves.

During his absence, the light had grown. The grey silhouettes around the clearing had become three-dimensional green trees – crab-apple and wild cherry. Their leaves had turned from anonymous grey to bright green, and the blossoms had shed their ghostly grey nightgowns, and donned their delicate, white dresses, ready to greet the new day.

Their beauty increased the piper's delight in the place, and his eagerness to bring his music to it. But his ambition was too important to be sacrificed for speed. Carefully, he selected the best reeds, and broke them to the correct lengths. He tested each one by gently blowing through it, smiling in satisfaction as he produced a series of clear notes.

As he did so, he was vaguely conscious of voices beyond the trees, voices whose weariness was banished by awed excitement.

"There, Mole. Do you hear it? You must hear it!"

"Yes, Rat. I believe I do. I truly believe I do."

"It is... wonderful. No words can describe it."

The light was brighter; the sky was still grey, but the first streaks of white were venturing across it as the piper completed his preparations. As he arranged the reeds, everything around him was still. In the trees, the birds were silent. In the bushes, the little creatures were too awed to move. Even the breeze had faded, so the leaves lay at peace. Nature waited, holding her breath. Only the background purr of the weir broke the expectant silence.

The piper put the reeds to his mouth, and began to play. The first notes soared across the clearing, and through the trees. He started modestly, playing tunes which he knew, resisting the temptation to burst into flamboyant melodies.

But the makeshift pipes urged him to abandon his reserve. Those pipes were not fashioned from the perfect reeds of his homeland. These pipes came from the reeds of a living river. They had not grown idly in a perfect meadow. They had battled for survival, and they were descended from generations of reeds which had also battled for survival. During winter spates, they had stood deep in swirling water. Under the onslaught of March gales, they had bowed but not broken. Those experiences were reflected in the notes they gave. Perhaps not as pure as the reeds from his homeland, but fuller, hinting at the richer lives they had led. They begged him to improvise tunes, and he was quick to accede.

As the reeds responded to his improvisations, he became more and more immersed in the music. He had never played such pipes. For him, the island, the river, the weir, the baby otter, faded to insignificance. The pipes, and the tunes he was conjuring from them, dominated his mind and his body.

He was unaware of the rim of the sun peeping over the horizon behind him, heralding another glorious summer day. He was unaware of the two little animals, mooring their boat, and creeping through the undergrowth of the island. Everything else was submerged under his absorption in the melodies he produced on those pipes.

As Rat and Mole crept through the bushes into the other end of the clearing, and stood, watching him in dumb awe, the sun rose high enough to send its first bright beams through the trees behind the piper, spotlighting them.

The sudden brightness, and the barely suppressed awe of the visitors, at last penetrated the piper's intoxication. His mind jolted back to the island, and he realised guiltily that the animals must have seen him. Fortunately, their instinct was to bow down and worship him. Seeing the tops of their heads, he took the chance of slipping away. His job was done.

That day became a copy of the one before – cloudless, with the white-hot ball of the sun tyrannising the countryside. At its blessed close, the woman returned to the river bank. Once again, she revelled in its beauty, black and silver in the moonlight.

As she approached the ford, she heard voices, so she peeped round the band of osiers. Tonight, there were two silhouettes on the spit of gravel – the same otter as the previous night, but now he was accompanied by another shadow the same shape, but smaller and plumper. Tonight, there wasn't the gloomy silence of

The Calling Of The Piper

a vigil, but excited laughing and splashing. The woman couldn't resist dallying in the shade of the osiers, watching the happy animals.

She would have liked to stroll farther along the river bank, but that would have to wait for another night. Now, she had a more urgent duty.

Back in her own lands in daylight, she left the palace, crossed the perfect, flower-studded meadow, heading for the knoll favoured by the piper. As she approached it, she wasn't surprised to hear his pipes.

As usual, the sound enchanted her. Once again, the tune, although without words, transferred its emotion to her mind, inspiring its own words.

She could not fathom the reason, but these tunes seemed to enthral her even more powerfully than yesterday's. She had come to speak to the piper, but she need not do so immediately; she couldn't bear to interrupt such melodies. She stopped, surrendering herself to them, and their unspoken message.

No matter whither I may roam,
   'Midst lakes and mountains grand,
I still prefer my home, sweet home,
   My own, my favourite land.
In Arcadia.

But if I seek a scene less mild,
   Where restless water flows,
I'll go where reeds and flowers grow wild,
   And the wind in the willows blows,
By the riverside.

At the House Called Beautiful
by Elizabeth Parkhurst

Dust swirled round the narrow parlour. The Chief Stoat's Lady picked up her broom with a sigh. Her Lord had gone out with a snarl of temper and a slam of the front door. From further down the Terrace she could hear the weasels having a quarrel of their own; a crash of glass, a high-pitched yelping of abuse, and then a sharp squeal of pain. A moment later there was a thumping, low down on her front door; she opened it to find the youngest weasel sobbing and holding his ear.

"Oh not again, young what's-yer-name!" she exclaimed. "Get in, sit down and let's have a look."

She lifted his paw gently from the wound, and drew a sharp breath.

"Oh dear, that's a bit nasty," she murmured. "Yer Dad should be more careful how hard he bites."

"That were me Gran. In a temper about Toad Hall. Still got all 'er teef. Ow, Missis, that hurts!"

"Hold still," she said. "Hmmm, I reckon that needs a stitch. Just let's wash that blood off yer."

She scurried out to the kitchen and came back with a kettle and a cracked china bowl. She dipped the end of a towel in hot water and sopped at the gory mess, more gently than one would have supposed.

The baby animal's protests had subsided. Like all the Wild Wood children he was a tough little brute, hardened to painful usage from friend, family and foe. He sniffed messily, and wiped his nose on his sleeve.

Lady Stoat rummaged in the dresser and produced a needle and thread.

"Right, now," she said. "This really will hurt."

She handed the weasel a bone to bite on, then deftly stitched up the gashed skin. She nipped the thread short with her own sharp teeth, took the splintery bone from her patient's mouth and replaced it with a piece of toffee.

"So what's all this about Toad Hall? I've not seen today's paper – is the trial over yet?" she enquired, as she tipped the bloody water out of the window.

"Oogff ngfff nnnfff – oh, 'ang on," mumbled the weasel. He removed his toffee and shoved it, wet, into his pocket, then beamed up at her. "Me Dad's up there now with the Master Ferret. They reckon ol' Toady's gone down for a lifer, so they're planning a massive squat. Good, eh? Mistress Ferret told Gran she's going to be Lady Ferret of Toad Hall and wear different diamonds every day she goes shopping. That's why Gran got the gin out and laid into the rest of us. Lord Chief Stoat come by, landed 'er one and sent me down here out the way."

"Oh well, glad he did. Ol' Fanny Ferret in diamonds?" she chuckled. "Hmm, I'd like to see that. Think yer Granny's quieted down yet?"

"If he ain't done her in he's knocked her out. I better get back. Thanks, Missis. 'Ere," he grinned suddenly. "What'll you do when we get to Toad Hall?"

"Wear diamonds every day when I *don't* go shopping," she laughed. "Now clear off, and watch it!"

"We all do, Missis!" said the baby weasel, retrieving his toffee and cramming it, now rather fluffy, into his mouth as he scuttled off.

Lady Stoat turned back to her sweeping. A house in the Wild Woods took as much work as Toad Hall, she was sure of that.

From the tiny front window she could see the whole neighbourhood. This was Number One, Daffodil Terrace. Further along the path were Bluebell Row and Cowslip Cottages. Didn't it sound nice and countrified, she thought bitterly. Cramped, dingy little holes they were, thin-walled and meanly built; draughty in winter, frowsty in summer and a fulltime job to keep clean. You couldn't keep your temper with 'em, hardly. No wonder the old 'uns drank and the kids played up and the menfolk were never home. As she swept, her thoughts turned again to Toad Hall...

"When we get to Toad Hall"... it was a story the Wild-Wooders told themselves year in and year out; a fantasy to keep themselves going, an impossibility shining bright amid the squalor. A fantasy of rich food on golden dishes, of beds piled high with feather quilts, of silk taffeta aprons to scrub the yard in and tiaras worn to go and fetch the coal. A fantasy of dainty picnics on well-kept lawns, with chilled drinks in crystal glasses, with bright rugs and well-stocked hampers – like that young Ratty when he went boating! It was a drudge's dream of being waited on by undefined yet willing drudges of one's own. "Maybe," said the dreamers, "the house would just clean itself, meals would appear bang on time and wash themselves up afterwards; windows would shine for the sheer fun of it and the lawn would grow to a precise quarter-inch then stop." You had to dream when your world was a nightmare.

This summer was different. Things had changed and the dream

At The House Called Beautiful

had progressed from a vague possibility to a worrying reality. Toad Hall, for the first time in its life, was empty. And empty, to the Wild Woods, meant "up for grabs". Fair do's, that were! Ol' Toady had no call to tangle with humans, no business taking to one of them nasty motors that made a noise and a stink and were a menace to all travellers. And stealing? Him being a rich gentleman, he'd no need to steal nothin'. Not like the Wild Wood, where you got by as best you could.

What else could the Wild-Wooders do? Their dreams had come alive, casting them off into a deep and uncharted current; could they navigate safely to shore? Could her Lord actually plan anything? With the lah-di-dah ferrets and them down-and-out weasels? She shook her head, took her sewing-box out again, and knelt to catch a split in the worn hearthrug.

The sun spilt golden shadows over the trees, and the late-summer dusk fell slowly. When she could see to work no more, she went to the fireside cupboard, cut a slice of bread and a slice of bacon, and set the frying-pan on the hob to be warming up. The bacon was for His Lordship, and half the bread was for her, dipped in the tasty, sizzling fat. He always had a hot meal to come home to at least.

"Can't complain at his feeding," she thought, as she laid the cloth and put out a jar of pickles.

He came home with a yell and a crash. Lady Stoat tried not to jump; nerves tried his temper. But tonight he was in tearing good spirits.

"Got a surprise for yer!" he grinned. "Get yer things, girl, we're movin' out!"

"Movin' out?" she gasped. The room swam. She had to sit down.

"Yeah, movin' out fer ever and ever! Come on – wot'yer sat there gawpin' at? Get yer clothes packed."

"Ain't we 'avin' tea first?" she asked faintly.

"Tea? Tea she calls it! A mis'able bacon butty, and she calls it tea. Don't make me laugh."

"Come on, love, I allus done me best with what we got..."

"And you've got your reward, my beauty! We're off to Toad Hall. Ol' Toady's gone fer good, so we're takin' our chance fer the good life. No more reasty ol' bacon fer you an' me, girl. It'll be Parma 'am on the finest, thinnest, whitest bread what's ever been made!"

"But...how?"

51

"We go up to the Hall and go and live there."

He spoke as if to a child, slowly and clearly. His joviality was fading. She frowned and bit her lip.

"Do you mean that?" she said. "Just walk in, you mean? What about Badger and his mates? He can get a bit funny, can Badger, I don't want him against us. Not with our kids to think of."

"Badger's getting past it" chortled Lord Stoat nastily. "He'll know which side his bread's buttered – there's enough old brandy in the Toad cellars to keep him well hibernated. We'll roll out the barrel and soon 'ave the ol' codger sorted out. And come what may, he'd never hurt the kiddies."

"He's got his friends, though."

"Oh yeah, so he has. I'm sure we're all terrified. A hippy-dippy poetical wimp of a Rat and a Mole who's so blind he's always falling in things and over things....do you know, he walked into a gatepost last week and actually begged its pardon! I nearly died!"

"There's Otter."

The Lord Stoat thought for a minute, scratching his whiskers. "Yeah, you're right," he said. "There is Otter. Well said. Still, he's a family man, him. Too bothered about 'is kids to act okkard. And we've already 'ad words with Badger and Mole. In the smoking-room, like the gentlemen we are." He grinned unpleasantly.

She stared. "Words?" she asked breathlessly. "How did you...?"

"Easy-peasy," he smirked. "Over the lawn we ambled, up to the French doors we strolled, an' there they were, two of 'em, snorin' their heads off by Toady's fire, with Toady's best Stilton on the table and a glass of Toady's best malt at their elbows. Disgraceful! So in we comes, our lot and the weasels, and liberates poor ol' Toady's house from them highly unlawful squatters. We shall have to move in while he's away, just to keep an eye on the place. It's our public duty." The Stoat guffawed, and his Lady managed a smile.

"It would be so nice to live somewhere decent. I just don't know what to think," she said, reflecting.

"You can stop thinkin' my girl, and start packin'," was the boisterous reply. "Pack all you really need and leave the rest. I'm takin' this blessed "tea" of yours to poor ol' Granny Weasel. Be ready when I comes back, or I just might leave you behind!"

He gave her a smacking kiss, grabbed the hot pan and slammed out. Quickly she rolled up her sewing-box in her best coat, folded the rest of her clothes into a basket with her mother's teapot nestling in the middle, damped down the fire and was ready when her Lord returned. He kissed her again and crooked

At The House Called Beautiful

his arm for her in a very lordly sort of way.

"Lord and Lady Stoat are now leaving!" he bellowed, and they stalked, heads high despite the bundles, down the length of the darkening Terrace.

Toad Hall, at first, was all they had promised themselves. It was a place of ornate but solid comfort, less fragile than Lady Stoat had secretly feared. But it was so big! So much empty, echoey space – and for what? Just for living in? Who could want all this room to themselves? The Wild-Wooders, who were used to dingy rooms and low ceilings, stood gazing around them, overwhelmed. Privately, each one felt an urgent desire to turn tail and flee; bravado and sheer pluck held them together. They were here now they'd made the decision, and there could be no turning back. Bags and bundles were dumped anyhow in the hall, and the occupation began in earnest.

There were arguments at first, mainly about bedrooms and hot baths, but soon the ladies were enjoying themselves immensely. Many of them had been in service and knew the ways of the rich; now they found larders hung with meat and game, and pantries full of pies, preserves and fine cheeses; there was bone china and there was silver cutlery; there were hot-house fruits and there was an excellent cellar. They produced banquets that fulfilled their wildest dreams, and fuelled even wilder nightmares. The old roof rang with song and shrill laughter. The Chief Weasel, who had a sharp and spiteful wit, wrote nasty new words to nice old tunes. His quick mind placed him at the head of the table, with the bigger, sturdier Stoat at his right hand and the educated but devious Ferret at his left. In those first, heady days they made a formidable team.

The housework was a different story. Coal had to be carried up endless stairs and ashes carried back down; short legs grew tired. Water had to be pumped and heated before anyone could have a wash; the range took hours of cleaning and black-leading. Shoulders ached and fingers were sore. Carven woodwork gathered dust; cobwebs were out of reach on the high ceilings; the spiders seemed to compete in festooning the chandeliers. Oak floors and wainscots needed constant polishing; silk hangings and small grubby paws did not mix. Children draped antique lace over antique tables to make dens, and then tried to light bonfires as if they were still out of doors. Fights, grizzles and yells echoed in once-tranquil studies and boudoirs; waxed corridors were buttered to make long, gleeful slides. The grownups, exasperated, slapped and scolded at random, then quarrelled among themselves over whose child had really done what.

As the season wore on, tempers wore thin. While the wives toiled, attempting to sink their own differences and share the labour, their lords lounged in the big leather chairs all day with their feet over the sides, drinking and smoking and telling loud jokes. Then they lounged through the evenings with their elbows on the big oak table, eating, drinking, smoking and telling loud jokes, and not once offering to lend a hand. The wives tried coaxing and cajoling and asking nicely for help or – at least – co-operation. It is hard to coax effectively when all one can see is a pair of slippers, a cloud of cigar smoke and a newspaper. Exhausted, they took to nagging their own husbands, criticizing each other's husband and generally getting cross. The tension became harder to bear than the actual work.

The bathroom was the chief battleground, for the mothers could never agree about bathing. How, they asked, could the Mistress Ferret need so much hot water? Did she really need a whole cake of soap and six clean flannels a day? Loftily she replied that her children were delicately bred and their fur was spotless, unlike some she could mention who never got washed at all. At this, Granny Weasel snarled that she could at least put all her children in the bath at once, unlike some she could mention whose brats were too fat to fit in a normal tub and "oughter be bathed in the fishpond". Mistress Ferret, preening her soft fur, suggested that the weasel children should be put into the fishpond and kept there; the old lady's temper flared into bad language. The Lady Stoat, who had been apprenticed to a laundress in her youth, was out of breath as she hauled a washing basket upstairs. Quietly she suggested that those who used the most should carry the most. This earned her a sneer from the Ferret and an approving cackle from Granny.

Left alone with a stack of linen to be sorted, she glanced into the gilt-framed bathroom mirror. She was tired. Her hard life had left her weathered and worn, but still comely; her new role was giving her new wrinkles, and her russet fur seemed to be turning grey. Here in the Hall she was living with, instead of beside, her neighbours. Back in the Wild Wood, they'd managed to rub along despite their differences; the womenfolk at least could turn away from trouble and close their front doors till tempers cooled and necessity had them back on speaking terms. The men, being men, sometimes bit chunks out of each other, but they were mostly chunks of fur; the squabbles were always over in a day or two. It was different here; there was no privacy, nowhere to hide, no respite from being seen at one's worst. Granny Weasel complained loud and long of being slighted – well, no wonder, considering the foul mouth and foul temper she had! And the Mistress Ferret,

At The House Called Beautiful

though an amusing and creative gossip, was vain beyond belief, and made a deal too much of her family's human connections. Lady Stoat shook her head and began sorting towels into the linen-press.

There was a cry from the garden, where the children's games were getting riotous; the Lady Stoat glanced out of the window, paused, then looked again as rich new colours caught her eye. The hedges were coming into full berry – fuller than usual in fact – and had ripened quickly over the last few days. This could presage a long, hard winter. She turned to the mirror and smiled; her reflection laughed back. Was she really greying with worry – or – could it be – would this be her season to shine? A hard winter would moult her into white ermine; by Yuletide she'd glitter like frost and shimmer like living snow. The poor old ferrets would look a bit beige and dingy beside a stoat family in their full winter pride!

She suddenly felt a lot better.

Not everyone shared her optimism. Days were drawing in, and food was certainly running out. Shopping had become a sad puzzle, for there was no actual money to be had, no hidden stores of gold; and the local shopkeepers knew them too well to allow them credit. Invoking Toad's name for the purpose resulted in the shopper being thrown bodily from the premises.

The Lord Stoat, on his own initiative, pawned the silver coffee-pot, which fed the children for another week. The kitchen gardens, once so productive, were now untended and unkempt; as the Chief Weasel remarked, if the Wild Woods took over the grounds, why, they'd all be less homesick! Vegetables bolted and ran to seed, for the Wild Wood had no tradition of gardening, and no-one could be bothered to learn. The fruit in the fine old orchards hung ripe unto harvest, and fights broke out over ladders and baskets and who had the right to climb first. The children swung nimbly in the trees, making dens and shelters, breaking branches in their careless play, gorging themselves with fruit until sick and queasy; throwing half-eaten apples at each other, at their elders and at the stained-glass windows of the Great Hall. It was obvious that, after the first fine extravagance, food would have to be rationed. Suspicion and selfishness replaced fun and feasting. Everybody was now watching everybody else as the old worries returned to ripen old resentments.

Granny Weasel was often to be found in the cellars. The vaults rang with her loud raucous singing and the children were told not to listen. She was, she claimed, checking and dusting the bottles, but the bottles were fast becoming empty, and she had to be helped to her bed most afternoons.

The Mistress Ferret, who had once been a head parlour maid, insisted on setting the sideboards and tables each day for afternoon tea. She was an excellent baker, and she worked wonders with her dwindling supplies, but she was sadly distressed by her housemates' reactions. Thin sandwiches, fragile biscuits and dainty cakes were gulped by the handful or used as missiles in youthful sport; the fine china got chipped and broken and the lace-edged napkins used as handkerchiefs, kites or pirates' flags. To her credit she kept her dignity, only retreating to the butler's pantry afterwards to cry in peace. Even there her privacy was not guaranteed, for the young stoats had found a squeaky floorboard, and spent hours trying to prize it loose with pearl-handled fish-knives.

"But, Missis," they would protest on being turned out, "if yer stamps on this bit it's all 'ollow underneath. Listen – bet there's a secret tunnel. That's where the treasure's been hid!"

"Out. Right now. The lot of you!" commanded Mistress Ferret. "If there was a secret tunnel the Master Ferret would know about it. And give over banging, I've got a headache!"

Operation Pantry Floor came to an end when the Lord Stoat pawned the fish-knives. Her vexation was mingled with relief at having one room, however small, to herself.

Lady Stoat now had the washhouse to herself every day, up to her ears in soap and bleach as she dealt with grimy, paw-printed towels and scrubbed wine and gravy off the huge damask tablecloths.

"How," she would grumble, "am I expected to keep my big lads in clean clothes when you lot won't even help me by eatin' a bit more tidy? Bloomin' Ferrets, with yer airs and graces, can't pour a glass without spillin' it – and I can always tell where you weasels 'ave sat, it's disgusting. You really do need someone to learn you yer manners!"

"Nothin' wrong with my kids' manners," snarled Granny Weasel. "It's you, getting all stuck-up and lah-di-dah like your fine friends the Festering Ferrets!"

In that she had just cause for resentment. The Mistress Ferret, convinced that diamonds would become her creamy-gold fur, had set the younger weasels on a fruitless search for the family jewels. The little animals, skinny and lithe, were made to squeeze under dusty wardrobes, into cupboards and presses, and through every box and bundle in the attics, only to emerge empty-handed, choking and miserable. Granny Weasel's temper erupted one hot day, and she flew snarling at the Master Ferret, who defended himself with a will. Gallantry was not part of the Wild Wood code;

At The House Called Beautiful

families joined in, and the fight grew nasty.

The youngest weasel ran to fetch Lady Stoat, knowing she could keep her head in a crisis. She dried her chapped paws on her apron and sent him upstairs to fetch a pair of the best sheets.

The Mistress Ferret appeared. The fight had run out of combatants, and the once-elegant animal was limping and splattered with blood. She leaned in the doorway, her head bowed.

"My stupid fault!" she gasped. "That fightin' was my fault, weren't it?"

"P'raps – but that Granny Weasel's the worst; can't keep 'er temper when she's had a few. You hurt, lovey?"

"The odd nip. Mostly off me ol' man, when I tried to pull 'im off Granny Weasel. She's an old lady, after all."

"She's got 'er family trained, though. Did you see them pile in mob-'anded? Wish my lot was that obedient."

Mistress Ferret snorted. "She's got 'em terrified of her, that's why!"

The baby weasel had returned, his arms full of bed sheets.

"Ah, here's me little helper," said Lady Stoat, patting his head. "What'yer found, Little'un? Ooh, Irish linen, that's just the job! Now fetch me my sewing-box, and mind the scissors. We'll need to cut this into bandages."

The weasel scurried off. The ladies exchanged a cautious smile.

"Best put the wounded in the morning-room," suggested Mistress Ferret, "plenty of daylight there, and a big fire."

"Good idea," agreed Lady Stoat. "It'll make the poshest field-hospital ever. I'll give me young'uns a shout; they can help set up some bedding."

It was late evening by the time the casualties were all cleaned, bandaged, stitched and bedded down by the handsome brick fireplace. The steady glow showed a dozen little faces, some drowsy with poppy juice and some still wrinkled in silent pain, but all snuggled into soft white pillows. The air was clean with scents of comfrey and lavender; but pervading all, urging itself upon the animals' sharp senses, was the smell of fear, anger and shock.

After tonight there could be no real peace.

"It's just not working," whispered the Master Ferret as his wife crouched at his bedside. "We could none of us stand each other in the Wild Wood, so why should we now in Toad Hall?"

"I don't know," she replied sadly, "I should have been so happy, but I felt bad because I wasn't. This is what we've dreamed of all these years, and now we've got it we can't cope with it – all the space and big rooms, all the baths and soap, all the lace and silver and the beautiful things and all the great long history of the place – all what we wanted when we lived in them poky little holes. What went wrong?"

"It was us what went wrong," sighed the Lady Stoat. "We dreamed and dreamed, and then we took the chance and acted out our dreams, but we just didn't think."

There was a tug at her apron. The baby weasel stood there, swaying on his little legs and yawning.

"How's me Gran?" he enquired anxiously.

"We'll have to see, my dear," she replied softly. "If she makes it through tonight there's a chance she'll get better. And then she'll have you fetching and carrying all day, so you'll need your sleep. Off to bed, now! This minute! Grrrrrr!"

She laughed and made a pretend growl at him, and he pottered away.

The days that followed saw changes at Toad Hall. Most of the mothers wanted their own front door, as they said, and their kids wanted what they were used to. They left very quietly by ones and twos. The weasels requisitioned a handcart, and bore their Granny home in a kind of dismal triumph. She would never walk again. However she could still give orders; the Hall could hear her right down the lane. The weasel menfolk soon made their way back.

As the year went on, Toad Hall became a fortress. It became known that Toad had escaped – done a runner – and with the connivance of humans! That in itself was an insult not to be borne by the Wild-Wooders. Toad, it was decided, must never return! Plans were quickly made; guards were mounted, troops were drilled and a crude discipline obtained. The Lord Stoat, free from his wife's influence, bore himself with a brutal swagger, and assumed command. He was a shrewd organizer, and knew his men. The stoats took over the outdoor patrols, with the quicker weasels as lookouts and sentries. The ferrets' despised human background now showed itself to advantage; they were all excellent shots. The Great Hall had now become a Mess in both senses; unswept fragments piled around the fine old chairs until carried off by commando-raids of mice, rubbish was flung pell-mell into the cluttered and smoking fire, beds were unchanged, sinks left to block up and overflow, ashes were never taken out and nobody bothered to wash. The stench was indescribable.

One fine cool morning, a weasel sentry reported to the Deputy Stoat.

At The House Called Beautiful

"'Scuse me, boss," he grinned. "Yer know that ol' washerwoman who's been hanging round on the off-chance. You won't believe what she's told me about tonight."

"What about tonight?" asked the Deputy.

"Well," said the weasel, "she reckons that we're gonna be invaded at the Feast. Ratty and Mole and ol' Badger have brought all their families and relations and got 'em all armed to the teeth. She said she knew for a fact that..."

A nearby window opened. The Lord Stoat had sharp hearing. He also had a bad head from the night before. He leapt over the sill, cuffed his Deputy to the ground and dragged the weasel into the conservatory.

"Right, lad", he snarled. "You were saying?"

The weasel, trembling with fear and importance, told his story.

"We're getting raided tonight, are we?" Lord Stoat's voice was ominously quiet.

"Yessir, yer lordship. Our Chief's birthday bash, tonight, innit," replied the weasel.

"An invasion force of moles, rats and badgers?"

"Yessir, yer lordship," smirked the sentry. "With weapons!"

"Weapons?"

"Weapons, yer lordship. You know – guns and knives and cudgels and – OW, that hurt!"

"Rats and moles did you say, lad? MOLES? A company of MOLES? An invasion force of timid, hen-witted, shovel-handed, short-sighted MOLES?"

"Well," shivered the weasel, "that's what the old girl said..."

"GET OUT! FAST!"

The weasel got out fast.

The Lord Stoat called his deputy.

"You heard all that," he barked. "What d'yer make of it?"

"Dunno, Chief. Could be all moonshine. Or gin, if I know washerwomen," shrugged the Deputy.

"Double the guard for tonight, Deputy. Specially the front door and the main drive. Better inform the Chief Weasel, too. Well, jump to it, man, I've got a speech to write!" snapped the Stoat.

The Deputy saluted and walked off. Had it been up to him, he would have guarded the back premises and the scullery yard and, thinking on what his young'uns had told him, he'd have put a few bright lads in the butler's pantry – but his ear still ached from that last blow.

Ma Weasel
by Ruth Sheppard

Big'un Weasel stood beside the kitchen range, his mouth watering with pleasurable anticipation of the fragrant bacon and the sizzling doorsteps of fried bread that Ma was carefully turning in the frying pan. Ma was speaking in her most formal, authoritative, maternal voice; Ma was displeased. Her rapid movements, accompanied by the banging of the large kettle of hot water that always stood at the back of the hob, and at ground level the swish of her many petticoats, issued a warning fit to make any self-respecting young weasel shiver in his boots. Big'un was already feeling sorry for himself but he resolved to just stand and take his medicine without first licking the spoon; he was in for a wigging, and he feared Ma's vituperative tongue.

Ma disapproved loudly. "Do you mean to stand there and tell me that you and that lazy gang of louts you always hang around with entered Toad Hall, in the absence of the gentleman owner, and took over the place? That you caused havoc in that beautiful residence, ransacking and destroying all Mr Toad's priceless possessions? I am ashamed of you, truly ashamed, and I never thought I would say that about my eldest son.

"How could you disgrace your poor mother in this fashion? I was in good service there for many years before I married your father, I'll have you know. Mr Toad's dear old mother, Lady Toad, indeed such a fine lady, was exceedingly kind to me, taking in this poor homeless girl, making a position for her. I was her lady's maid, looking after her exquisite gowns; how I loved the satins, the delicate Nottingham lace she was so fond of, hanging them carefully in her closet, and putting the shoe trees into her dainty kid leather slippers. I am proud of that time I spent waiting on that gentlewoman, and it was my privilege to see the gentry with all their costly jewels, their beautiful gems. She treated me more as a daughter than as a serving girl, and you and your good-for-nothing, hobble-de-hoi friends unlawfully enter that lady's beautiful dwelling, now the home of her dear son, and you create uproar, and damage the beautiful furnishings, the treasured and priceless portraits.

"And you expect me to stand here, cooking your breakfast, and let you get away with such grossness. Well, young ne'er-do-well, you will not get off scot-free this time. I won't stand for it; I simply will not tolerate the dishonour you have brought upon the good name of this respectable weasel family.

"You will call on Mr Toad this very morning, and you will grovel if that is necessary, and you will attempt to make good as much of the appalling damage as you can, and you will not return home until I hear from Mr Toad that this has been done.

"I have known him since he was a mere baby, and for all his bluster he is a gentle and forgiving soul. I know he is a hothead, but underneath all that false show of exuberance there beats a heart of pure gold. He will probably let you off lightly. I will not."

Big'un hung his head even lower and, in a cowardly manner he knew would appal his mother, began blaming his accomplices.

The young weasel said, "Uncle thought up the plan, and, well, he is the Chief Weasel. I didn't dare answer him back, or openly defy him, even though I knew you would be disappointed in my behaviour. I am so sorry, Ma. I promise I will do anything you ask of me to make amends. And Mr Badger and his friends, well they did come at us with swords and pistols, and some of the young weasels were badly hurt, even some of the younger stoats, and at least one of the ferrets had blood on his neck. I know our behaviour was wicked, but they were not blameless either."

Ma retorted angrily, "Don't you dare try to blame your shocking behaviour on other animals. They did not twist your paws to do it, did they? You acted of your own free will. You will go up to Toad Hall this afternoon and offer any assistance you or any of the other young weasels are able to give. And I will deal severely with that younger brother of mine. Honestly, doesn't he know that to be elected Chief Weasel is the highest honour that can be placed upon one of our breed? I cringe when I think of the shame he has brought on the sacred memory of our Wild Wood ancestors." Ma continued, as she furiously batted bacon and fried bread with a set of tongs, "I don't want your little sisters and brothers to hear this sorry tale. You are supposed to set them a good example, not a diabolical one. The Wild Wood has always been the loveliest place in the world to live and I will not let you spoil it for them – for any of us. How will this family ever live down such a shameful blight on our good name?"

Big'un did not enjoy one morsel of his breakfast, even though Ma was renowned throughout the Wild Wood for her tasty dishes; and bacon and fried bread were by far his favourite foods.

Ma continued to cook huge plates of breakfast for her large family of little weasels, but as she thumped the pans on the shining hob the light of battle also shone in her eyes, and even Big'un felt a touch of compassion for that venerated gentleman, the Chief Weasel, who would be obliged to eat humble pie when his angry big sister caught up with him.

Littl'un, the smallest member of the whole, large, extended

Ma Weasel

weasel family had been hiding behind the cushions on the day bed. He had long ago realised that this was the best hiding place, if you wished to learn the secrets of the strange, terrifying world of grownups. He had seen Pa giving Ma an affectionate kiss before he left for work each morning, and yesterday he had watched Ma shorten the hem of his pretty sister's best gown as she stood and slowly circled, on newspaper spread on the kitchen table, while Ma, her mouth full of pins and with a wooden foot-long rule in her hand, had measured exactly the distance from the table to the bottom of the hem.

He cuddled up close to Ma's patchwork counterpane; he knew because Ma had told him frequently, from his earliest days, that this was made from scraps of fabric Ma had gleaned from her time as a lady's maid, and each pane represented a gown that demonstrated the rich fabric of life in Toad Hall. This was a snippet from Lady Toad's ball gown, when they attended a grand reception at the palace, and that stunning black and white piece in the corner there was from Lady Toad's Ascot suit. Just look at that dear snippet of crimson velvet, at the bottom there; Mr Toad's sisters had party dresses made from that when they were young. Ma's normally sharp dark eyes would mist over and her glance become soft as she remembered the fine gowns of her youth, although not even one of them had been hers. He knew the most prized snippets were the corner panes, once snowy white, now showing the yellow edges of age and much handling; these were Ma's treasured memories of Mr Toad's sisters' wedding gowns. One had married an ambassador to a country in the distant reaches of the Empire, the other made do with a very rich husband. The present incumbent of Toad Hall was unmarried, but always stated that was because he had not met the right lady yet.

Ma continued to elaborate on the charms of the current Mr Toad and closed her eyes and her ears to the commonly held view that he was a gossip and a fool, however well-intentioned he may be. To Ma he would always be the precious baby toad she had sung lullabies to all those years ago.

But Ma was seething, as Littl'un well knew. He could tell by the haste with which she undertook her daily chores, how she noisily bounced the washed pans down on the hob, so that they would not dry rusty, and the way she called her daughters to come briskly and help with the housework. He felt a brief pang of pity for his stylish, dashing uncle, the Chief Weasel, the darling of all the young weasel maidens, a hero to the young bloods, he who would feel neither stylish nor dashing when Ma had finished her harangue.

Littl'un considered it pertinent to hide under the safety of Ma's counterpane just a little longer; he had no wish to arouse Ma's ire, fearing she may accuse him of snooping on a conversation that was none of his business. He did not envy his big brother his trip to Toad Hall.

Big'un dawdled through the tidy village where the weasels had lived since time immemorial, past the cluster of tiny cottages which leaned against each other for support. Weasels are social creatures and thrive in close harmony with their own kind, but they keep themselves to themselves and have no wish to be noticed by other animals; their cottages blend into the countryside. Here on the border of the Wild Wood, where the heartsease-edged pastures end and the glorious, green wood begins, the village had grown over eons of time until it seemed to have now become as one with the pastures and with the Wild Wood.

Big'un dreaded that his interview with Mr Toad could place him before a magistrate, as it was rumoured Mr Toad's own activities had so recently done for that gentleman himself.

Big'un knew he was guilty, and a feeling of intense embarrassment caused him to walk with his eyes lowered. The swaggering young vagabond that had joined so willingly in the antics of a wild gang of miscreants was a reformed creature as he skirted the stubble pasture, keeping to the protective shadow of the Wild Wood, on his way to Toad Hall. He promised himself that from this day forward he would never disgrace Ma again.

As he approached the noble mansion, his refined nostrils took in the fragrance of freshly split deal and the sharp odour of new paint; the thuds of hammering and the rhythmic peal of sawing hung in the early morning air.

When he introduced himself to Mr Toad that gentleman refused to believe ill of the pathetically sorry young creature. He truly admired Ma Weasel, and he was sure that her son was merely a mischievous youngster who had overstepped the mark. Mr Toad's eyes softened as he recalled being rocked to sleep while Ma Weasel had sung lullabies about golden slumbers, and her gentle paws had stroked his scaly cheek. All his life Mr Toad had felt secure in his comfortable home, amongst a loving family and with his many friends. Ma Weasel had been part of that security when both of them were many years younger than today. He made a mental note to give the young weasel a small gift for his mother, in remembrance of Mr Toad's own mother, who had always thought Ma Weasel to be a jolly fine servant girl. He was well aware that young ones will get up to mischief given half a chance; his own history most surely illustrated that point.

Mr Mole and Mr Rat were not nearly so ready to forgive; and Mr

Badger snorted down his snout and lumbered out of the room, totally unprepared to listen to such pathetic nonsense. The weasels had always been nuisances as far back as he could remember, which was some considerable time. This young jackanapes was just another unpleasant member of the weasel clan.

Mr Rat suggested, carefully counting the tasks on his claws, "Perhaps Big'un could give a hand with the sawing, after which he could remove the broken furniture to the fence line where the carrier's cart will collect it late this afternoon. Then perhaps he could paint, polish, clean the windows, hang the washing, iron, make beds, peel the potatoes, and clear the back garden of deal shavings and paint pots."

Mr Mole finally added that, if he had any time left after that, then Mr Toad needed some firewood chopped and the kitchen grate blacked.

Mr Badger, of whom Big'un was terrified, stalked off to supervise the renovations of the conservatory, with a cross "Humph, I shall believe it when I see it. Young weasel, I just hope none of your scatterbrained friends are hiding in the woods, just waiting to attack us harmless old animals." Big'un was duly shocked at the suggestion. Moreover, Mr Badger was a very large animal, and Big'un doubted that he was entirely harmless, although Big'un realised respect was due because of Mr Badger's obviously great age.

Mr Toad said, "Young weasel, do join me in a scone and some blackberry preserve before you commence your labours. And under no circumstances must you tire yourself out. Ma Weasel would never forgive me if I sent you home exhausted. Oh, and I must tell you about my brief introduction to the horse dealing industry, it is such an adventure and your mother will so enjoy listening to the thrilling details. Also, she would love to hear the exciting tale of my wrongful imprisonment at the hands of stupid oafs. I sneaked out when no one was looking of course, and claimed my rightful freedom. Oh no, they were not able to keep Mr Toad prisoner against his will. I fooled them all, which was amazingly easy to do."

Mr Badger's glowering countenance confirmed to both raconteur and listener that such fanciful storytelling was highly inappropriate. Under Mr Badger's withering glance Mr Toad retired to his study to arrange payment for the workmen, and Big'un left hurriedly in the direction of the broken furniture piled in the back garden.

The sun had settled behind the western hill, and the birds were busy tucking their young into cosy nests before Big'un had finished his many chores. During the afternoon he had been joined by a number of his contemporaries, sent to Toad Hall by their ashamed mothers, who, at the urging of their angry neighbour, had cleared the village street of youngsters. Each young weasel had been sent on his way with the kind of maternal admonition that was often referred to amongst the mothers as receiving "a flea in the ear".

With good grace the youngsters had joined Big'un in the many tasks of appeasement he was required to perform, so that the setting sun saw a neat and tidy Toad Hall, with most of the broken walls patched and repainted, and glass shining in the formerly shattered windows. The interior of the majestic mansion shone with huge applications of spit and polish. The carrier's clattering cart, loaded with its pile of broken furniture, was long gone in the direction of the town.

Mr Toad would not allow the young weasels to leave his home without hospitably offering them a hearty drink of lemonade and some doorsteps of newly baked bread spread liberally with best butter and blackberry preserve. He had secretly hoped that someone would propose "three hearty cheers for Mr Toad," but no-one had, and he wasn't sure how to drop the appropriate hint. Besides, he knew that this would rouse the disapproval of Mr Badger again. He called Big'un to one side and gave him a small brooch – not valuable, but pretty and memorable – as a gift for his dear mother. Mr Toad had also managed to find a length of fine lace stuffed away in one of Lady Toad's old cabin trunks. Oh, they had travelled far and wide in the old days! He was sure that Big'un's young sisters might just be able to use the lace, as he knew that Ma Weasel would have trained her daughters to be, above all, fine needlewomen.

Mr Rat and Mr Mole waved the young workers on their homeward journey. Mr Rat said, "You really should spend more time beside the river; your woodland is so deep and mysterious, and the beauty and the freedom of the open waterways will teach you much about another way of life, different to the dark secretive Wild Wood."

Mr Mole said, "I hope you young scoundrels do not abuse the good faith Mr Toad has obviously placed in you; it is truly marvellous that he feels you are worthy animals, so please do not prove him wrong. You must all toil towards bringing the good name of weasels to its former dignity."

Mr Badger said little. It was not that he did not think the young weasels capable of repairing the damage to their family name; it was more that, in his day, young blinders would not have dared to behave in such an outrageous fashion because they would have feared the disapprobation of their parents. He despaired of the younger generation. Sometimes he feared that the world would come to no good. He told himself, however, that he was prepared to be pleasantly surprised.

The loyal friends stood outside Toad Hall's gatehouse, waving their handkerchiefs at the departing clan of weasels, resolving that for the rest of their lives they would never be prepared to draw arms against another animal.

Trudging away from the river towards the Wild Wood, the young weasels strolled arm-in-arm, sometimes singing marching songs, as it was a lengthy distance, and sometimes just talking quietly amongst themselves, acknowledging they were to blame for the damage they had caused and that they would not be so easily led in the future. They still had their angry mothers to confront; it was not a pleasant thought. Mr Badger, Mr Rat and Mr Mole were "child's play" compared with the parental ticking-off that awaited them. Weasel mothers were well-known throughout the Wild Wood for refusing to brook ill-behaviour in their offspring. The young weasels were too tired after the day's toil to consider frolicking in the countryside; so it was a restrained and orderly pack that slowly wended its way through the gloaming.

Soon they came to the village, where the chamomile scented pastures edged upon the silent, looming gloom of the Wild Wood. Eventide had settled over the woodland, and the flower-strewn walks between the beeches and elms were now the murky territory of the owls. The stillness of new darkness, when all daytime creatures seek their rest, reigned until the nightjar's rowdy protest broke the silent peacefulness.

Lamplight gleamed through the casement windows of the cottages, throwing elongated shafts of golden radiance at regular intervals onto the darkened village street, but Big'un noted that his uncle's house by the village green was in darkness. No light showed. That powerful leader, the Chief Weasel, had retired early, to metaphorically lick the wounds inflicted on his overweening arrogance by his older sister's vitriolic censure, and to compose a personal apology to Mr Toad. The Chief Weasel still regarded that gentleman as an overbearing snob and a dandy, but he shamefully admitted to his sister that he and his cohorts had no right to enter Mr Toad's property and he was aware that he must acknowledge his responsibility as their leader. He did not imagine for one moment he would be supported in this matter by the Chief Stoat, or indeed the Chief Ferret. The realisation of this home truth represented an important catalyst in his life; he must learn to stand on his own feet if he were to be a competent leader, and if that meant acting independently, then so be it.

Big'un could hear his sisters singing a popular ditty in harmonious unison, as they sat beside the lamp and hemstitched towels to add to Ma's ever growing stock of spotless household linens. Littl'un, who had been put to bed early, grizzled softly in his darkened bedroom. He had wanted to stay up long enough to hear of his big brother's adventures at Toad Hall. Sometimes life for a young weasel was so unfair!

The next morning Littl'un rose early, but he did not eat his breakfast. Ma thought her youngest son was sleeping late; life in the family had been overpowering during the last few days, and she reckoned that it may have taken its toll on the smallest family member.

But Littl'un refused to be thwarted. If he was to take his place in weasel society eventually, he would need to know of every action and every reaction that occurred in the vibrant life of the weasel village. Some day he planned to be Chief Weasel, and today was not too soon to start learning the ways and means. One day he would be the equal of Mr Toad, frightening Mr Badger, and those two likeable gentlemen, Mr Rat and Mr Mole. He would visit Toad Hall by invitation, and would bring his Ma interesting tales of the life of her old home, which he knew she loved so much.

Unbeknown to Ma, he had tucked himself safely out of sight, under Ma's counterpane. He intended hearing every word that was spoken while the family breakfasted, even though he knew Ma would admonish him that it was none of his business, and that eavesdroppers never hear well of themselves.

After breakfast, his two middle sisters set to with brooms, followed by much dusting and polishing, and his youngest sister seated herself on the front doorstep to shell a basin of peas and to watch the world go by, the door standing open to air the cottage and to allow the morning sunlight to brighten the rooms. She suddenly exclaimed in great excitement, "Ma, we have visitors!"

Littl'un awoke with a start. He really had not intended to doze off. Well, he must be careful to stay alert. They had few visitors at the cottage. He must ensure he missed nothing.

Ma straightened her snowy mob cap, hid the stray kiss curl that would escape no matter how she tried to keep it in order, made sure her apron was still pristine, and went to welcome the visitors to her parlour. Her two daughters, busy cleaning in their duck overalls, quickly slid out of sight. It was a capable housewife who welcomed Mr Rat, Mr Mole, and Mr Badger into her spotless, orderly cottage.

They accepted the offer of morning tea, served on the willow pattern china that Lady Toad had given Ma Weasel as a wedding present, because she had loved it so much. Somewhere at the back of the larder was hidden a tin containing almond buns, fresh as if taken from the oven that morning. Snowy napkins, edged with the lace she learned to crochet in her days at Toad Hall, lay beside the dainty plates.

Mr Rat hurrumphed, "Dear lady, it is well to find you in such fine fettle; and your husband, may we conclude that he also enjoys excellent health? We have inflicted our company on your good self because we wish to discuss the future of that young scallywag."

Mr Rat continued, "He just cannot go round causing mayhem the way he did two nights ago. He will be arrested, and no good will come to him. It is a dreadful life for a young weasel in gaol. Bread and water, you know, and no sunlight or fresh air." Mr Rat seemed well-versed in the day-to-day details of prison life.

Mr Badger said, "Time to learn a smidgeon of responsibility for his own outcomes, he cannot always rely on others. He must be accountable for his own actions." Large Mr Badger looked extremely uncomfortable in the tiny parlour. He just did not fit.

"As I am sure you know, Mr Toad is fond of motor-cars," said Mr Rat. Yes, Ma had seen one once, when she went down to Pangbourne to visit her sister. She was aware that Big'un was knowledgeable about motor-cars, and enthusiastic too. She just reckoned that it takes all sorts to make a world. Big'un had said everyone would have a motor-car, way ahead in the future. She doubted it.

"The trouble is," continued Mr Rat, "because of well...laws...Mr Toad is just not permitted to drive motor-cars himself."

"He actually needs the services of a chauffeur," said Mr Mole, taking up the main narrative.

"Your eldest son seems a bright chap, in spite of his recent misdemeanours," Mr Badger pontificated from his comparative great height. "Mr Toad was unable to accompany us today as he has a prior engagement." Actually the friends had almost been forced to imprison Mr Toad in Toad Hall; he had spluttered and argued, and said that he knew Ma Weasel was longing to see him, as they had not met in a long time, and he knew how much she yearned for his delightful company and his witty, sparkling conversation. The three friends had decided during a previous meeting that the company of Mr Toad, with his kick-ck-cks and poop poops, would not aid the serious nature of their interview with Ma Weasel. Mr Toad had stayed willingly in the end, with his works ledger opened before him, but only because they threatened to tie him up and lock him in.

Mr Badger said, "He would, of course, be expected to treat his employer with humility and respect, but we are sure, dear lady, that you have taught him appropriate behaviour in the presence of his elders. He would be provided with a uniform to wear during motor-car journeys, and overalls to keep himself clean while he maintains the motor-car. Mr Toad has a large number of tools in his spacious garage." Mr Badger waved his paw airily and continued, "Undoubtedly your son would understand the mystery of motor-car tools. I must say that for myself, I do not."

Mr Badger continued, "He would receive the appropriate wage, which would, of course, be paid to your good self, so that you could undertake a savings plan for his future." He edged uncomfortably towards the oak settle. He would have liked to sit down, but he was not at all sure the settle would withstand his weight.

Ma Weasel was rendered speechless. There was little left for her to say. Her Big'un with a career! She could just imagine Big'un in a grey melange uniform, with a peaked cap. Oh, she would be the envy of all the other weasel mothers. Thankfully, some good appeared to have resulted from the shameful antics of the weasel gang. And he would have the privilege of a home in Toad Hall – that was the best thing of all. Oh, she loved that beautiful mansion.

It was decided that at Michaelmas Big'un would commence in Mr Toad's employ. There was the slightest hint that Mr Toad may need maids in the future, and Ma Weasel grew inches taller with pride as she considered the idea of her daughters as maids; maybe they would be sewing maids or parlour maids, and if that fine gentleman ever did marry, then maybe even a lady's maid. She would revisit her girlhood vicariously through her beautiful daughters. Her family's future appeared before Ma Weasel in a lovely, comfortable daydream, edged with a rosy glow.

Littl'un was exceedingly hungry, but he could hold out; now was not the time to interrupt such important proceedings with babyish pleas for titbits. His future flashed before him as a rosy vision. He would be the Chief Weasel, with family contacts within Toad Hall, the finest house in the county. Perhaps one day he could have his own motor-car, and even employ his own chauffeur. He hid further beneath the patchwork counterpane; he had so much to think about, being the leader of the well-respected weasels, famous throughout the Wild Wood; that was a daydream that needed patient consideration. Littl'un promised himself Ma Weasel would be justly proud of her youngest son, and the good name of the Weasel clan would continue forever.

Encore
by Jennifer Moore

It was summer once more. The river gurgled lazily beside verdant green banks, lolling along with a sparkling joy and an easy contentment. Fat insects buzzed drunkenly across its path, weaving in and out of the swollen-headed bulrushes.

The Mole lay back in the boat, staring dreamily up at the cerulean sky, making pictures from the thin wisps of cloud that hovered in the blue.

"That one looks a little like a dragonfly. A white misty dragonfly. Or maybe it's more of a hammer. What do you think Ratty?" said Mole.

"Hmm?" came the vague reply. As the Water Rat drew the oars rhythmically through the water his mind was otherwise occupied, trying to find a suitable word to rhyme with "Otter" that would do his old friend justice. But it was a hot, lazy afternoon, and his head felt so delightfully heavy and warm that the rhymes just weren't coming as easily as they should. All he could think of was "rotter", which wasn't the right kind of rhyme at all. "Potter", he mumbled to himself. "No that's no good. Otter simply isn't the pottering kind. Stotter... totter... wotter. Yes that might just do it."

And now the weather's hotter,
  We know where we'll find Otter,
There! Quick as a flash
  With a lightening splash,
Diving beneath the wotter.

No, no, that's no good at all. Nobody says wotter. At least, nobody with any sense."

"Hello there," said a sleek head surfacing alongside the boat in a stream of bubbles. "Watch where you're going with that thing, Ratty. You're all over the place today."

"Ah Otter," said the Water Rat, sitting up a little straighter in his seat. "Sorry, old chap. Lost in thought. I was thinking about you in fact."

"Hello Otter," said the Mole, heaving himself back up into a sitting position. "A glorious day isn't it? We were just on our way to see Toad."

Otter grinned. "Don't tell me he's up to his old tricks again. What is it this time, then? Motor-boats? Horse riding? Ballooning? What's the latest? I must say it's been very quiet around here since his latest adventures. That stunt with the stoats and weasels seems to have taken it out of him rather. But I suppose it was only a matter of time."

"No, nothing like that," said the Rat. "I believe he's kept to his word this whole year. A reformed creature is old Toady."

"He did have the tennis court built last month," piped up the Mole. "But the game proved a little energetic for his liking." He lowered his voice: "Between us three, I think he fancied the white shorts would make him look sporty and dashing." The animals shared a smile as they shook their heads. It was an indulgent kind of smile such as a mother might give a child who is truly sorry for a minor misdemeanour. "Dear old Toad," sighed Mole.

"We're actually on our way to ask him a favour," said the Rat. "Badger wants to borrow that old gypsy caravan of his for a family of hedgehogs who are currently homeless. Turns out they'd been living in a...", his voice dropped to a low whisper, "bonfire." A collective shiver ran through the three animals, despite the warm sun beating down on their fur. A nice cosy fire in the hearth is one thing, ideal for toasting marshmallows and warming oneself on chilly winter nights, but a bonfire is another creature altogether.

"Thank goodness they got out in time," said the Otter, suddenly filled with an irrational yet urgent desire to check on his own family. "Must be off," he added, turning swiftly in a tight circle and disappearing back into the water with a speed and grace that never failed to impress the Mole, leaving only the telltale trail of bubbles in his wake.

The two friends continued on down to Toad Hall in companionable silence, clouds and poetry all but forgotten. The Mole was thinking of the two young hedgehogs he had met at Badger's house on that first terrifying trip into the Wild Wood. Of course they were both a good deal older now, but he shuddered nonetheless to think of two such young creatures in mortal danger. The Water Rat, meanwhile, was attempting to steer his mind away from unwanted thoughts of vicious flames licking at dry wood, by concentrating on his plans for dinner. Both he and the Mole had declared themselves so full after their huge luncheon of French bread, cheese, potted ham (two plates worth for Mole), salad, gherkins, fresh raspberries and apple pie and cream to follow, that for a time it seemed as if their appetites might never recover. But as he forced himself now to conjure up a suitable dinner menu – a light tomato salad, perhaps, with maybe a cold sausage or two on the side, and just the teensiest sliver of leftover pie – the Rat felt his still full stomach stretch and smiled a little in anticipation.

Encore

They glided gently up the creek towards Toad's boat-house and moored. Clambering back out of the boat onto dry land, they caught sight of a pair of puffed-up peacocks strutting across the emerald green lawns towards the deserted tennis court.

"Looks like Toad's taken up bird-keeping," smiled the Mole. "Maybe Otter was right. Perhaps he's slipping back to his old ways after all."

"Nonsense," said the Rat firmly. "I have every faith in him. Trust me, Moly, if you'd known him as long as I have, you'd realise he's a completely reformed character. Twelve months it's been now without the merest sniff of a new obsession. He's really turned over a new leaf this time."

"Apart from the tennis court and peacocks of course," said the Mole quietly to himself, not wishing to argue the matter out loud and risk offending the Rat. "Although I suppose a healthy interest in new projects is no bad thing in itself. All things in moderation and all that..."

Inside the great house all was quiet save for a muffled banging sound coming from the banqueting hall. The two friends followed the soft thuds and the occasional theatrical cough through the great doors, to find themselves face to face with what appeared to be a stage. The near end of the hall had been given over to neat rows of plush red velvet seats, all facing towards the heavily draped platform at the far end.

"Toad?" called the Mole, studiously avoiding his companion's eye lest his expression should appear too I-told-you-so-ish. "Are you there? It's me, Mole," he added, somewhat redundantly, "and Ratty. There's something we want to ask you."

The stage curtains parted an inch or so. Toad's left eye peered carefully out at them.

"Just the fellows I want to see," he boomed. "Take a seat, why don't you? Front row. I'm just putting the finishing touches to my costume."

The Rat sighed heavily as he sat down. The Mole, guessing what was on his friend's mind, did his utmost to cheer him up.

"I'm sure you're right Ratty. This is nothing like the old days. This is...." He opened up his arms and turned around to take in the whole room, as if hoping to find the right word in one of the far corners. "This is nothing like motor-cars," he said at last. "At least no one can get hurt in a theatre. It's just a bit of harmless fun, that's all."

"I wouldn't count on it," muttered the Rat grimly.

"Really," went on the Mole, trying hard to recall his own

73

The Wind In The Willows Short Stories

thoughts on the subject, "a healthy interest in new projects is no bad thing in itself. All things in moderation and all that..."

A series of strangled trumpet notes sounded somewhere off-stage.

"Applause if you please," came the Toad's voice. The audience of two obliged with a half-hearted smattering of handclapping, as the Toad pulled back the curtain with a flourish. He was sporting crimson velvet knickerbockers with matching buttoned waistcoat and a starched ruff, stretched tight around his fat neck. In the crook of his left arm he was cradling what appeared to be a frog's skull.

"To be, or not to be," he cried. "That is the question..."

"The question," interrupted Ratty with a weary shake of his head, "is why you are wearing that ridiculous get-up? And exactly whose head is that you're carrying?"

"I think you'll find that's two questions actually," beamed the Toad, "but I'm more than happy to answer them both. As soon, that is, as I've finished my piece. I've been practicing all morning, so do be quiet and let me finish."

"Here we go again," sighed Ratty bitterly. "Otter was right. Same old Toad. If it's not boats, it's caravans. If it's not caravans, it's motor-cars. If it's not motor-cars, it's..."

"To be, or not to be?" cried the Toad again, slightly louder than before, "that is the question: Whether 'tis something ta da da something, the slings and arrows of outrageous fortune or... Oh bother and blast it! I've gone and forgotten it now. You've broken my concentration."

"Isn't that a shame?" said the Rat, a little meanly. "Oh well. On to business then." His dismissive, unfeeling manner took the Toad a little by surprise, but perhaps it was not as astonishing as all that. After all, no one likes to be made a fool of, not even a creature as kind and fair and generally well disposed towards his fellow animal as the Rat. At that precise moment he was struggling bravely to keep in check his less than charitable thoughts towards the stage-struck Toad. What he wanted desperately to say, in fact, was, "You are an ungrateful wretch. To think that I stuck up for you! I told them you were a changed animal, but you're still the same self-centred creature you always were." But he calmed himself down with a few deep breaths and forced himself to remember the real reason for their visit. "Mole and I," he said at last, "have come to ask you whether..." He stopped short, noticing the Mole's peculiar trance-like expression. "I say, Moly old chap, are you feeling all right? Did that last helping of potted ham disagree with you?"

Encore

"Oh my," sighed the Mole. "Oh my!"

"What is it?" asked Ratty. "Whatever's the matter?"

"That speech," said Mole, wiping away a tear from the corner of his eye. "Those lines. I've heard them before. My great uncle was an actor you know. He used to tell me such wonderful tales of his life on the stage." He gave a long, passionate sigh. "I'd forgotten until now. He promised to take me to the theatre when I was bigger only he, only he..." The Mole fell silent, staring sadly at an unseen spot upon the stage.

"There, there," said Rat kindly. "Don't go upsetting yourself, there's a good fellow." If he was at all surprised by his friend's unexpected revelation, he was a polite enough creature not to show it. After all, it is not the done thing to delve too deeply into an animal's past. The present is, for many, all that matters and, indeed, all that should matter, so long as one is willing and able to learn from one's mistakes along the way. Unlike the Toad.

"You mean it's in your blood?" gasped Toad. "But that's marvellous. You must come and help me. You can be my right hand Mole. I've got a list of jobs that need doing right here in fact." He pulled a long scroll of paper out of his waistband.

"That's quite enough, you unfeeling creature," Ratty told him sternly. "Can't you see the poor fellow's upset?"

"He was blinded by the spotlight," sniffed Mole. "You know how weak our eyes can be in bright light. He didn't see the trapdoor until it was too late."

"There, there," repeated Ratty. "Perhaps it's time we got you home," he said. "Too many sad memories here. You'll have to find someone else to humour you this time I'm afraid, Toad."

"Oh no," said the Mole. "I'll be fine. I was just a little overcome, that's all. I'd like to hear more. All those stories," he sighed wistfully. "Doomed heroes and bloody battles. Star-crossed lovers and great kings. Talking statues and–"

"The adulation of the audience," piped up Toad. "The smell of greasepaint, the roar and swell from the orchestra pit, the splendid speeches, the finely stitched costumes...ah yes, dear Mole. The theatre is the thing."

"Not motor-cars then?" goaded the Rat. "No more poop poop?"

"Certainly not," said Toad. "Noisy, vulgar things. I was blinded for a while but I've seen the light." He laughed. "I've seen the spotlight, you might say."

Mole sniffed again.

"You are quite possibly the most insensitive creature I've ever met," scolded Rat.

"A figure of speech," said Toad airily. "Moly here knows that, don't you? I think you'll find us theatre folk understand each other."

"He doesn't mean any harm," said the Mole.

"No," sighed the Rat. "He never does."

The Rat and Mole saw very little of each other in the days that followed. Rat had been helping to clean out the old caravan and settle the hedgehogs into their new home, while the Mole was up to his whiskers in theatrical preparations. The poor fellow was too exhausted by the time he arrived home each evening for much in the way of talking, although he was too generous a soul to even think about complaining. The Toad, it seemed, was keeping him extremely busy ordering programmes, painting scenery, overseeing the costumes, organising a small ten-piece orchestra and even coaching the extras, who kept forgetting their lines.

The Toad's own part in the preparations, meanwhile, appeared to be largely managerial. As he had explained to the Mole on more than one occasion, he didn't want to risk over-exerting himself physically before the opening night. As the undisputed star of the show (having failed to secure a worthy enough understudy), without him there would *be* no production.

The Mole himself was more than content with his promised two lines. He practiced them over and over in the mirror each morning before setting off for Toad Hall and another long day of chores. The other bit parts were to be taken by an assortment of stoats and weasels. It appeared that Toad was more than ready to overlook their having taken over his house in his darkest hour, and was currently employing forty or more of the most artistically inclined amongst their number, in a series of roles ranging from walk-on parts to High Court judges.

On the morning of the grand opening Mole was awake with the dawn, his stomach knotted tight with nerves and excitement.

"Oh my," he whispered to himself, wriggling his toes in anticipation as he lay listening to the soft gurgle of the river. "It's finally here. Tonight's the night." He lay there a few minutes more, thinking about his Great Uncle and how proud he would have been; about Toad's tales of thunderous applause and standing ovations; about the bagginess of his costume after too many days spent chasing around on errands and not enough time spent picnicking with the Rat. At last he stretched himself out as far as he could with one last excited wriggle that rippled through from the tips of his toes to the tip of his nose, before climbing out of bed.

Encore

"Oh my," he said again. "So much to do." He took a deep breath. "I need to pressmycostume, practicemylines, pickuptheprogrammes, rounduptheweasels, rallythestoats, checkthelighting, rehearsethemusicians, invitethepress, flowersforToad... Oh my. Oh my. Not a moment to spare."

"Are you all right Moly?" asked the Rat, as he entered the parlour a short time later to find the Mole attempting to press his waistcoat with a cold iron, muttering wildly under his breath.

"Ah yes, Ratty. All under control. Just practicing my lines one last time. *Who's that dashing young fellow racing past at the speed of lightening? Why, I believe it's the irresistible, irrepressible, irreproachable Mr Toad.*"

"Irresponsible Mr Toad, more like," sighed the Rat. "Irresponsible and irredeemable. I suppose he's got you doing all the hard work again, hasn't he, while he swans around in those ridiculous knickerbockers, lording it over everyone like he's the star of the show?"

"Oh, but he *is* the star," said the Mole earnestly. "He's got more lines than anybody. It's to be a dramatisation of his own adventures. Without him there'd *be* no show."

"A dramatisation of his adventures?" repeated the Rat.

"Oh yes," said Mole. "It *was* going to be Shakespeare, but Toad was worried the audience might be a little..." he dropped his voice to a guilty whisper, "...a little bored."

"Whereas *The Life of Toad* will be a thrilling spectacle for all, I suppose?"

"You mustn't be too hard on him, Ratty. After all, we didn't let him have his speech last year at the homecoming banquet. Not even one little song. And he's been working so hard on the script."

"Very well," sighed the Rat. "So long as it's clear that the only reason Badger and I are attending the performance is to support you. Speaking of which, why don't you let me finish pressing that while you have some breakfast? Can't have you rushing round all day on an empty stomach, can we?"

The Mole gave a grateful sigh. "Thank you, Ratty."

Having very little to do himself, the Rat dedicated the rest of the day to helping Mole with his errands. Together they made light work of Toad's list – with enough time to spare before Mole's dress rehearsal for a late lunch on the lawns of Toad Hall. A promising morning had ripened into another beautifully hot, blue-skied afternoon – perfect picnicking weather in fact, although it was not, in the event, one of their finest: A growing sensation of nervous excitement was playing havoc with the Mole's appetite (it was as much as he could do to manage four sandwiches, two gherkins, a slice of pie and an apple) and the peacocks laid siege to the picnic basket, making off with the last sandwich and a sizable piece of plum-cake, while the Water Rat's back was turned.

"I'd best be off then," said Mole when at last they had finished clearing away. He was hopping anxiously from foot to foot. "I'll see you and Badger after the show."

"Best of luck," said the Rat warmly, adding under his breath, "something tells me you're going to need it."

"It's 'break a leg'," the Mole told him.

"I'm sorry?"

"That's what you say to actors. For luck."

"Well it doesn't sound very lucky to me."

"No," agreed the Mole, thoughtfully. "I don't suppose it does. Still, I'm sure we'll be fine. It's going to be a memorable night. I just know it."

"Unforgettable, I fear," murmured the Rat.

"Oh, and thank you for today, Ratty. You've been such a help."

"No problem old chap," smiled Rat. He stood there a while, watching, as his friend tripped his way across the lawn towards Toad Hall, a peculiar bounce in his step. "I just hope, for your sake, this doesn't turn into another of Toad's disasters."

Mole had reserved front row seats for the Badger and Rat. They took their places and sat in silence, staring around the hall in wonder. Vivid murals had been painted along the wall panels – each depicting the Toad in a different scene of heroism, from the daring rescue of a beautiful maiden from a dragon's jaws, to a one-eyed, one-handed battle against the Spanish Armada. Beneath this last panel stood an elderly weasel, handing out programmes with a look of world-weariness. The heavy wooden shutters in the windows had all been drawn for the occasion, blocking out the soft evening sun. The hall was illuminated instead by an enormous chandelier above their heads, which sent its fractured light bouncing off the heavily draped stage to wonderful effect.

"Scarcely recognise the place," grunted the Badger.

"No," agreed Rat. "Toady's really gone to town this time."

"Won't last of course," Badger sighed.

"It never does. I can't say I'll be sorry when this one's over with. He's been running poor old Moly ragged."

"Too soft-hearted for his own good is Mole," said Badger in

Encore

such a fond tone that the statement seemed more like praise than criticism.

"Shhh, shhh, they're about to start," hissed the old weasel as the chandelier's lights were extinguished and the hall was plunged into darkness. From somewhere behind the Badger and Ratty came the sound of bodies tripping and bumping on chair legs, accompanied by a wounded chorus of "ow's" and "ouches".

The orchestra pit erupted in an excitable fanfare, violins skittering wildly above a loud trumpet call, as the heavy curtains parted to reveal the Toad spotlighted in the centre of the stage. He gave a deep bow and another and another.

"Get on with it," hissed a sharp voice from the back of the audience.

The Toad drew himself back up to his full height.

"Ladies and Gentleman," he boomed. "Thank you so much for coming to what promises to be a wonderful night. An extraordinary night. A night you will remember for the rest of your lives. A night to tell your children of and your children's children and–"

"Get on with it," the voice called again.

"Indeed," smiled the Toad, graciously. "So without further ado I give you 'The Marvellous Adventures of Mr Toad'." He gave another low bow and swept off the stage as a young chorus of stoats filed out of the wings singing:

May we present to you tonight
   Each glorious episode,
Each marvellous adventure
   Of the brilliant Mr Toad.

It's time the populace realised
   Just what a debt is owed
This modest champion in our midst –
   The heroic Mr Toad.

Through fearsome dangers dreadful
   Our plucky hero rode,
So lend an ear and raise a cheer
   For adventurous Mr Toad!

The Rat glanced down at his programme to see *Act 1, Scene 1 – Toad Hall – The Toad Outwits his Captors. The roles of Misters Toad, Rat, Mole and Badger to be played by Mr Toad.* When the lights went up again Toad was lying in the centre of the stage wearing a doleful expression.

"Oh have mercy on this hapless Toad," he cried. "Why, Badger, must I be kept here, a prisoner in my own home?"

Toad then leapt to his feet and stepped back addressing the spot where he had lain.

"Because I am a mean and pompous Badger," he announced in a gruff voice, "who cannot stand the thought of a fellow having a harmless bit of fun with his own motor-car."

Beside him Rat could feel the Badger stiffening with suppressed anger.

"And I," said the Toad now, raising his voice to a foolish squeaking pitch, "am just a simple Rat who does what he is told. If Badger says I am to guard you and keep you from a life of deserved happiness then that is what I shall do."

Rat snorted. "I don't talk like that. He sounds nothing like me."

"And I," went on the Toad, "am a mere Mole. It pains me to see such a marvellous creature kept so low but what can I do? I am of no consequence."

"That's not in the script," came the Mole's off-stage cry. "None of that is in the script."

"It is the actor's prerogative to improvise should the mood take him," replied the Toad airily. He dropped back down to the floor and raised a hand to his brow. "But what's this?" he said, returning to character. "The Mole and Badger are leaving Ratty in charge? Why it will be a small matter to outwit him! I shall feign illness and make my escape while he is fetching the doctor."

"Of all the ungrateful..." growled Rat. "He's making a laughing stock of us all."

"If his poor father were here today..." said the Badger with a sad shake of his head.

It was not, of course, the Toad's intention to bring distress to his friends, but simply to cast himself in the best light possible. It had occurred to him, somewhere between the dress rehearsal and the opening song, that an escape from well-meaning friends with one's best interests at heart is not as dramatically effective as an escape from tyrannical associates. There is, after all, nothing particularly heroic about a hero who tricks his dearest companions in an ungrateful act of deceit. As ever, the Toad did not pause to dwell on the consequences of his actions, but simply dived in headfirst, flinging out insults with a gay abandon in order to lend his own part in the story the sympathetic valour which was so lacking in the original.

Encore

Toad was not, however, the only actor to have decided upon some last minute alterations. The Mole, in his anger, was heard to cry, "*Who's that ungrateful creature racing past at the speed of lightening? Why, I believe it's the irresponsible, irredeemable, irritatingly obnoxious and conceited Mr Toad,*" in the wake of Toad's on-stage motor-car, to great applause from his friends in the front row. The stoats and weasels meanwhile dispensed with the script altogether in the second act, joining together in an additional rendition of *The Song of Mr Toad*, to the uproarious laughter of the audience:

May we present to you tonight
   Each ridiculous episode,
Each overblown failing
   Of the sorry Mr Toad.

It's time the populace realised
   Just what a debt is owed
By this foolish, flighty jailbird,
   The worthless Mr Toad.

In women's rags upon a nag
   Our plucky hero rode,
So lend an ear and spare a jeer
   For Washerwoman Toad!

"That's not in the script!" shouted a red-faced Toad. "I changed the story, remember? I don't want the whole world to know how I dressed up as a lowly washerwoman and forgot to bring any money with me!" The audience, which appeared on closer inspection to be made up almost entirely of Wild-Wooders, erupted in a fresh roar of laughter.

"Washerwoman Toad!" they chanted. "Washerwoman Toad!"

"Be quiet the lot of you," squealed Toad, fighting to make himself heard over the shouting and clapping. "We haven't got to the best bit yet."

"I think you'll find the performance is over," said Badger, rising to his feet and joining the Toad on stage.

"But it's–" spluttered Toad.

"It's over," repeated the Badger firmly. "Ladies and gentleman, thank you for coming. I'd like you all to leave now."

The long year since Toad Hall's triumphant recapture had done nothing to dull the Badger's fearsome reputation amongst the Wild-Wooders. The shouting and laughter died down almost at once and the audience began to disperse, dutifully filing back out of the hall with only the quietest of giggling and muffled whispers of "Washerwoman Toad".

"It was all going so well," said the Toad sadly, fingering his costume in a forlorn manner. "Don't you think so Moly?"

Mole shuffled sheepishly out onto the stage. "I'm so sorry," he told the Badger and Rat. "I had no idea he was going to say those things. I'd never have agreed to..."

"It's all right," said the Badger kindly. "We know that. Although I must say I enjoyed your lines immensely."

Mole smiled gratefully. "I don't think he meant anything by it, you know," he whispered to Badger. "He just got carried away."

"We know that too," said the Badger. "But we'll let him sweat a little while longer shall we?" Indeed the Toad could barely meet his friends' eyes and scurried off at the first opportunity to "help with the clearing up".

"I think I'm through with the theatre," said Mole, once he'd changed back out of his costume. "I don't know what my Great Uncle would have made of tonight's performance. It was a bit of a disaster."

"He'd have been very proud of you," said the Rat, loyally. "As are we."

The Mole yawned. "It's been a long day," he said. "Do you suppose Toad would mind very much if I left him to it? I feel very weary all of a sudden."

"Of course," said Rat. "Let's get you home shall we?"

"I think we should leave Toad to do his own dirty work this time," agreed the Badger.

"Speaking of Toad, what on earth is he up to now?"

Mole and Rat turned to see Toad standing on a chair in the orchestra pit, sporting a long blonde wig, much to the delight of the weasels crowding around him.

"Yes," they heard the Chief Weasel saying, "that's more like it. You look just like an opera star now. A fellow of your stature and fine singing voice is wasted on traditional theatre. I believe you have the makings of a true operatic sensation."

"Do you really think so?" replied the Toad excitedly.

"But of course. All that's missing is the outfit. Something long and flowing."

"Like a dress?" piped up one of the younger weasels.

Encore

"Precisely. You don't have a dress to hand do you?" the Chief Weasel asked.

"No," said Toad. "But I could get one ordered first thing tomorrow. In blue perhaps. The opera eh? I always fancied myself as a bit of a singer you know." He tried a few tentative arpeggios.

"Wonderful," mocked the Chief Weasel. "You're a natural."

Toad swelled. "Well it would be a shame to let all this go to waste," he said, sweeping his arm across the hall.

Rat gave a loud sigh and Badger shook his head wearily.

"Shouldn't we say something?" asked Mole anxiously. "He's making a laughing stock of himself."

"Oh Moly," smiled the Rat. "Dear, good-natured Mole. Since when did telling Toad anything do anyone any good? Least of all Toad?"

Mr Toad's Wedding
by Martin J. Smith

One morning in late March, Mole was busying himself tidying up the entrance to the home he now shared on a fulltime basis with his friend the Water Rat. He hummed to himself as he worked, revelling in the warmth and at being able to exert himself after the long, dark winter.

He heard the loud splash of an oar hitting water and then an even louder cry. He glanced out over the river and saw the Water Rat waving so wildly that he looked likely to pitch himself overboard.

"You'll never guess the news," called the Rat. "Never in ten thousand years."

Mole put down his broom and watched as his friend tied up the boat and leapt up the path.

Ratty waved his hands in the air with excitement. "Guess my news, come on try to guess."

"You have bought a new boat," said Mole.

The Water Rat shook his head.

"Toad has bought a new boat, or a car, or a locomotive."

Again Ratty shook his head.

"It's even more wondrous than that," he said. He sat down on the little bench by the side of the door and shook his head slowly, as if he couldn't truly believe the thoughts whirling round his own head. "Toad has just told me that he is going to get married."

"Married," cried the Mole, clapping his hands in joy.

Ratty looked at him askance. "I'm glad that you think it's a cause for celebration," he said.

"Don't you?"

"Not at all. Marriage is not for the likes of us. Not for animals meant to be lifelong bachelors. Marriage is for females and suchlike. And most of all, marriage is not for someone like Toad."

Mole looked out over the river. In the depths of his heart stirred a little twinge of envy. It must be wonderful to fall in love, he mused, to make a gallant proposal, to be shyly accepted and to plan a whole new life together. But he took one look at his friend's disgruntled face and decided to keep these thoughts to himself.

"Has Toad said who he wants to be his Best Animal?" Mole asked.

At that Ratty leapt up, his face now alight and beaming. "As a matter of fact, yes, he has. He has asked me. Isn't that grand?"

"Oh yes, it's absolutely grand," cried the Mole, shaking his friend's paw vigorously. "And absolutely the best choice possible."

"I agree," said Ratty. "In fact I'll get down to my speech right this minute."

Mole smiled fondly at his friend as he plunged into the house, all doubts and reservations about the wedding seemingly quite banished.

"Married," said the Badger in astonishment when they broke the news to him that afternoon. "To a female?"

"To Natalia Natterjack, to be exact," said Ratty. "She lives in Natterjack Manor."

"Never heard of her," said Badger. "Wish I never had." He poured them all a cup of tea. "Does the poor young creature know what she's letting herself in for?"

Ratty shrugged.

"And the other news," said Mole, "is that Toad has asked Ratty to be his Best Animal. Isn't that splendid?"

Badger growled. "Not if Toad changes his mind. Custom decrees that in those circumstances the Best Animal has to marry the bride."

Ratty's cup fell to the floor. "You can't be serious," he said. "Badger, tell me you're not serious."

"It is a most serious matter," said the Badger. "Who ever heard of a marriage between a Water Rat and a Toad?"

Ratty turned a stricken face to Mole.

Mole had never known Ratty so quiet as they walked home that evening. Despite Mole's best efforts, Ratty could not be shaken out of the deep gloom he had been plunged into by Badger's words. But the next morning he had regained his ebullient self and was whistling merrily as he made the fifth revision to his speech.

At lunchtime a telegram was delivered to their door. It was from Toad. "Natalia taking tea this afternoon," it read. "Do come. Toad."

So Ratty and Mole put on their second-best clothes, thought better of it and changed into their best ones, combed their hair and rowed, with a mixture of anticipation and trepidation, up to the boat-house belonging to Toad Hall.

"Do we curtsey when we are introduced?" asked Mole as they got close.

Ratty snorted. "Certainly not. She's only from a Manor. We

Mr Toad's Wedding

don't bow to Toad after all, and he lives in Toad Hall."

They tied up the boat and strolled up to the lawn in front of the Hall. The garden table had been moved from its habitual position in the middle of the lawn and placed instead beneath the shade of a beech tree. Toad could be seen busily spreading butter on a scone. Next to him, her head further sheltered by a parasol, was a creature who could only be Miss Natalia Natterjack.

"Good afternoon, Miss Natterjack," chorused the two friends.

Toad's fiancée glanced up and bestowed upon them a girlish giggle.

"Isn't she a peach," cried Toad springing up and pumping both their hands. He turned to admire Miss Natterjack and sighed with passion.

"Have you ever seen such a well-turned ankle?" he asked. "Or such beautiful skin? And as for her sweet, sweet mouth and her eyes." He beat his fist upon his breast. "Oh I could drown in those large, lustrous eyes."

Ratty plumped himself down at the table. "Delicious looking scones," he said, helping himself to two.

"I think she's a peach," Mole said to Toad. "You're a very fortunate animal."

"I am indeed," said Toad. He placed a hand in his waistcoat and positioned himself behind Miss Natterjack. "You know, I often think it's high time you fellows thought about finding two nice young ladies and getting yourselves married. Even a chap like you, Ratty, could find someone."

Ratty spluttered, spraying scone all over the tablecloth.

"Oh yes, I do," continued Toad. "Hear me out. Falling in love seems to somehow round out a fellow's life. Since I have met Natalia I have learned to see myself through her eyes. I realise that I am a much more splendid fellow than I had hitherto believed."

Ratty and Mole exchanged knowing glances but said nothing.

"Natalia has convinced me," continued Toad, "that I have so much to give to the world; to teach, to inspire. I am made to be a husband, to become even more of a pillar of the community than I am already, to offer my humble talents as a gift to my friends and fellow citizens. Marriage is the state to which all should aspire."

He puffed himself up and looked even more seriously at Ratty and Mole. "I must say that I am rather shocked at the tardiness which you two have displayed over the matter. You're not getting any younger you know, and you hardly have the advantages which I have been blessed with."

"You're so right, my precious darling," simpered Miss Natterjack. "How did you get to be so very, very clever?"

Toad waved away her comments with becoming modesty.

Ratty snorted loudly and reached for another scone.

"Have you set a date for the wedding?" asked Mole, to change the subject.

"On May Day," announced Toad. "What other day could be more fitting than that?" And he beamed a huge smile of smug satisfaction.

So the weeks wended by. Toad Hall became a magnet for every tradesman in the vicinity. Some were responding to requests from Toad. Even more, however, were seizing the opportunity to pronounce to him that what they had to sell was absolutely essential to the success of the wedding and that he should buy two, or better still, three of their wares. Toad invariably bought half a dozen.

In the meanwhile, Toad and Natalia composed exhaustive lists of guests that simply had to be invited. When Ratty, Mole and Badger called to see how plans were progressing, the list had grown to include five hundred and twenty eight names. "Will they all come?" Mole asked Toad.

"Of course they will," said Toad in astonishment. "Who could bear to resist the high spot of the season?" Then he tapped his chin pensively. "The only conceivable absentee might be my cousin Chevalier Vicomte Tallyrand Toad. He is travelling the South Seas in search of the last surviving Dodo."

"Does such a beast exist?" asked Mole.

"Tallyrand likes to think so," said Toad. "But he has been on the quest for six years without success. He does get such odd notions in his head, poor chap."

"Do you want a poem as well?" called Ratty from the hammock. Scattered all around were discarded sheets of paper, yet more drafts of the famous speech.

"If you can stretch to it, dear Ratty," said Toad. "Perhaps a paean of praise to Natalia would go down well."

Natalia raised a fan to her face and gave a look of surpassing coyness.

"Paean of praise," muttered Badger to Mole. "I never thought Toad could get more foolish but he has proved me wrong."

Suddenly Ratty let out a huge yawn and threw down his pen. "I say chaps," he said, "why don't we take advantage of this gorgeous weather and go for a scull on the river?"

Mr Toad's Wedding

"Capital idea," cried Toad. "I'll get changed into my sculling togs." He pulled off his cravat and jacket, flung them to the ground and was just about to hurry up to the Hall to change when Natalia called out.

"But Toady, darling, you're surely not going to go out on the river and get all hot and messed up. Surely?"

Toad stopped in mid-stride and stared at her in some bewilderment.

"What do you mean, light of my life?" he asked.

"Well the river is such a dreadfully dank and dirty place," she said. "You're bound to get mud and weeds and creepy crawlies all over you."

"Of course he is," cried Ratty. "That's the fun of it."

Natalia glanced at the Rat for a moment and then turned once more to Toad. "Besides," she continued, "we need to go over the wedding list to check if there is anyone we've missed out."

"Missed out," cried Toad. "But we've got five hundred guests already."

"Quite," said Natalia. "With that number we really must have missed out quite a few. Cousin Matilda had six hundred guests at her wedding."

There was a long silence. Then Natalia said, "You really must stay with me, darling Toady, and complete the wedding list."

Toad blinked his eyes, nonplussed. He turned to his friends, then back to Natalia, then back to his friends once more. He was caught between adventure and duty, between fun and fiancée. The three friends saw the torment in his face and watched, mesmerised, as he began to hop on each foot, first towards Natalia, then towards them.

Natalia patted the chair which Toad had just vacated. He turned a piteous look on the others, picked up his cravat and slumped down.

Natalia gave what she believed to be a gracious smile before raising her fan to her face. Yet, to the eyes of the three friends, this movement was not swift enough to conceal a smirk of triumph. A cloud crossed over the sun and a cold wind blew.

Three days later, as Mole was snoozing in the afternoon sun, Ratty marched up the garden path and threw the latest version of his speech on the ground. Mole opened one eye. "Something the matter?" he asked.

"Something the matter?" cried Ratty. "I should say there's something the matter. Here am I trying my hardest to write a speech that will make this foolish wedding memorable and I am forced by Toad to lay down my pen to attend to his latest whim."

Mole sighed, opened the other eye and sat up. "Latest whim?" he asked mildly.

"Toad has decided," said Rat, "or maybe Miss Natterjack has decided, that we should spend the next week rehearsing the wedding; every move, every step, every speech."

He threw his hands up in the air. "I have told him time and again that my speech is still in the midst of creation. It is impossible to guarantee its exact length at this juncture, so what on earth is the point of rehearsing the wedding."

He sighed and shook his head sorrowfully.

"Perhaps he doesn't understand the demands of poetry," Mole said, pouring his friend a glass of lemonade. "He is more a creature of action than of thought, after all."

"Well there may be plenty of action," said Ratty. "Mother-in-Law Natterjack is arriving today and, from what I gather, she is a creature of very decided opinions."

Mole smiled, closed his eyes and prepared to resume his nap.

"I'm afraid there's no time for a siesta," said Rat. "Toad has summoned us all to the Hall. The first rehearsal is at three o'clock sharp."

At ten to three Ratty and Mole tied up their boat and made their way up the path to Toad Hall. The lawn in front of the hall was thronged with animals. In the middle, deep in conversation, were Toad and Badger. Ratty and Mole made their way through the crowd and joined them.

"What a marvellous turnout," said Mole, looking about him. "There must be hundreds here."

"But not the leading ladies," said Badger. "There doesn't appear to be any sign of Natalia and her mother."

"Don't be so gloomy, old chap," said Toad anxiously. "They will be here any minute, mark my words."

"Have you met your prospective mother-in-law?" asked Ratty.

"Not yet," said Toad. "But I have heard that she is a lady of exquisite breeding, sweet temper and decorum."

"Let's hope so," growled Badger ominously, "for your sake."

Toad stared at Badger, his eyes widening visibly. "What do you mean by that?" he asked.

Badger harrumphed and put his nose in the air.

"Badger?" asked Toad. He touched Badger's arm anxiously.

Mr Toad's Wedding

"What do you mean old chap?"

"Well," said the Badger mournfully, "you know what they say about young females and their mothers?"

Toad shook his head miserably.

"It is a well known fact," continued Badger firmly, "that all young females grow to be the exact replica of their mothers, in looks, attitude and behaviour. So you had better hope that Natalia's mother truly is as sweet-natured and well bred as you have been told."

At that precise moment a large motor-car swept up the drive. In the back were two females of the Toad disposition.

"The Natterjacks," gasped Toad, thoroughly flummoxed by Badger's words.

Mole brushed his hand across his fur while Ratty ostentatiously pulled out the manuscript of his speech and began to study it.

The motor-car pulled to a halt and out hopped an elderly frog in well-pressed chauffeur's uniform. He opened the far door and Natalia emerged, giggling and blushing, arrayed in a dress of spring lemon, with tassels, baubles and lace fluttering from almost every surface. She held out her hand to Toad who kissed it with a flourish.

Then he turned a nervous face to the other occupant.

The chauffeur opened the door, placed a small step on the ground for ease of exit and proffered his hand in assistance. It was immediately slapped away and, with a deep grunt, an imposing figure hopped out onto the lawn.

"May I introduce Mother-in-Law Natterjack," simpered Natalia to Toad.

The huge shadow of Mother-in-Law Natterjack towered above Toad. He visibly quailed. She was a head taller than her daughter but in girth four times her size. The warts upon her stupendous head had long multiplied past the two or three which were considered comely for female toads, studding almost every part of her face so that her complexion resembled a pineapple. Her huge eyes were a deep yellow, as though they had sat in her head too long over the summer and were beginning to turn stagnant. She opened her mouth and a long, leathery tongue lolled out and wetted her face.

She turned to Toad and her eyes widened in horror. "A Common Toad," she declaimed. "I had not realised you were a Common Toad."

She inflated her body immensely and looked accusingly at her daughter, who shrank beneath the glare.

"Madam, I am the owner of Toad Hall," spluttered Toad, stung into voice despite his dismay at the sight of her.

"I know that," said Mother-in-Law Natterjack. "I can see that, I can see that quite plainly. Do you take me for a fool?" She raised a pince-nez to her eyes and studied him carefully. "But I can also see, at the very first glance, that you are certainly not a Natterjack Toad but one of the Common ilk. I had expected better for my daughter."

She snorted and established herself in Toad's favourite basket chair.

Toad looked at her in consternation and stretched himself to his full height.

"Common ilk," he cried. "I'll have you know that I can trace my family back for one hundred generations."

"I don't doubt it," said Mother-in-Law. She coughed into her handkerchief. "But all Common, Mr Toad, all Common."

Toad spluttered. "Not all. Although we have no Natterjack in our family, let me tell you that on my mother's side, the French, we have Midwife Toads, Painted Toads and Yellow-Bellied Toads. My cousin, Chevalier Vicomte Tallyrand Toad, is a Western Spadefoot Toad no less, and hails from Monte Carlo."

"Foreigners," grunted Mother-in-Law. "Can't abide them. Stink of garlic and talk with a lisp." She dabbed her cheek with a handkerchief. "Natalia neglected to tell me that, in addition to being a Common Toad, you have antecedents from beyond these shores."

Toad opened his mouth, working it furiously. But to the astonishment of all who knew him, not one word uttered from it.

"Come away," said Mole quietly, taking him by the arm. "Let's escape for a little stroll."

The four friends walked off towards the hall. Toad's mouth was still opening and closing wordlessly.

"This is terrible," he moaned at last. "What a truly awful mother-in-law. This is the worst thing that could happen to me."

"Not the worst," said the Badger.

"What do you mean?" asked Toad. "What could be worse?"

"What did I tell you?" said Badger. "Like mother like daughter." He placed a paw upon Toad's shoulder. "My condolences."

A thin scream struggled out of Toad's mouth.

The initial, unfavourable start to the wedding rehearsal speedily went downhill thereafter. Toad was agitated and kept standing in

Mr Toad's Wedding

the wrong place, Natalia was fretful and every few minutes burst into tears, Ratty was uncooperative and barely took his eyes from his speech, Badger glared at everyone as though he had a mind to whack all and sundry over the head, while Mole was nervous and kept bumping into things. And Mother-in-Law Natterjack stared like a basilisk at the whole proceedings. She would not stand up, she would not take part, she would not applaud when she was required. She remained rooted to Toad's chair, croaking disdainfully and inflating the pouch beneath her chin until it dwarfed even her stupendous head.

"I'm worried that she might pop," whispered Mole nervously.

"Let's hope she does," said Ratty callously. "Just make sure that we are far enough away to avoid being spattered."

Finally, with everyone having missed their cues, with hardly anyone in the place that he or she should have been, with most of the smaller animals having burst into tears, the parson finally called a halt to the rehearsal and proceeded to lead the assembly in a half-hearted rendition of *All Things Bright and Beautiful.* Then all the creatures, great and small, dejectedly slunk off home.

"Not you fellows," called Toad frantically. "Please don't go. Stay for tea with Natalia and Mother-in-Law Natterjack."

Ratty's eyes widened in horror and he glanced towards the river and escape.

"We can't leave him now," whispered Mole. "He needs us."

"Mole is right," said Badger mournfully. "We shall have to gird ourselves to the company of both daughter and mother-in-law."

So the three friends returned to a very relieved Toad and took tea. It was a most dispiriting meal, eaten for the most part in silence. At the end of it, there remained untouched plates of sandwiches, cakes and even scones.

"What a dreadful waste," snorted Mother-in-Law. And she shot out her tongue and scooped all the cakes and scones into her cavernous mouth. Ratty, Mole and Badger took one look and fled to the river.

"I feel so sorry for poor Toad," said Mole next morning over breakfast. "What a terrible animal his mother-in-law has proved to be." He spread ginger preserve thoughtfully over a thick slice of toast.

"Absolutely," said Ratty. "And if Badger is right then Natalia will grow to be exactly like her. I said that marriage was not for the likes of us or Toad."

"I can't believe that Natalia would change into something quite so...quite so...well...quite so gruesome," said Mole with a force that surprised even him.

Ratty wagged a piece of bacon at his friend. "You keep a grip on yourself, young friend," he said. "I do believe that you are developing a soft spot for Miss Natterjack and where on earth might that lead."

Mole blushed. "Well at least it won't be me who may have to end up marrying her," he said. "That privilege belongs to the Best Animal." And tight-lipped, he spread a second slice of toast with even more ginger preserve.

Ratty chuckled to himself and put six more rashers of bacon into the pan.

"I tell you what," Ratty said after a while. "Why don't we go over to see Toad? I expect he needs cheering up." He gave such a broad grin that Mole's tetchiness was quite dissipated and in good spirits they headed off to Toad Hall.

They found Toad on his lawn, staring anxiously at the wedding programme. He looked extremely fraught but, at sight of them, he brightened up considerably.

"I was just about to have elevenses," he cried. "Come and join me."

High in the sky, unseen by all, a large round object moved slowly towards them.

Mole and Ratty sat at the table. Sweet and plain biscuits, hot muffins with plenty of butter, plain and current scones were soon being assiduously consumed along with hot cups of coffee.

Then, all at once, the bright sunlight was dimmed. The three friends glanced up in surprise. Hanging in the sky above their heads was a huge red and yellow balloon. Suspended beneath it was a sturdy wicker basket with three heads just visible above the top.

At that moment, a ship's anchor was hurled out of the basket, embedding itself in the middle of the croquet lawn. The basket settled beside it and the balloon gently subsided and collapsed. A figure dressed entirely in crimson leapt out of the basket and held wide his arms.

"Mon Cher Toad," he cried. "I have journeyed hither across deserts, mountains and the seven seas. I have suffered thirst, hunger and sleepless nights. I have fought off the military of three countries and the navies of two, not to mention brigands and ne'er-do-wells without number. And why? To answer the summons of my little cousin Toad to his nuptial feast."

He placed a monocle in one eye, scrutinised Ratty and Mole

Mr Toad's Wedding

then gave a low and lordly bow. "I am Chevalier Vicomte Tallyrand de Toad, Legion of Honour, Croix de Guerre, Knight of St. John. To whom do I have the pleasure?"

"Rat," said Rat.

"Mole," said Mole.

Tallyrand looked bemused for a moment, then clapped his hands. "Well you look robust fellows, if I may say. Go help my servants secure my chariot of the air." And he gestured them to the balloon.

"Oh no, old chap," stammered Toad. "No need for that. I've got plenty of my own people for that sort of thing. Ratty and Moly are my closest friends."

"My deepest apologies," said Tallyrand bowing once again. "How could I mistake such charming friends of cousin Toad for mere domestics or gardeners?"

"I should like to have a garden," said Mole. "But the river is quite enough for me."

"You own a river?" said Tallyrand. "Then I shall delight to spend time fly-fishing with you."

"Nobody owns the river," snorted Ratty. "It just is."

"Your friend has a fine sense of humour, no?" said Tallyrand, sitting himself on Toad's chair. "The river just is," he laughed, as he helped himself to a sandwich.

Toad pulled up another chair and poured his cousin a cup of coffee. "It's absolutely marvellous to see you Tallyrand," he said. "I didn't think you would actually get here." His eyes blinked wide in admiration. "And even more now that I've heard about your brave adventures and the mountains and navies and brigands."

"And did you capture the last Dodo?" asked Mole.

Tallyrand shook his head sadly. "Alas no, my friend. I saw him, I saw him as clear as I see you here today. I crept up to him, net in my left hand, rifle in my right. Which to use? I could easily have shot him – Bang! Bang! – for I am a deadly marksman, Olympic medallist and big-game hunter. But really I wanted to capture him, for glory and for science. My moment of inner debate proved fatal."

"Fatal?"

"Fatal. For the Dodo seized his chance, poked his immense green tongue at me and, laughing with delight, flew away."

He wolfed down a second sandwich and sniffed at the coffee. "Have you any champagne?" he enquired.

Later that morning, as they rowed back along the river, Ratty shook his head and tutted. "I don't like him," he said. "Not one little bit."

"Don't you?" said Mole. "I know he's rather full of himself, but I'm sure that at heart he's as decent and good-natured as Toad."

Ratty blinked his eyes in surprise and patted Mole on the arm. "Well if you think that…" he said.

The next day the two friends received a message to meet at Toad Hall for luncheon. "Do you suppose that cousin of Toad's will still be here?" asked Ratty as they approached the boathouse.

"Undoubtedly," said Mole. "Look at all the trouble he took to get here."

Ratty shook his head at the innocence of his friend.

To their delight, they found Badger sitting in the morning room, his head deep in a newspaper. At that moment the clock struck one and the dinner gong sounded. The three friends ambled into the Banqueting Hall where lunch was to be served. To their surprise they found Tallyrand sitting in Toad's seat and looking very comfortable indeed. They nodded hello and took their places. Soon afterwards Toad hurried in, full of chatter and good cheer. Without a second glance he threw himself into Tallyrand's lap. Tallyrand laughed drolly as Toad scrambled off in embarrassment. "Terribly sorry, Tallyrand old chap. Usually sit there myself and didn't see you."

"No need for apologies," said Tallyrand. "Find yourself a seat." He waved his hand airily.

"Thank you," said Toad.

The other animals exchanged silent glances.

In honour of Tallyrand the meal was entirely French. They started with Salad Nicoise, followed this with Rainbow Trout with shrimp sauce, then little lamb chops cooked very rare with herbs and potato dauphinoise. There were cheeses to follow and finally a crème brulee. Toad had selected his finest wines to complement the food.

Throughout the meal Tallyrand regaled them with his many adventures. He told them about the novels and poems he had written, about his marvellous plays, some of which he had acted in, about his wonderful chateau with improvements designed by himself, about his discovery of the sources of the rivers Amazon, Ganges and Zambesi. He told them of his commission to bring law and order to the wild lands of eastern Tartary, his discovery of the lost section of the Silk Road and his rescue of a Siamese princess from pirates in the South China Sea.

Mr Toad's Wedding

"Returned her to Bangkok on the day of her wedding," said Tallyrand. "And now, dear cousin, shall we discuss yours?"

He took a sheaf of paper from his pocket. "I assume, naturellement, that I am to be Best Animal, and I have taken the opportunity to compose a speech complete with poem."

Ratty's mouth gaped in astonishment. Mole and Badger exchanged concerned glances. Toad clapped his hands in delight.

"Marvellous, Tallyrand, marvellous," he said. "Let's hear your speech."

Ratty sat stunned and silent as Mole rowed home after lunch. It was only when they reached home that he finally spoke. "Toad had asked me to be Best Animal," he said. "And now he has completely forgotten." He hung his head in despair.

All the next day, Ratty did nothing but stare at his speech and sigh. Mole became more and more fretful at his friend's reaction. He wondered whether to send for a doctor, to seek out Badger's advice or go to Toad Hall to remonstrate with Toad and seek to reverse the decision. But finally, as the sun was setting, Ratty glanced up and managed a wistful smile. "At least there's no longer any danger of my having to marry Natalia," he said.

By the following weekend, Ratty had quite recovered his ebullient spirits. "I was a clot," he said to Mole. "As if Toad can be blamed for being inconsistent, forgetful and vain? What else could I expect him to be? I shall enjoy the wedding all the more for having no Best Animal responsibilities."

The next day was May Day and the long anticipated wedding. It was a glorious morning with a deep blue, cloudless sky. A gentle wind soothed the languid heat, and the smell of wildflowers filled the air.

The river was thronged with excited animals making their way to Toad Hall, Ratty's and Moly's boat to the fore. It was so warm that Ratty took his suit jacket off and, as he did so, Mole caught a glimpse of what could only be his Best Animal's speech, poking out from a pocket. He decided not to make any comment.

The lawns of Toad Hall were crowded with tables laden with food, hundreds of animals resplendent in their very best clothes, and a large marquee where the ceremony was to take place. Ratty and Mole took their places at the front, next to Badger, and were soon joined by Toad in a magnificent light grey silk suit, cummerbund and top hat.

But handsome though he undoubtedly looked, he was completely eclipsed by his cousin. Tallyrand promenaded in the full eighteenth century costume of a Vicomte of France. His shoes were jet black with silver buckles, on his legs he wore sheer white tights, and his crimson suit was made of the finest French silk embroidered in cerise and cream. A tricorn hat with ostrich feather sat rakishly upon his head. He flourished a walking stick made of ebony, and hanging from his belt was a deadly rapier.

"I don't think I could have quite matched that," Ratty whispered to Mole.

"Maybe not. But I bet your speech is better," replied Mole.

A chamber orchestra played light summer melodies as Toad and Tallyrand took their seats. Then, the music slowed. All of the animals shifted expectantly in their seats and the orchestra launched into *Here Comes the Bride*.

Tallyrand turned and glimpsed Natalia for the first time. Ratty and Mole saw him start and rub his eyes, saw him straighten, saw him take a deep breath. Then he gestured one of his servants over and whispered something quietly in his ear.

Toad began to hop from foot to foot as the music swelled. Natalia joined him and he beamed upon her. She never noticed. For she had caught sight of Tallyrand, resplendent and swaggering. Her eyes widened, she blushed and she sighed deeply. Behind her sounded the deep belch of Mother-in-Law Natterjack.

The ceremony began. The parson seemed to have become quite flummoxed by the exotic appearance of Tallyrand. He missed out a number of words and pronounced others in totally novel ways. But eventually he dithered his way to the final part of the ceremony.

He took a deep breath and called out, "Are there any here present who object to the marriage of Mr Toad and Miss Natterjack?" Mole tensed, fearing that Ratty would leap up to try to save Toad from the marriage.

But it was not Ratty who moved.

No sooner had the parson uttered the words than Tallyrand leapt towards Natalia, swept her in his arms and gave her a passionate kiss. "You're beautiful," he cried. "I cannot help myself. I must spirit you away to my magnificent chateau."

"Chateau?" said Natalia. She stared for a moment at Toad, thinking swiftly. Her eyes swivelled from Toad to Tallyrand and back again. Then she flung her arms around Tallyrand and kissed him equally passionately.

"Sorry dearest Toad," she said over her shoulder, "but true love cannot be denied."

Tallyrand seized Natalia by the hand and they fled out of the

Mr Toad's Wedding

marquee. All of the animals, and most of all Toad, were astonished into immobility.

Then Mole cried: "He's stolen the bride. After him!"

The spell was broken. Led by Mole, Toad and Ratty, the congregation surged out of the marquee in pursuit of Tallyrand and Natalia.

In the distance they could see Tallyrand's servants feverishly inflating the balloon, and Tallyrand and Natalia getting closer and closer to it. The pursuing animals put on a spurt but they were just a little too late. Tallyrand and his servants lifted Natalia into the basket before leaping in after her.

Tallyrand waved his arm as the balloon began to ascend. "Sorry Toad," he called. "I am totally smitten. Adieu."

But he had spoken too soon. Toad saw four guy ropes trailing from the basket and he leapt for one. Mole grabbed the other and Ratty the third. The balloon paused in its ascent for a moment, then regained its strength and began to drag the animals across the lawn.

"Hang on lads," cried a deep voice. Badger plunged through the crowd and grasped hold of the fourth rope. His great strength halted the balloon. But neither balloon nor friends had sufficient power to win this match, and the balloon hung immobile between earth and sky.

Then, with a raucous cry of, "Wait for me," Mother-in-Law Natterjack burst into view. She moved with tremendous speed and, judging the distance to a nicety, she leapt into the air, scrabbled for the basket and hung on for dear life, her body hanging out of the basket in a most alarming manner.

Her additional weight proved fatal to the struggle and the balloon began to sink to the ground. Toad glanced up. He could see the basket slowly getting closer. But more than that, he could see the scarlet bloomers of Mother-in-Law Natterjack as she clung on to the basket.

Suddenly he cried, "Let go of the ropes, let go of the ropes."

His command was so peremptory that the other animals obeyed. The balloon, released of its bonds, leapt into the air like a thing newly free. In moments it had soared far above the Hall and was heading away to the south and to France.

Toad turned a satisfied face to his friends. "I take back all that I said, Ratty. You were right. Marriage is not for the likes of us."

The Toad Rush
by Margaret Bulleyment

The Water Rat lay curled up in that blissful state between sleeping and waking. This was the magical moment of the day when he heard his beloved river for the first time, as it lapped quietly at his door. He turned over in bed, yawned and reached down for his slippers. There was a loud splash, as his paw tried vainly to locate the familiar footwear.

He shot up in bed and gazed in disbelief at his possessions floating around the room. Sometimes his cellar flooded in the winter, but never had the water reached his bedroom. The river was in trouble.

Trying not to panic, he waded outside to his boat which was riding high on the muddy water. The osiers and reeds along the river bank had disappeared and little groups of ducks and moorhens were swimming around, looking bewildered.

The Rat cast off quickly and with strong strokes headed downstream. Knowing the river so well he could row its usual course, but anyone unfamiliar with its twists and turns could get dangerously entangled.

Taking the usual river's curve, he glanced behind him and lost stroke in his shock. Stretched across the river was a huge dam of mud and reeds, and beyond it, where the river bank surfaced, was a tower of branches with a doorway in the front. Someone, emerging backwards from the tower, was singing; someone large and brown, with thick shiny fur and an enormous tail.

The Rat rowed as near as he could and took a deep breath. "What on earth do you think you're doing?" he shouted at the shiny back.

The stranger turned, displaying the largest and sharpest front teeth the Rat had ever seen.

"Well, howdy sir. You must be Mr Water Rat. I've heard so much about you," drawled the stranger. "Mighty pleased to make your acquaintance, sir. It's Beaver, sir. Beaver at your service."

"What? Who?" spluttered the Rat, completely wrong-footed by the stranger's amiability. Quickly, he recovered his customary composure. "Who's been talking about me?"

"Our good friend Mr Toad," replied the Beaver. "I was expecting to meet you at his lunch today, but we were fated to meet before then."

"Now look here, old chap," the Rat replied frostily. "I don't know what Toad's been telling you, but my best friends are not in the habit of flooding my entire house. It is, to say the least, extremely bad manners. As is building a....monstrosity like this," he waved a paw in the direction of the dam, "on our river. We river-bankers have a code of conduct, don't you know and you've breached it."

"I'm mighty sorry about that, Mr Rat, mighty sorry, but we all have to live together in our different ways and this is my way. But seeing as you're obviously gonna be a good friend and neighbour, I'll see what I can do with my dam for the moment. Now you return home and I'll see you later at Mr Toad's." The Beaver nodded to Rat and disappeared back into his lodge.

"Make sure you do something immediately, or I'll not be responsible for my actions," said the Rat. Bristling with anger, he headed back upstream. The Rat was not in the habit of being told what to do on his river by newcomers, and Toad should have told him about his despicable, new neighbour.

By the time he reached home, the flood had begun to subside and he could at least walk through his front door. He needed to get ready for Toad's luncheon and, although the last thing the Rat wanted was to meet the obnoxious dam-builder again, the Mole had also been invited and would be waiting for his friend on the other side of the river. The Rat got ready as best he could in his muddy circumstances and rowed across the receding river to meet the Mole.

"What a beautiful summer's day," said the Mole, stepping gingerly into the boat from the muddy river bank. "It must have rained really hard in the night, but look at it now. Just perfect for a pleasant luncheon with friends. I've been looking forward to it all week."

"Hrmph," replied the Rat, jabbing at his oars, so the boat rocked.

"Are you all right Ratty?" said the Mole. "You look a trifle flustered."

"Flustered's not the half of it, Mole," replied the Rat, and he proceeded to tell the Mole about his morning's encounter.

"I'm sure we can sort it out over one of Toad's excellent luncheons," said Mole. "It's too beautiful a day to get upset."

Mole's enthusiasm was infectious and, by the time they tied up at Toad's boat-house, Rat was beginning to feel his old self again. As the two friends crossed the lawn and mounted the terrace steps, Toad, clad in a bright green silk waistcoat and brandishing a wine glass, hailed them from the conservatory doors. His other arm was around the shoulders of a brown, shiny character, dressed in what looked like blue workman's overalls. The Rat, no

The Toad Rush

hostage to fashion himself, shuddered.

"Ratty, Moly," effused Toad beaming from ear to ear. "It's so good to see you, chaps. Come and meet my new friend, Beaver. Beaver, old chap, this is Mole and this is...oh you've met, haven't you...you've just been telling me. I'm sure you and Ratty are going to be the very best of friends."

"Good to meet you, Mr Mole, sir," said Beaver, pumping Mole's paw enthusiastically, "and you too, Mr Rat. I hope our little misunderstanding this morning is forgotten."

"Of course it is, Beaver old chum," said Toad. "We're all good friends here. It's just a pity you'll miss Badger and Otter today, but they're up river for a few days with the Great Council."

"That sounds very important," replied Beaver, looking suitably impressed.

"Well, chaps sitting around jawing is not my kind of thing, don't you know," said Toad. "I'm more of an action man, myself, but Rat and Mole went last summer and..."

"Very valuable it was too," cut in the Rat. "The River-bankers formed the Great Council some years ago after the Wild-Wooders tried, unsuccessfully, to move permanently into Toad Hall. We decided to meet every year with River-bankers from other parts and exchange news. At the time of the Toad Hall incident, we didn't know that something similar had happened upriver with another group of weasels, stoats and ferrets. If we'd known..."

"Yes, yes, Ratty, it was a bad business," the Toad broke in, "but that was years ago and since then the Wild Wood has been very quiet and masses of the nasty little blighters have moved out to the town. It's practically deserted these days. Now let's forget those horrid times and concentrate on our luncheon." Toad waved a paw at the huge conservatory table spread with cold meats, pies, pickles and salads, all framing a magnificently dressed pike, its evil eyes replaced with parsley and capers.

"Now, Moly. Take a seat next to Beaver. I'll sit the other side and Rat can sit opposite." Toad waved his glass at Witherspoon the butler, who glided swiftly around the table, seated everyone and disappeared.

"Been here long, Mr Beaver?" asked the Mole, helping himself to a generous spoonful of pickle. "Do you come from far away?"

"I've just moved in Mr Mole, but I've come from a river, a very long way away," Beaver replied.

"He's far too modest," said Toad, eagerly attacking the pike. "He's been telling me wonderful stories of his homeland and all the exciting adventures he had to get here. Where he used to live sounds a fantastic place."

"Why did you leave?" said the Rat, rather rudely, his plate still empty.

The Beaver fixed his eyes on the pike, and then said quietly, "Too many of my relatives were being made into hats."

"Oh, I say," muttered the Mole.

"I didn't mean... I'm sorry." The Rat shifted uncomfortably in his seat.

"Well you're among friends here, old chap," said Toad standing up and patting Beaver on the shoulder. "Let's have a toast to our new friend. To Mr Beaver and may–"

There was a splintering crash as a huge rock shattered the conservatory roof, peppering the pike with shards of glass.

"Ergh!" shrieked Toad, falling backwards.

The Beaver leapt to his feet, sprinted through the doors, down the steps, hurled himself straight through the dense hedge and disappeared from view. Fast footsteps scrunched on the gravel, followed by the sounds of blows, then an angry voice, screams and shrieks, before the Beaver burst back through the hedge, dragging a cringing weasel in each powerful paw.

"These nasty little critters wanted to spoil our lunch," bellowed Beaver, banging the two terrified weasels together, like a pair of cymbals. "What do you want me to do with 'em? Dump 'em in the river?"

The Rat was busy hauling the shocked Toad to his feet, while the Mole tried hopelessly to salvage the remains of the luncheon. "Whatever you like old chap," whimpered Toad.

The Beaver marched down to the river, a weasel under each arm, and unceremoniously hurled the shrieking creatures into the water. "If I see you two again, you'll be a pike's lunch," he bellowed. He strode back to the conservatory, a gleam of satisfaction on his face.

Toad was beginning to recover. "Beaver, you're a hero. Just the kind of chap to have around in a crisis. Now, I've had a thought. How would you like to come and live here in the grounds of Toad Hall? There's a stream that leads off the river, which you can dam to your heart's content, and, in return for the superior services of Toad Hall, perhaps you wouldn't mind using your strongman tactics occasionally with the odd poacher or Wild-Wooder?"

"That's a very generous offer Mr Toad, sir. I don't mind if I do," replied Beaver. The two animals shook paws, as the butler ushered in a bevy of maids bearing brooms and dustpans.

The Toad Rush

"Now," said Toad decisively, "let's go and sit calmly on the terrace. I have a proposal for you all. In fact, it's why I invited you."

"Why do I have a sinking feeling about the word *proposal?*" the Rat whispered to the Mole. "I think we've had enough excitement for one afternoon. What on earth were those Wild-Wooders thinking of? They've been awfully quiet lately."

"Don't know," said the Mole. "Probably just some stupid prank."

Seated on a comfy terrace chair with a fresh glass in his hand, Toad seemed to have almost forgotten the disastrous lunch. "Now as I was saying earlier, Beaver has been telling me some very interesting stories about the river he came from. Lots of people visited his river and guess what they did?" He looked at the Rat and the Mole, his head on one side. His two friends looked blank.

"They panned for gold."

Instantly, the Rat's face changed. "No, Toad. I know exactly where this is going. We're not panning for gold."

"Oh Ratty, you always spoil things," said Toad petulantly. "It'd be great fun and, if there's four of us, we'd have far more chance of finding some. Then we could form–"

"You cannot really believe that we'll find gold on our river," the Rat retorted. "Don't be so ridiculous, Toad."

"If I may say something, Mr Rat, sir," Beaver said politely. "Where I come from, many good-hearted men of common sense, like yourself, doubted they would find anything, and when others made it rich they were not very happy."

"I'm not interested in making it rich," said the Rat. "I just don't want people digging up bits of my river because of some half-baked idiot's idea."

"It's only going to be us four, Ratty, old chap, and it would be good fun for this afternoon. I'll ask Witherspoon for a picnic hamper to make up for our lost luncheon."

"It might be fun, Ratty," said Mole whispering. "We only have to sit on the river bank while Beaver and Toad amuse themselves. You know I like picnics."

"Oh, all right," said the Rat grudgingly. "Just don't expect me to join in."

"Oh, wonderful, then it's all arranged," said Toad. "We're going to be rich."

"You are already, Toad, remember," said Ratty.

"Well," the Toad looked a little shamefaced. "One or two horses have let me down lately and..."

"Oh, Toad, you're not...?"

"No, no, old chap. But striking it rich might be fun."

Almost immediately, the Rat regretted his decision. The Beaver disappeared and returned carrying all manner of shovels and pans, which he loaded into the Rat's boat until it was listing dangerously.

"Beaver and I'll go in my boat," said Toad. "You two chaps bring the equipment and we'll see you there."

By the time the two friends arrived, Toad and Beaver had already set out the picnic under the willow trees and, while the Rat and the Mole tucked into the salmon sandwiches, Beaver shoehorned Toad into a pair of blue overalls that matched his.

"I say now, don't I look the part," said Toad, adding a broad brimmed hat to his outfit and eagerly grasping the armful of equipment the Beaver handed him.

He waddled down to the water's edge. This little backwater on the town side of Toad Hall was still on Toad's land, but it was more gravelly along the river bank. The ducks and moorhens, so plentiful near the Rat's home, were not to be seen.

The gold-panners crouched in the shallows and, as the shadows lengthened, earnest instructions about *tipping pans* and *swirling gently* floated on the warm breeze.

"He can't come to any harm, Ratty. You know that," said the Mole laughing. "He'll soon get bored, and at least the equipment's cheaper than carts, cars and planes."

"I suppose so, but I must say I resent that arrogant Beaver getting his feet under Toad's table," replied Ratty. "Why don't we leave them to it and have a quiet nightcap at my place. The water should have drained away by now." The two animals bid farewell to Toad and Beaver and headed back downstream. "By tomorrow, Toad will have found a new interest," said the Rat. "Any guesses what it'll be?"

The Rat woke with a start, turned over and groaned. He and Mole had spent the previous day cleaning, drying and tidying up after the flood, and every muscle ached. He stretched out a paw, found his slippers instantly and reassured, drifted back into sleep. He woke again to a frantic knocking.

He wandered to the front door to find a dishevelled Mole on the doorstep and Portly, Otter's son, pulling away from the landing-stage. "He's off to collect his father and Badger," said the Mole, stumbling through the door, "but he brought me the news first."

The Toad Rush

As Portly lifted a paw in farewell, a noisy motor-boat cut straight across his bows, nearly tipping him overboard. Weasels, dangling from the lethal craft, screamed with laughter, as Portly rocked dangerously in their wash.

"What news?" said the Rat, gazing out at the river sleepily. "It looks awfully busy this morning."

"Busy? It's frantic! It's mayhem!" shouted Mole, "Toad's found gold and the river's gone mad!"

"What?" The Rat was wide awake now. "But he couldn't have... It's a trick, and that Beaver's at the bottom of it."

"Beaver or not, Portly said there are hordes of Wild-Wooders and all sorts of animals descending on Toad Hall, to see what they can find too."

The Rat wasted no time and soon the two friends were in the Rat's boat, bound for Toad Hall. "I've never seen the river so crowded," said the Rat, in horror, deftly avoiding a drifting boat. The Mole peered over its side as they slid past and a drunken stoat lying on the bottom brandished a bottle at him. "Where have all these Wild-Wooders appeared from?"

"I don't know," said the Rat between gritted teeth, "but we're going to find out."

As they rounded the bend, a tangled mass of boats, animals, picnic baskets and shovels was surging over what had been Toad Hall's landing-stage.

"Mr Rat, Mr Mole," someone shouted above the din. The Mole recognised one of Toad's footmen, waving at them. "Mr Toad has saved you a mooring here," the footman bellowed, as the Rat tried desperately to ship his oars in the crowded water.

The Rat and the Mole disembarked and struggled onto what, two days ago, had been Toad's beautiful lawn. Now, it was a flattened patch of scrubby brown and green, across which snaked an enormous queue of jostling, pushing and shouting animals. In the shrubbery, a couple of stoats were already exchanging blows.

"This way, sirs, Mr Toad is anxious to see you," the footman shouted, hustling them forward.

"Not as anxious as we are to see Toad," muttered the Rat, cuffing a stout ferret who had objected to the Rat's queue-jumping.

The ragged line continued up the terrace steps to where the conservatory table, so recently covered with food, was now piled with papers, ropes, shovels, pickaxes and gold pans. Toad was sitting at one end, still wearing his blue overalls, but now sporting a green eyeshade and writing frantically.

He handed the weasel, standing beside him, a large sheet of paper. "Make your mark on that, old chap. That's your pitch certificate. It lasts a day. You hand it to Mr Beaver when you arrive at the river bank. Collect one item from each pile on the table and embark from the landing-stage."

The weasel pressed his paw onto an ink pad, then onto the sheet, handed Toad a wad of bank notes and made his way down the room, collecting his equipment.

"What's going on, Toad?" shouted the Rat.

"Just the fellows, I need. One sec, Witherspoon!" Toad's butler appeared magically at his master's side. "Can you look after things here for a few minutes?"

Leaving Witherspoon in charge, Toad steered his friends to his study. "Now then chaps. I've had the most amazing good luck, and I'm happy to share it with you. Would you like to join the Toad Gold Company I've formed with Beaver? You don't have to put much money in, but I know that, in spite of your remarks yesterday, you'll want to be part of this, now I've struck it rich."

"If you think for one moment we would have anything to do with Beaver, or this..." began the Rat.

"The animals are buying pitches on your land and buying their equipment from you?" said the Mole thoughtfully.

"So, even though there's no gold, you'll have still made money," snapped the Rat.

"Well, yes," said Toad, "but it's not like that. Beaver's got it all organised. If we let people try their luck here now, they will not trouble us later. I would never have thought of that. Beaver's such a good businessman. Anyway, there is gold. Do you want to see it? It's in my safe."

"And I suppose you've had your *gold*," the Rat emphasised the word, "verified by a jeweller?"

"Two actually," replied Toad. "Beaver and I went to town yesterday. I've got the certificate to prove it. This isn't a trick. It's genuine."

Toad pulled an impressive piece of paper out of his overall pocket and flourished it in the air. "There you are. In fact, Mr Browning and his assistant said they would come down and verify all the claims for us at once. It's only going to be for a day, Ratty, then we can do all the panning ourselves."

"But you're still prepared to have hordes of Wild-Wooders, and goodness knows who else, traipsing all over our river causing chaos, just to make money. Toad, I'm ashamed of you. Come on Mole." The Rat turned abruptly and walked out.

The Toad Rush

"You've gone too far, Toad. I'm sorry," said the Mole, following his friend out of the door and shutting it firmly behind him.

"Right, so let's go and see our friend, Mister Beaver," said the Rat grimly, pushing through the throng and heading back to his boat.

"No, Ratty," said the Mole. "We can't confront him; he's too powerful, and what can we prove? I'm not sure what his trick is anyway, but everything rests on Toad finding gold in the first place, so let's go to town and find that jeweller."

Neither animal went near the town unless there was a very good reason, so the Rat knew that the Mole had thought very carefully about it. "All right, old chap, that's a sensible idea. P'rhaps I was a bit hasty."

As it was, after the chaos at Toad Hall, the jetty in the town seemed almost peaceful. The two animals disembarked, and asked politely for directions to Mr Browning's jeweller's shop. They found themselves in the old town square, where black and white, half-timbered buildings leaned lop-sidedly against each other.

"That's Mr Browning's shop," indicated a portly gentleman with mutton chop whiskers. "The one on the corner, behind all that scaffolding. What a mess! No wonder poor old Browning's ill. You weren't expecting to find him there, were you?"

"Was he ill yesterday?" asked the Mole.

"Good lord, yes," replied the gentleman. "He's been ill a month. The renovations should have been finished weeks ago but, if you employ those lazy weasels, you're lucky to get the job finished at all."

"Mole, I am beginning to think you're right," said the Rat. "Where is everyone? Let's take a look around the back," he added, disappearing down a tiny alleyway between the jeweller's and a draper's shop.

The Mole followed him slowly, emerging into a courtyard dominated by a dilapidated hut, surrounded with untidy piles of wood and tools. A gate opened out on to the side road, where a horse and cart were standing.

"Be careful, Ratty," Mole whispered, drawing him back into the shadows. "If it's open, someone must be around. Listen..."

The Rat's ears twitched but the Mole had already grabbed him, dragging him down behind a pile of rope, as two smartly clad weasels, one with a bandaged paw and the other with a limp, stumbled through the gate. Both clutched a heavy wooden box with brass fastenings.

There was a sharp intake of breath and Mole's paw tightened

109

on the Rat's.

"Oh, I say Mr Browning," said the smaller weasel, mockingly, "this is jolly heavy, don't you know?"

"Atkinson, my dear old chap, you're so right," replied the taller one, in an exaggerated tone. Then his voice roughened, "but it'll be worf all the bruises, to see that ugerly Toad right back where 'e belongs."

They burst into raucous laughter, kicked open the hut door, slammed their burdens to the ground and started singing "*Toad he went...*"

"I remember that song," whispered the Rat, "but since when did weasels wear suits?"

"Two days after ending up in the river," replied the Mole.

The Rat shifted uncomfortably and clutched the rope beside him. "Mole, I think we need to get a little tied up here. How long is it since you practised your knots?"

"Too long, Ratty. Let's go," said the Mole, grasping one end of the rope.

Grabbing the other end, the Rat dashed in front of the hut, bellowing and screaming as he did so. The hut door burst open, spilling out the weasels, who tripped headlong, sprawled in a tangle on the ground and lay moaning. Swiftly, the Mole and the Rat ran rope rings around them, securing them tightly.

This time, the weasels really were terrified. "There's enough rope, to roll 'em back, Mole," suggested the Rat.

"True, Ratty, but I could manage a horse," replied the Mole, "if you could manage the prisoners' cart."

Fortunately the prisoners were scrawny and the tiny side street deserted, so, only half an hour later, the weasel ring and the heavy boxes were on the bottom of the Rat's boat, and the two friends could begin the long row back towards Toad Hall.

By the time they arrived, exhausted, at Toad's landing-stage, it was dusk and the throngs of hopeful gold-panners had dispersed. "You stay here with the prisoners, Mole," said Rat. "I'll go find Toad and see what's happened to our friend, Beaver."

As Rat wearily approached the steps to the terrace, wails of anguish echoed out of the conservatory doors. "No, officer, no. There's been a misunderstanding."

Quickening his step, the Rat burst into the conservatory, as a portly policeman attempted to drag a weeping Toad out. "Ratty, old chap, tell them I'm innocent."

"Innocent of what?" said the Rat, looking around the assortment

The Toad Rush

of uniformed policeman crowding the room.

"I 'ave just arrested Mr Toad for circulating counterfeit bank notes," said the sergeant of police. "'E is now haccompanying me to the town, where a magistrate is hawaiting 'im."

"Before you do that, sergeant," said the Rat, "I think you might be interested in a parcel in my boat. The contents of the parcel have an interesting story to tell. Perhaps you could send some of your men to fetch them. You'll also find two boxes containing counterfeit money and something I believe called," he finally turned to look at Toad, "fools' gold."

As the sergeant dispatched his men down to the landing-stage, Toad wiped a grimy paw across his face. "Oh, Ratty, I knew you could do it," he blubbered.

"I haven't done anything yet, Toad," said the Rat tersely.

His face pale, Toad sunk moaning onto the conservatory floor.

The sergeant took out his notebook as the weasels were rolled in. "Names?" he barked at them.

"They don't have proper names in the Wild Wood," sniffed the Toad.

"Mr Browning and Mr Atkinson," replied the Rat, trying not to laugh.

"Mr B... Oh no." The Toad sank down again.

"Wild-Wooders appear to be quite talented actors and masters of disguise," said the Mole, stepping over the weasel ring, "particularly for those who want to believe in them."

"We're not from the Wild Wood," burst out Browning weasel, trying to sit up. "We're brothers from the town."

"We're all listening," said the Rat, with the satisfaction of one who had already heard the story.

"Our Dad was from the Wild Wood. He was Chief Weasel at one time."

At the mention of that name, Toad gave a little cry.

"'E was a very talented actor and singer, and when we were little 'e used to sing us *The Ballad of Toad Hall*. It told of 'ow 'e and his friends had lovingly rebuilt and looked after a dilaperidated and abanderoned criminal 'ome."

"What?" Toad leaped angrily to his feet. "How dare you?" he shrieked.

"Sit down and be quiet, Toad," said the Rat.

"When one night," continued the weasel, warming to his audience in spite of his circumstances, "a hundred bloodthirsty

The Wind In The Willows Short Stories

badgers, six boatloads of rats and a troupe of Die-hard Toads stormed their home, right in the middle of one of our old Dad's spectacular song and dance routines, and brutally drove them out!"

Toad was shrieking uncontrollably by now and struggling with the policeman guarding him. "Let me at 'im." The policeman sat down heavily on his prisoner.

"So we grew up plannin' to get our own back one day. Lots of our mates from the building site had parents who'd left the Wild Wood too, and we was drinking in *The Railway Tavern* one night, when we met Beaver. 'E masterminded the plan 'cos 'e'd done it before. 'E's the one that took Toad's real money. We're just hinnocent victims, out for a merry prank."

"You need to find our friend Mr Beaver, sergeant," said the Rat, "but I suspect he's long gone."

"Wrong, my friend," said a booming voice right on cue and the burly figures of the Otter and the Badger appeared at the top of the terrace steps, a bedraggled Beaver sagging between them.

"There's only one thing an Otter hates more than a Beaver and that's a dishonest one," continued the Otter. "We heard all about his antics at the Great Council and we only just got here in time to catch him, due to Portly's sterling efforts." Portly smiled modestly from behind the Beaver's bulk.

"Beaver, how could you?" mumbled the Toad, from under the policeman.

"Some creatures will do anything, if the price is right," growled the Badger, looking straight at Toad.

"'Ow do you spell Atkinson?" asked the sergeant, licking his pencil. "P'rhaps we'd better just take the prisoners away. Release Mister Toad."

Toad's handcuffs were removed and locked securely onto the Beaver's burly forepaws. "Tell me my friend," said the Rat quietly, "do you come from a river far away?"

"No, I escaped from captivity," said the Beaver wistfully, without a hint of a drawl. "It looks like I'm returning, but that's life. For one moment, I was enjoying your river. P'rhaps one day I'll return."

As the policemen marched their charges off, Toad climbed slowly to his feet. "Thank you, old friends. I've been a stupid, greedy Toad, but I promise I'll..."

"You'll be back to your old tricks by tomorrow," interrupted the Otter, "but, as I hear Badger and I missed a rather spectacular lunch, the least you can do is invite us all, next week."

The Toad Rush

"Perhaps a simple picnic might be better," whispered the Mole diplomatically in the Otter's ear. "I think Toad might have lost a lot of money."

"A picnic's a splendid idea," announced the Rat, "just so long as there are no other activities."

"Tomorrow then, my friends," said Toad. "We'll celebrate my deliverance from the jaws of prison. Hurrah!"

The Rat woke slowly, to hear the soft lapping of the river at his door. A picnic beside the river on a summer's day – what could be more perfect?

"Ratty wake up!" The Mole's voice interrupted his reverie. The Rat stumbled to the door and opened it to his old friend. "While we were busy apprehending criminals," announced the Mole, "Toad made a big win on the races. Now he wants to buy the horse, so we're all invited to a shareholders' luncheon."

"No, Mole," said the Rat, picking up a basket from beside the door. "We're going for a picnic. Just you, me and the river."

An Unexpected Uncle For Toad
by Jessie Anderson

It was going to be a perfect summer day – blissfully warm, long and lazy. Although it was only mid-morning a heat haze was already shimmering over the river, larks were singing as they soared into the blue canopy overhead and the Water Rat, stretched out on the river bank, doing nothing in particular, felt contentment seeping with the sunshine into his soul.

This was a day for being rather than for doing, he thought, or for not doing anything more strenuous than messing about in his boat. But it would be very pleasant if a friend like Mole, for instance, should happen along to share in the messing. They might even go for a picnic on the river. His thoughts, drifting along as lazily as the river below him, were interrupted by the sound of small feet pattering along the tow path behind him. "Hullo Mole, old chap," he called out cheerfully without turning round, for he had recognised his friend's footsteps. "Have you come to share this blue day with me?"

"Oh Ratty, I'm so sorry," said the Mole, slithering down the bank to sit beside his friend. "Why are you unhappy?"

"Me, unhappy?" said the Water Rat in surprise. "Far from it. I couldn't be happier and now we can enjoy the day together."

"But you said it was a blue day," said the puzzled Mole. "And when people say they're blue it usually means they're unhappy."

"No, my friend," replied the Rat. "I'm not blue – just the day; and blue is the perfect colour for a perfect summer's day. Look at the sky; isn't it the most beautiful blue; and there's a kingfisher sitting on that branch overhanging the water. Have you ever seen anything more brilliant than the blue of his feathers? Watch those dragonflies darting like small blue flames over the pool by the far bank. And the pool itself looks as though a piece of sky has fallen into it. Oh yes, blue is the happiest summer colour – I shall write a poem about it."

"You're right, of course," agreed the Mole. "When you put it like that – you being a poet and all – I can see that blue is the perfect summer colour." Then he added as an afterthought, "I'd always thought of gold, myself, as the colour of summer."

The two friends argued lazily and amicably for a few minutes about the relative merits of blue and gold until the Mole said, rather anxiously, "Ratty, you aren't going to write your poem now, are you? I thought we might be going on the river."

Since the Mole had, with the Water Rat's encouragement, come to enjoy his days on the river and had even achieved some skill at rowing, he was always eager to join his friend in an excursion – particularly if a picnic was going to form part of it.

"Don't worry, old chap," the Water Rat reassured him, "I don't feel a poem coming on at the moment. Besides, when I do get around to writing it, I shall be remembering this perfect blue day all over again – that's twice the enjoyment." He began to scramble along the bank towards his home.

"Come along Moly," he said. "We'll just get a few things from my store cupboard to make a picnic and then we'll paddle down the river to Toad Hall. How does that suit you?"

"Oh Ratty, what a splendid idea," replied the Mole enthusiastically. "Not just the picnic, I mean," he added hastily in case his friend should think he was only interested in the food which the Water Rat always provided so lavishly. "I think Toad would be glad of a visit. I ran into him the other day and he seemed a bit unhappy."

"I know what you mean," said the Water Rat looking serious. "Toad has never been his old exuberant self since we got Toad Hall back for him from those rascally weasels and stoats."

"Perhaps Badger was a bit hard on him then, don't you think?" suggested the Mole. "Telling him he had to stop boasting and showing off and all that sort of thing. But that's part of being Toad. It's just the way he is."

"Yes, it is," agreed the Rat. "And we like him in spite of his boastfulness. But you must admit life's been a lot more peaceful since he gave up all his wild schemes."

"You're right," sighed the Mole. "It still makes me shudder when I remember his craze for motor-cars and all that led to. All the same, a quiet Toad isn't the Toad we know, and it's a bit worrying."

"You mean, you think he may be planning some new outburst?" asked the Rat anxiously. "And this is just the calm before the storm?"

"It wouldn't surprise me," replied the Mole. "Well, the best way to find out is to visit him."

They had reached the Water Rat's home and it didn't take them long to pack up the picnic hamper which Rat always kept ready to hand for just such an expedition as this. Mole, who lived rather more frugally than his friend, always delighted in unpacking the Rat's picnic hampers and today he was experiencing the added delight of helping to pack one, carefully stowing away jars, bottles and packages as Ratty handed out more and yet more supplies

An Unexpected Uncle For Toad

from his well-stocked larder. There were bottles of beer, a large slab of cheese, oatcakes and buttered bread rolls, mouth-watering pickles, ham and tongue, an apple tart, several slices of plum pudding and, finally, some hard-boiled eggs.

Knives and forks and little pots of salt, pepper and mustard were stowed into convenient corners. Then, over the top of the feast was laid a red and white checked gingham tablecloth with napkins to match. (Even on a picnic Rat liked to observe the basic rules of civilised dining.) Then, with the lid secured firmly, the two friends carried the heavy hamper between them down to where Ratty's boat was moored.

They made their way upstream allowing the little blue-painted boat to glide lazily past banks from which wild roses, meadowsweet and cowslips sent out the heady scent of summer. Before long they reached the landing-stage for Toad Hall, their friend's very grand residence. As they made the boat fast, the front door of the Hall opened and Toad came slowly down to meet them. And what a woebegone Toad it was. Gone was the ebullient welcome which they had always received on previous visits. Rat and Mole looked at each other apprehensively.

"Hullo Toad," said the Water Rat. "We've brought a picnic to share with you. You don't want to be stuck indoors on a day like this."

"It's very kind of you Ratty – and good to see you too, Mole," said Toad in a flat, lifeless voice. "Come up to the house will you. I've a guest I'd like you to meet."

The two animals, by now thoroughly alarmed, followed their friend up the grand stone steps, flanked by two stone lions, at the entrance to the Hall. Mole had never quite got over his nervousness at entering Toad's very imposing home. And today his whiskers twitched with more than his usual nerves; he had a feeling that something was very wrong. He glanced towards Ratty and saw that he was looking far from his usual confident self. If he hadn't known how courageous his friend could be he would have suspected him of wanting to turn and run.

"Come into the drawing room," said Toad, still in the same dead voice as he opened the great oak door into the splendidly appointed room where their gaze was instantly fixed on the figure lounging in the great armchair by the French windows. It had been, they knew, the favourite armchair of Toad's father. Today it was occupied by a large, fat and very ugly-looking toad.

"This is my uncle – my father's elder brother," said Toad with a marked lack of enthusiasm. "These are my good friends Ratty and Mole."

"Pleased to meet you, lads," said Uncle Toad expansively, waving a cigar at them. "Any friend of my nephew is a friend of mine – you'll always be welcome here."

"We always are welcome here already – as Toad's friends," said the Water Rat rather sharply.

"We don't seem to have heard about you before," said Mole placatingly. He thought Ratty was making his disapproval rather too plain. "After all," he said to himself, "Toad's uncle deserves to be treated with respect even if he does seem to be taking too much on himself."

"No, I'm not surprised at your ignorance, my friends," said Uncle Toad. "I've been abroad for many years and rather lost touch with my family." His expression, as he eyed their friend Toad was difficult to read. It looked, Mole thought, like a mixture of cunning and bravado. The old toad took his time over lighting his cigar. Then, having settled himself more comfortably in his chair, he continued, "I decided it was time to return to my roots and to settle down. I've had enough of wandering."

"You must have had an interesting life," said Mole. The conversation was getting really difficult, he thought – and neither Ratty nor Toad was helping. "Where abroad have you been?" he finished lamely.

"Oh, here, there and everywhere," said Uncle Toad vaguely. "Places you've probably never even heard of."

The Water Rat roused himself. "How about our picnic," he said. "Are you coming Toad? And you too, of course, Sir," he added reluctantly, "if you'd care to join us."

"Thank you, but no thank you," replied the elder toad. "It's been a long journey to get here and I think I need some time to recover." He smiled at Toad, but his smile didn't reach his eyes. "You go on the picnic, my boy. After such a long absence I need to familiarise myself again with the Hall. Then I think I'll move my belongings into the master bedroom, if that's all right with you."

"Whatever you say Uncle," said Toad meekly.

By this time the Rat was seething with fury, which he barely managed to control until he, Mole and Toad made their way to the landing-stage. "Why on earth are you letting him behave as though he owned the place?" he demanded.

"That's just it Ratty," said Toad miserably. "It seems he *does* own the place." He gulped down a sob. "You see, he's my father's elder brother, so by rights Toad Hall belongs to him."

The two friends looked aghast at Toad. "Where's he been all this time?" snapped Ratty. "I don't recall your ever mentioning an uncle."

An Unexpected Uncle For Toad

"Yes, my father did have an older brother," admitted Toad, "but as far as I know he went abroad before I was born and died there years ago – although it looks now as though he didn't. Die, I mean."

"Very odd, if you ask me," remarked the Rat. "Why didn't he return while your father was alive?"

"Beyond me," said Toad miserably. "And there's nothing I can do about it. Now Toad Hall is legally his."

"Never mind Toady," said Mole trying desperately to think of some way to comfort his friend. "He's so old he won't live much longer and then Toad Hall will be yours again."

"No, it won't," gulped Toad. "He has a son. He's coming to join him here soon, he says. And he's the rightful heir. Whatever will happen to me?"

As a picnic it wasn't a great success, despite all the good things in the hamper. Both Rat and Mole felt it would be bad form to appear to be enjoying themselves while their friend was in such distress.

At last, feeling very low-spirited, they bade a sad farewell to Toad and, as they rowed miserably downstream, a cloud obscured the sun, and a chill wind, blowing offshore, made them shiver. Ratty's bright blue summer day had turned a dismal grey. Silently they tied up the boat, heaved the hamper up to the Water Rat's home and began unpacking the remains of the picnic.

Suddenly Ratty stood up straight with a determined look on his face. "I don't like it at all," he said fiercely. "There's something very far wrong here and we're going to find out what it is." He grabbed Mole by the paw. "Come on Moly. No time to lose. We're going to see Badger."

"I'm happy to see Badger at any time," said Mole. "But I'm not sure what you think he can do."

"Badger was Toad's father's old friend," said Ratty. "He knew the whole family for many years and I think he may well know something that will help our friend Toad. Now, come on."

The Badger was just sitting down to his supper when the Mole and the Rat rang his front doorbell. "Come along in," said Badger in his hospitable way. "You're just in time to join me for a bite to eat."

The friends accepted gratefully for, because of Toad's unhappiness, they had done far less than the usual justice to their picnic. Mole, particularly, was always happy to be in Badger's comfortable underground home. It was much less grand than Toad Hall and, to Mole's way of thinking, less intimidating and more homely

The Wind In The Willows Short Stories

and cosy – rather like his own Mole End, in fact, only more spacious.

The three friends settled down happily to a very generous supper and it wasn't until they had finished and were sitting contentedly in Badger's comfortable armchairs that their host at last said, "Now tell me what brings you here. I can see you have something on your minds."

"Oh Badger, it's Toad," exclaimed Ratty and Mole together.

Badger sighed. "Toad is it?" he said. "I might have expected it. What's he up to now?"

"This time it's not what Toad has been up to," wailed the Rat. "It's what his uncle has been up to."

Badger gave a grunt of surprise. "His uncle," he said. "He doesn't have an uncle. He did have, but he died some years ago."

"That's what Toad thought," said Mole. "But it seems he's still very much alive and ready to claim Toad Hall as his own."

"That's a lot of nonsense," snapped the Badger, bristling angrily. "Toad's father was my oldest friend and he told me when and where his brother died. I don't want to go into all that now, without talking to Toad first, but you can take it from me this Toad is no uncle to our friend. He's an imposter."

"Oh Badger," said the Water Rat smiling hopefully. "That's wonderful news. But how can you prove it?"

"Just leave that to me," said the Badger. "All you need do is bring Toad along here tomorrow – without uncle – and we'll make our plans."

"But how shall we manage to get Toad here without his uncle?" asked Mole nervously.

"Easy," said Ratty confidently. "As chairman of the local residents' association, Badger has called an urgent meeting of the committee – that's you and me, Mole, and Toad – to consider ways of improving home security, because of your concern over the increasing number of burglaries in the district."

"Well done, Ratty," said Badger smiling. "I didn't know how concerned I was until you mentioned it. That should do the trick. Just make sure you get Toad here tomorrow."

Rat and Mole lost no time in returning to Toad Hall with Badger's message. They had a scary moment when Uncle Toad announced that he should come to the meeting as well. He'd become quite anxious, he said, about the lack of security at Toad Hall.

"It's wide open to any number of undesirable characters," he

An Unexpected Uncle For Toad

said pompously. "I've had some experience of security matters and I shall be only too happy to give you the benefit of my expertise."

"Oh Uncle," said Toad with a well-assumed expression of regret, "We'll have to do without your help this time. Have you forgotten about your appointment with the bank manager tomorrow?"

"How stupid of me," said Uncle Toad, looking rather put out. "I must open a local bank account to have my funds transferred from abroad. And I'm also desperately in need of some new clothes suitable for Toad Hall. My nephew here has kindly advanced me some money to go shopping for them." Then he added, with a sly leer in Toad's direction, "It's very trusting of you, Nephew, but then, what's yours is mine, as the saying goes."

Ratty looked ready to explode with rage so Mole, to calm things down, said innocently, "You'll be using the Toad family bank, of course. You'll not have any problem opening an account there."

"Which one..." began Uncle Toad before stopping in mid-sentence and finishing hurriedly, "the family bank, yes, of course." The danger, for all concerned, was avoided for the moment and Toad was free next morning to join his friends for their visit to Badger's home.

"Badger will know what to do," said Toad as they made their way next day along the little country lanes with their riot of wild flowers. Bees were buzzing about their business amongst the clover; butterflies hovered over violets and buttercups and birds chirped happily in the hedgerows. Toad's spirits rose to match the brightness of the day and he began to skip along merrily.

"Badger always knows what to do," he continued. "Why didn't I think of asking him?"

"Well, now's your chance," said Ratty rather huffily as they arrived at the familiar green painted door with the neat brass plate bearing the inscription, "Mr Badger" on it. "Really," he thought, "Toad might be a little grateful for our support."

Badger had been impatiently awaiting their arrival, so the door was opened almost immediately. "Come in, come in," he said in welcome. "Now, Toad, your friends here have told me about your present predicament, so let's get straight down to business. What do you know about your uncle?"

"Hardly anything," replied Toad. "All I know is that my real uncle went abroad before I was born and died there years ago. And apart from dying that's what this uncle, or whatever he is, claims he's been doing."

"Balderdash," shouted Badger fiercely.

"Balderdash," murmured Ratty to himself. "What a splendid word. I must remember to use it in a poem some time."

"Balderdash," repeated Badger, even more fiercely. "And piffle," he added, for good measure. "Your real uncle never went abroad in his life. And your father always knew where he was."

"That's quite astonishing," said Toad thoughtfully. "He never talked about him and always shut me up if I asked any questions. How is it you know all this?"

"Your father trusted me with information he didn't always want to share with others – even you," said Badger. "What I'm going to tell you now is something your father said was to be kept from you unless circumstances made it imperative that you should know. I think that time has come."

The Mole and the Water Rat looked at each other uncomfortably. "If this is private," said Ratty, "we'll leave you alone."

"No, no," said Toad hastily. "You're my friends and whatever I have to hear I'd rather hear it with you to share it."

"Well," said Badger heavily, "you must know there are good and bad sorts of people everywhere. There are good moles, like our friend here and, I've no doubt, bad moles; good badgers and, I daresay, bad badgers, although I haven't met any." Toad began to fidget, so Badger continued hurriedly, "There are good toads, like your excellent father and, sadly, there are bad toads, like your uncle. Not to put too fine a point on it, your uncle was a scallywag and a rascal."

Toad began to look relieved. "Oh, for a moment I thought you meant really wicked," he said. "This sounds more like a bit of high spirits getting him into trouble – the sort of thing I'm quite capable of myself."

"You don't need to remind us," said Badger severely. "No, Toad, this was more than high spirits, although it probably started out that way when he first ran away from home. Then he got into bad company and minor offences became real crimes. He always kept in touch with your father, mainly because he so often needed him to pay his debts or bale him out of prison. Eventually his life became a series of periods in and out of prison. He was there when he died and your father, unable to rescue him yet again, was with him at the end."

Toad, completely overcome, kept muttering brokenly, "I didn't know. I didn't know. Why didn't my father tell me."

"Your father was a very proud toad," said Badger. "He felt his brother had brought shame to an honourable family name. So it was easiest to try to wipe out the memory of your uncle's misdeeds

An Unexpected Uncle For Toad

by saying he had died abroad and refusing to talk about him further."

Toad said nothing at all for quite a few minutes as he tried to come to terms with this revelation. At last he said, "Then who is this – this person who claims to be my uncle?"

"I'm not sure," said Badger slowly. "But I'd hazard a guess that he is one of your uncle's prison mates with whom he became friendly and to whom he probably boasted about his wealthy background. Perhaps when your uncle died he had the idea of using this knowledge to his advantage and it's taken until now to find the right opportunity."

"And how are we going to prove he isn't who he says he is," asked Toad unhappily. "He's got so much information about my family that he could have anyone fooled. I certainly believed him."

"He'll trip up eventually," said Badger.

"The sooner the better," urged Toad, "or he'll have me out of Toad Hall before I can call for help."

"We'll be there Toady," said Ratty valiantly. "We'll help all we can."

"You certainly will be able to help," agreed Badger. "You'll be needed as witnesses when the imposter confesses – as he will, if my plan works."

"I knew you'd have a plan, Badger," said Toad quite like his normal, cheerful self. "How very clever you are."

"You are going to be your Aunt Arabella," said Badger surprisingly.

"My Aunt who?" said Toad. "I haven't got an aunt of any sort."

"You have now," said Badger firmly. "What's more, she's very fond of her nephew and she's coming to visit."

"I don't want to be my Aunt anybody," protested Toad. "And I positively refuse to dress up again. It was absolutely humiliating pretending to be that frumpy old washerwoman."

"But this time," coaxed Badger, "you'll be an elegant and very dignified lady. Ratty, Mole and I will collect a splendid wardrobe for you. You'll be a tremendous success – and you know what a superb actor you are." This appeal to Toad's vanity was as successful as the crafty Badger had known it would be.

"Well, if you're sure there's no other way," said Toad.

"There isn't," said Badger firmly. "And remember, you're not to get carried away. You must stick to the story I'll outline for you. Otherwise we'll never get a confession."

Badger had made his plans very carefully so that, by the time the trio arrived the next day at Toad Hall with an impressive array of garments collected from various elderly female relatives for Toad, all they had to do was follow Badger's instructions. Fortunately Uncle Toad was taking his after-lunch nap when they arrived and they had ample time to prepare the scene. When Uncle Toad, resplendent in his new clothes, eventually swaggered into the drawing room an unexpected gathering confronted him.

He had already met the Water Rat and the Mole, but he didn't feel too comfortable about the fierce looking Badger. And who on earth, he wondered, was this overdressed, old lady in the shapeless fur coat and the ridiculously large hat obscuring her face?

The Rat took charge of the introductions, explaining that Toad had been called away by the gardener to discuss plans for the new rose beds. "This is Toad's oldest friend, Mr Badger," he said. "And this is Toad's Aunt Arabella, who, of course, is your sister." At this Uncle Toad started nervously.

"What a happy reunion this will be for you," put in the Badger maliciously.

"My dear brother, I wouldn't have known you – but then it's been a long time, hasn't it?" fluted Toad in what, he thought, was a suitably tremulous voice for an elderly aunt. Only the seriousness of the situation prevented Ratty and Mole from laughing out loud. Trust Toad to put on a good performance, they thought.

"And where have you been all these years, brother dear?" quavered Toad. "When I heard from my nephew that you'd come back from the dead, as it were, I couldn't wait to meet you. What a lot we shall have to talk about – recalling those happy early years together."

The old Toad shifted uneasily in his chair. Where on earth did this pesky old woman, fit in? he wondered. Why had there never been any mention of her? There was nothing for it. He'd just have to bluff it out. That's what his wits were for, after all.

"You'll be wanting to know about Albert," said the pesky old woman.

The old toad managed an inquiring smile. "I was just about to ask," he said. (Was Albert her dog, her son, her husband, or what? he wondered frantically.)

"Sadly, Albert died three years ago," said Arabella, wiping away a tear.

"That's a relief," muttered Uncle Toad. At least he wasn't going to have to face Albert as well.

"What did you say, brother? You'll have to speak up – I'm a little hard of hearing," said Toad, by now thoroughly enjoying himself.

An Unexpected Uncle For Toad

"I said that's a real grief," replied the old toad. "How much longer is this ordeal going to continue?" he thought to himself.

"What chums you and Albert were," smiled Toad, happily immersed in his role as Arabella. "And the mischief the two of you used to get up to – you can't have forgotten that time with the elephant?"

"What time – what elephant?" Uncle Toad felt he was beginning to lose his grip on reality. The afternoon was turning into a nightmare, and it seemed unlikely ever to end, with more and more "memories" being produced by this dreadful sister. Would she never stop saying, "You must remember, brother dear; you can't have forgotten..." on and on?

The perspiration was pouring down Uncle's face as the garrulous Arabella prepared for the final blow. "It nearly broke my heart when you ran away," she said. "But what helped to ease the pain was the remembrance of your last few precious words to me before you left." The old Toad made a supreme effort to look suitably affected. Then Toad released his sharpest verbal arrow. "Say them to me again, brother dear," he murmured. "Just once more, to make an old woman happy."

The interloper knew he was cornered, but he made one last feeble effort to save his skin. "Not in front of these people, Arabella," he muttered. "That moment was too private to be shared. I can't do it."

For Toad the moment had come. "Can't do it!" he roared, snatching off the ridiculous hat. "No, of course you can't, you fraud." He jumped out of the enveloping fur coat and shook his fist in Uncle Toad's face. "You can't repeat the words because they were never said. There never was a sister Arabella, or an Albert – or an elephant either. You are an imposter!"

For one moment it looked as though the rascally old toad would make a run for the door. Then, as he saw the large and powerful Badger barring the way, he thought better of it. He shrivelled like a balloon from which all the air had escaped. Finally he burst into tears. "I'm sorry," he sobbed. "I was a fool to think I could get away with it. I became friends with your uncle in prison and he told me endless stories about his home. When he died I had the idea of impersonating him, but I couldn't do it while your father was alive because he knew only too well that his brother was dead. Besides, he would have recognised me from his visits to the prison." He wiped the perspiration from his brow, before continuing. "After he died I had a fair stretch of another prison sentence to serve, so I had to wait until now..." His voice trailed away miserably.

"And you were going to steal Toad Hall from me," shouted a very angry Toad.

"And why not?" snapped the imposter with some return of his normal confident manner. "What have you done to deserve it? You were born into it – no effort required on your part. I've had to steal and plot and cheat for everything I've had. Nothing came easily for me."

"Did you ever consider trying a stint of honest work?" inquired Badger dryly.

The old toad began to weep again. "Please, please don't have me sent back to prison," he pleaded. "I'm too old; I'm not in good health, and I'm really sorry about deceiving you. I'll give you back the new clothes."

Toad decided it was time to be magnanimous. "You may keep the clothes," he said grandly. "They're not to my taste. I prefer understated elegance myself."

Badger, Ratty and Mole managed not to smile as they thought of Toad's well-deserved reputation for sartorial excess.

"Now go – and don't ever come back," said Toad, enjoying this moment of high drama. The imposter scuttled away quickly in case Toad should change his mind. That was the last they ever saw of "Uncle". "Now," said Toad, "let's celebrate." He was his old ebullient self again. "Wasn't I clever as Aunt Arabella?" he demanded, puffing out his chest.

"I think the clever one was Badger who thought up the whole scheme," said Ratty a little reprovingly.

Toad, good-hearted fellow that he was, was instantly contrite. "Yes, of course, Badger," he said. "I owe everything to you and to my good friends, Ratty and Mole, for sticking by me through this terrible ordeal." A broad, beaming smile spread over his face. "So let's open the champagne and drink to friendship."

Below The Waves
by Belinda Beasley

"It's stopped raining, Mole," said the Water Rat, peering through the steamed-up window of his back parlour.

At that very moment the sun shot a beam across the bow of the boat tied up outside, illuminating it as if in celebration; a thrush stood to full-breasted attention in the branches above and burst into joyous song; and a dozen mayflies sallied forth, from wherever it is that mayflies go when forced by inclement conditions to leave the airy dance floor which is theirs for so short a time, and started waltzing once more.

"Huh, makes a change," grumbled the Mole. "I expect it'll start again any minute."

The sunbeam faded a little at this unenthusiastic reception.

The Rat pushed open the little glass pane on its squeaky hinges and sniffed the air.

"You might be right of course," he said soothingly, wanting nothing to ruffle Mole's fur in anticipation of his own forthcoming suggestion, "but the sky looks quite clear now and the sun is out again," – the sunbeam brightened a little to reinforce the Rat's point – "and everything will be dry in no time; and my boat is waiting; and... O, Mole! Please let's go out!"

Because the Rat so wanted to *go out*.

Much as he loved his own back parlour – and a back parlour has many attractions: in certain harsh weathers for example, or when a chap needs a bit of peace and quiet, or when he feels the call to get on with poetry things – the simple fact was that the Rat's animal nature cried out for water and fresh air, if not constantly then at least regularly. He was of the honest opinion that several hours in a back parlour, when everything outside was so progressive and thrusting and full of energy; when the hedgerows were full of daylight fireworks, exploding with larkspur and poppies; and the shallow river beds burgeoned with bulrushes, was enough to drive even a sensible animal to distraction.

He also thought there was nothing more glorious than getting soaked to the skin by a summer shower.

The Mole, however, was a little fed up with being out and getting wet. In fact, the Mole was even a little fed up with water! Oh, he loved the water in the river all right – water which spangled in the sunlight and gleamed in the moonlight. The water in the river quickened his pulse and brought out the poetry in his soul. He loved *that* water, gliding along on a swift current, first mate in Ratty's boat. He loved the *water-travel* aspect of water, sitting at the helm and imagining himself a great mariner, exploring the Barbary Coast (wherever that was). Oh, yes! Water in the river was alright, where it stayed sensibly between banks and kept its mind on where it was going, but the past solid fortnight of rain was a different matter altogether!

It was rain at its most moody and difficult. It was on-again, off-again rain that couldn't make its mind up whether to stay or to go and then rained again before the first lot had had a chance to clear off. It soaked through umbrellas and hats and overcoats and galoshes and found its way into ears and between toes and soaked through fur and skin and into the very *bones* of everything. And it had taken its toll on the Mole and on his good humour.

However, even if the bold, adventurous spirit in the Mole was feeling a little damp and grumpy, the congenial one, as always, wanted nothing more than that his friend should feel happy. So, he pulled himself together with an effort.

"Yes let's go out Ratty. It would be lovely to get some fresh air."

The overjoyed Rat leapt to his feet and scuttled about getting this and that – no time for a proper luncheon basket today as time was of the essence, but they could take several packets of sandwiches and cake wrapped in greaseproof paper and some lemonade and a pork pie and a couple of apples in each pocket and a couple more because they were bound to feel peckish and that tin of anchovies that he'd been saving for the ducks as they didn't really like cheese sandwiches and preferred something a bit exotic.

The Mole, meanwhile, fetched his mackintosh.

Soon they were ready and, as they went out into the sunshine, where the light was sparkling like a thousand, tiny, mullioned windows off the leaves of the beeches, the Rat chased his tail with happiness at the very thought of getting into his boat and onto his beloved River, for, even when he was going about on dry land and foraging through the driest meadow, the chinkling music of the River's sighs and splashes played faintly in the farthest corners of his mind. Now, as he flung back the tarpaulin covering his boat (for he believed in keeping the rain off boats, if not off rats), a feeling of great peace and contentment swept over him, and he felt himself a very blessed rat indeed.

The Rat hung the tarpaulin from a branch of the beech tree,

while the Mole clambered into the boat and made his way to the prow, where he perched himself facing forwards and sniffed the air like a portly and amiable figurehead. Then the Rat untied the painter from the landing-stage, climbed in and pushed off, and the little ship drifted out into the current.

After the morning's rain, the outer world was cheerful and friendly, as if cleansed of all malice. An azure sky gazed down at them, thoroughly amiable, and the newly washed air was kindly and warm, while a gentle breeze came along from time to time, like a gracious host, to make sure that they were comfortable. The silky surface of the water mirrored fringed banks, which shone with vegetable gold and the air in the meadows beyond was coloured with birdsong. It was a day when nature was eloquent and the earth was rosy.

Neither animal spoke for some time, which was their usual habit whenever setting off in the boat, as the River was a familiar friend with whom silence was the floodgate of the heart. There was only the slosh of the sculls as the Rat paddled lazily, watching a lark above the meadow and wandering deep within his own thoughts. Naturally, this meant that the boat continued upstream on a meandering course, drifting this way and that, and quite often into the bank, whereupon the Mole would push them away with his paddle and they would again take up the current.

They spent a couple of hours simply wandering the main river until a rather loud rumble from the Mole's stomach signalled the need to stop for lunch. At the thought of food, the Rat pulled on the oars more energetically than he had all morning and soon swung the boat into a backwater in search of a quiet mooring.

Overhanging willows forced the Mole down from his seat in the prow and he and the Rat had to lie low several times to avoid being knocked out of the boat altogether, but at last they came into a clearing, then into a wider stretch of water, where the Rat declared a particular spot on the bank excellent for mooring, and they docked.

"I wonder where the ducks are today," said the Rat, stowing his sculls in their rowlocks and clambering out and onto the bank where the Mole was already laying out the provisions on his mackintosh.

"Perhaps it's not wet enough for them now the rain's stopped," chuckled the Mole, and the Rat realised happily that his friend's spirits had been fully restored to their usual good-humoured state.

The Wind In The Willows Short Stories

After lunch, once the last crumbs of cake had been brushed from the Mole's waistcoat and the apple cores tossed into the river for the benefit of any tiny creatures who fancied a bit of fruit, they both felt full and round and sleepy. The Rat lay back and tried to think of a word to rhyme with "anchovies", with which to annoy the ducks when he finally saw them, and the Mole lay on his full stomach and gazed out at the River.

They had docked in a pleasant place, but now he saw that the backwater to which they had come was a darksome passage roofed with branches and banked with mossy stones and tree roots. The tangle of trees cast the water in a dim light broken only by the occasional shaft of sun piercing the leaves. Here, the River was soft and quiet and the only signs of the current running through it were leaf islands trapped at the water's edge and the occasional, floating log drifting past.

The Mole had recently been reading about the Amazon and he wondered now whether the jungle was anything like this. It would be an adventure to go to such a place, but he wasn't sure how he would feel about crocodiles (his blood ran cold at the very sound of the word in his head), which he understood were a menace to small creatures. At that moment a glint of sapphire buzzed past as a dragonfly skimmed the surface of the water, itself menacing a small creature and sending it into everlasting night.

The Mole watched the dragonfly and wondered if they had them in the Amazon jungle and thought it would be a shame if they didn't. Then he tried to imagine he was in the Amazon...and he listened to the sounds in the trees around and above and pretended to himself that the wood pigeons were parrots (which he had never heard). So rapt was he in his fancy that for some minutes the quiet river *was* the mighty Amazon and the log a little way downstream *was* a crocodile.

He was shunted forcefully out of his dream, however, on realising that the log was clearly moving under its own volition...and heading straight for him! He quickly sat upright and, for a horrible, heart-stopping moment, he felt such an unimaginable terror that the Rat, in sympathetic response, felt his own heart suddenly race and, fully alert, he sat up too and saw something so strange that he rubbed his eyes in disbelief.

An eel, as straight and stiff as one of Ratty's sculls, was heading straight for them – an eel standing on its tail (or on what the Rat supposed was its tail and it was brought home to him in an instant that he had no idea where an eel's head stopped and its tail began), an eel upright on a log, like no eel he had ever known, and moving rapidly in their direction! The Rat felt a sudden rush of dread that revenge for the many eel

Below The Waves

suppers he had enjoyed was about to take its course.

The Mole and the Rat were frozen with fear and wonder as they faced this twin terror of crocodile and eel-monster. They had just got themselves under control enough to realise that they needed to turn tail and run when a round door on top of the log suddenly opened and Toad popped out.

"Surprise! Oh the look on your faces! What a picture! Bet you never thought to see old Toad pop up like that! In the middle of the river too! Just what you'd least expect!" said Toad, gleefully.

"Actually, Toad, I'd expect anything from you," said the Rat a little testily at Toad's blatant disregard for animal-etiquette which forbade scaring the living daylights out of one's fellow creatures, except for culinary purposes. Toad, oblivious to anyone's moods except his own, ignored this and pointed to the erect eel.

"Periscope," he said. "Cleverest thing. Can see everywhere. In all directions and no one even knows you're there. It's all done with mirrors. DOWN PERISCOPE!" he yelled imperiously into the hole from which he'd popped, and the erect eel looked inquiringly about, wriggled slightly and descended into the log with some ceremony.

The Rat and the Mole looked at each other and then at Toad.

"Well," said Toad, "don't you want to know what I'm up to? You usually do."

"Is it sensible?" said the Rat

"Is it safe?" said the Mole.

"Will it keep you out of trouble?" they said together.

"Yes, yes, yes," said Toad irritably, "it's all of those things and very much more besides. It is the most wonderful, beautiful, glorious thing. The world has opened up to me before my very eyes. Why, the wonders I have seen and I've only been out for fifteen minutes! You really can't imagine. Well you can, Ratty, because you see it all the time but do you really see, I ask myself. O, how quickly we become blinkered to the marvels around us. Has familiarity perhaps made you inattentive? Perhaps even bred contempt?"

Bemused, the Rat stared at Toad. "What are you going on about, Toad?" he asked.

"The River of course," said Toad. "I can now swim about the River just like you and Otter and all the rest. And the beauty is, I don't get wet!"

"Can't see much point in swimming if you don't get wet," said the Rat cheerily, "but come on Toad, explain what you mean, old chap, because I don't know about Mole here, but I'm no wiser than when you popped up out of that log a minute ago."

"Log!" cried Toad, greatly offended. "Log! This is no log, Rat! This is watercraft of the highest order. A vessel of surpassing ingenuity and a feat of engineering. This, Gentlemen, is a submersible!"

The Rat and the Mole looked at him blankly.

"An underwater boat," he added, exasperated.

"Underwater what!" gasped the Rat.

So Toad launched into a long and complicated explanation of his new plaything (though *he* didn't call it that, of course). He told them about the comfortable quarters below deck – compact and convenient in every way. He told them how it worked, and about the propeller which moved the craft, and how the propeller was operated by a dynamo system pedalled by Burly, his new under-butler (and Otter's nephew) – "A marvellous young fellow and bound to go far!" He told them how the 'sub' (for that's what he called it) had been delivered that very day and lowered into the water with quite a lot of trouble, as it rolled around alarmingly at first, but how he had worked out (with some help from Burly) that they were trying to put it in upside down and the machine was simply trying to right itself, proving what a remarkable invention it was – "As if it had a mind of its own!" He went on at length about the little portholes for viewing and what he had seen so far, which included quite a lot of weed because he hadn't realised he'd steered them into a backwater. But then again, he'd not realised that weed could be so interesting! Finally, he explained that he'd decided to try out the periscope and what had he seen but his two friends staring at him in astonishment from the river bank. He finished his lecture by inviting them on board.

"One at a time, mind you, as it's a two-animal craft and I have to be there to show you around. Burly would have to get out, but I'm sure he wouldn't mind...could probably do with a break. You could take over the cycling and we could go downstream a way. How about it?"

The Mole had been very interested in all that Toad had to say about the submersible, punctuating Toad's speech with little words of encouragement, such as, "Oh my!" and "Astonishing!" and "No, really?" but the Rat had been silent. Now he spoke up.

"You've gone too far this time, Toad," he said quietly. "It's unnatural, swimming underwater in a machine."

"That's just what the ducks said," said Toad cheerfully.

Below The Waves

"One of them stuck his head down just as we were going past and he and I came face to face through a porthole. I could tell he was shocked, so we surfaced and I came up to talk to him – like I'm doing to you now – and to explain and what-have-you, but he wouldn't let me get a word in edgeways. Before I knew it all his relatives and neighbours were there and everybody was making a dreadful racket and quacking nineteen to the dozen. They said exactly what you just said, 'it's unnatural, swimming underwater in a machine'."

"Well, they're right," said the Rat.

"Poppycock," said Toad. "Pure poppycock. That's a very blinkered view. Very parochial, if you don't mind my saying so Rat." The Rat did mind but Toad went on. "I can't see how swimming about underwater, propelled by a bicycle is very different to swimming about on top of the water, propelled by oars!"

The Rat had no answer to this but he still felt it was wrong.

"So, how about it, Mole?" said Toad, "D'you fancy a trip below the waves?"

The Mole did indeed fancy a trip below the waves and said timidly he had always wondered what it would be like underwater – above water being so glorious and all. The Rat was, unfortunately, somewhat sarcastic about it and said there was more to the experience than what you could see from inside a sardine can, and the Mole thought that perhaps he should decline in the interests of friendship. However, it was finally decided that the Mole would have a go, while Ratty and Burly visited the Otter to catch up on river gossip.

The longsuffering Burly came up, clearly glad for a rest, and the Mole went down, and Toad closed the hatch (as he called it). The Rat and Burly stood on the bank and watched as the submarine rocked a little in the water. Then they heard Toad's voice echo "Going Down!" in an unnecessary sort of way, as the submersible descended with a "gloop" into the bosom of the deep.

What struck the Mole on arrival into the confines of the underwater boat was that it was indeed very confined. Being an underground creature by nature, if not so much taste these days, he was used to operating in small spaces, but even he found the conditions cramped. And the air! Toad had assured him that air was pumped into the submersible at all times from canisters and he saw them fixed reassuringly along both sides of the vessel, but there was clearly nowhere for the stale air to go once it had been breathed in and out several times. He was about to comment on it but Toad said, "Ah, the air's freshened up now we've had the hatch open for a bit," so the Mole let the subject drop.

Nonetheless, despite these drawbacks, he had to admit it was very impressive. Brand-new and gleaming, and with everything shipshape and in its proper place (Burly's doing, as Toad was an untidy creature), it had a naval bearing which the Mole could not help but admire. The porthole windows sparkled inside their shining, brass frames. Maps and charts were carefully filed and labelled in tin boxes on the shelves on one side and food and drink carefully filed and labelled in tin boxes on the shelves on the other. Halfway along the vessel was a striped, Toad-sized hammock and beneath the porthole at one end was a large wheel, which Toad explained was the rudder and should only be operated by the Captain (himself, of course).

In the stern was a rather uncomfortable-looking, sit-up-and-beg bicycle, which Toad called the 'engine'. He helped the Mole onto the seat, which was very bony even to the Mole, and adjusted the pedals, which had to be fully extended to fit the Mole's rather short legs. Then he went fore and stood at the wheel and shouted, "Stand by!" and, after a moment, "Full steam ahead!" which the Mole understood to be his signal to start pedalling (though he thought "Start pedalling!" would have been more appropriate) and they were off.

It took the Mole a few minutes to get the hang of pedalling while, at the same time, breathing and keeping his seat. At times the craft rocked disturbingly and, after about ten minutes, this, combined with the stale air and extreme exercise, began to make him feel dizzy. He had worked up quite a sweat and had still not properly seen anything out of the portholes, as he didn't have a very good view of them and besides, there seemed to be nothing but weed and green bubbles.

"Toad?" he enquired politely, "Do you think I could get down and have a look out of the window for a bit? See what's out there?"

"Of course, of course," said Toad absentmindedly, pulling down a chart from a shelf and laying it out on a small table. "It might be a good idea to stop for a minute anyway, while I get my bearings."

Bells should have rung for the Mole at this point, but he was a trusting animal and so all bells remained silent as he went up to a porthole and pressed his nose against the glass for a better view.

Below The Waves

At first, the Mole was very disappointed. There seemed to be nothing to see except swaying reeds. A watery gleam suffused everything and, although the sunlight glittered above and cast long, pale floodlights through the water, the River appeared deserted and all was eerily quiet. There was only the sound of Toad muttering over his maps and the sighing of reeds rhythmically sweeping the outside of the vessel. Yet, as he watched, the Mole felt himself drawn into the scene before him. Unable to turn away, his eyes adjusted to the strange, distorted perspective and, gradually, he saw that, what he thought was the mere play of light and shade, was some sort of living gossamer that floated away like a ghostly nymph. Strange half-shadows came towards him, then turned away before he could identify them, and a trout (a leviathan at such close quarters) swam nonchalantly past the porthole, turning this way and that in search of food, and caught the Mole's eye and (it seemed to the Mole) smiled to itself. A fat eel suddenly wriggled among the reeds and a shoal of tiny fishes – glittering with all the colours the Mole knew – shot out and made a fast escape. Creatures grotesque and wild glided on the riverbed, half-seen, half-hidden by weed and mud-drift and yet all the more fearsome for that. All the time, the water was softly ebbing, back and forth, back and forth.

"So, this is Ratty's other world," thought the Mole, dreamily wondering if the Water Rat's below-water life was what gave Ratty his poetic bent and explained his interest in...

Suddenly, the Mole's musings were cut short by the violent rocking of the vessel and the noisy falling from shelves of maps and charts and tins of provisions. Then a hurricane of water and innocent river creatures hit the starboard side full on. The Toad cried "Hold Fast!" which was correct, and "Batten down the hatches!" which was unnecessary, as there was only one and it already was battened down, and "Swab the decks!" in his confusion.

Up above, a steam-launch was making its unconcerned way up-river, full of sunshine holidaymakers come out to play, laughing and chattering and finishing a late lunch. Someone on board suggested opening another bottle of champagne and everybody cheered.

Down below, the little submarine, having been battered by the general wash, was now caught in the backwash, where it started spinning furiously, and the animals found themselves thrown to the sides. The Mole valiantly tried to reach the engine, thinking to get the propeller going again and move into calmer waters, but he was unable to get even to his knees. Toad simply gripped the Mole's arm and held tightly while dodging tins of sardines and pressed ham.

Up above again, those on board, gaily steaming back to town after a simply glorious time on the River, cheered as another bottle of champagne was found and quickly opened. The cork flew gracefully through the air and hit the water, while everyone laughed happily, completely oblivious of any impending tragedy for the two little animals below them.

As the steamer chugged into the distance and the wash subsided, the creatures of the River righted themselves and resumed what they were doing before the steamer had come along and thrown everything about. Gradually, the submersible slowed in its watery pirouette. The Mole pried Toad's fingers from his arm and got unsteadily to his feet. The combination of steamer-wash and neglect of both steering and propulsion had driven the vessel to the surface. The Mole tried to get his bearings by looking out of the portholes but it was hopeless: everything was just green and bubbling and full of infuriated fishes darting back and forth collecting belongings, which had been swept away into the eel-haunted reeds.

"Any idea where we are, Toad?" said the Mole. "We ought to get this thing pointed in the right direction." But Toad simply moaned and looked decidedly green, even for a toad.

"Not to worry," said the Mole, who was very worried indeed but could see that Toad was in no condition to navigate. "Why don't I have a look through the periscope? See if I can see what's what?"

"Up periscope," croaked Toad weakly, reluctant to give up his captainly status.

"Right you are," said the Mole and pushed the instrument surfacewards and looked through the eyepiece.

It was worse than hopeless. Although the periscope showed that they were indeed above water, it was impossible for the Mole to tell exactly where. In every direction, he saw only river bank with trees, or river bank without trees, or river without bank, but nothing that he could identify. He pulled the periscope down again.

"Can't see a thing," he told Toad, with forced cheerfulness. "Where were we before?" Scarcely was the question out of his mouth than he knew it was futile. The bells, which had been so still and peaceful previously, now jangled harshly, and he realised that he and Toad had been lost for some time and now they were doubly lost.

"Never mind," he said kindly, because Toad now looked even greener. "I think the best thing would be for me to go up and

Below The Waves

have a proper look."

Unfortunately, just as the Mole opened the hatch and the air struck him, and he thought, "O my! How wonderful to breathe fresh..." a second steam launch thundered past, full of merry passengers. The Mole was just in time to see a giant wave from the steamer's wash cannoning towards him and, though he had very little experience of waves, his entire life dashed past and he clearly saw himself potentially concluding it in a submersible with water on the inside as well as the outside. Quick as a flash he ducked down, pulled the hatch behind him, and locked it swiftly into position. No sooner had he done so than he was thrown from the hatch ladder and landed in a heap next to Toad, and no sooner had he done that than the vessel began to do acrobatics in the water, and all that had once been so shipshape took the final step to becoming a completely rough and unordered mess.

The Mole had no idea where he was in relation to everything else but suspected that wherever it was it wasn't where he should be. Suddenly, there was a loud 'Clunk!' and he was vaguely aware of a shriek from poor Toad before he himself tumbled into darkness.

Now, what seemed to the Mole to be a silent, mostly deserted, ghostlike place is, to those who inhabit it, a veritable hurly-burly, and the interior of the main river is as busy to its small denizens as the high street of any large city is to the urbanites who frequent it. There is a continual chatter in the water as the watery throng goes about its business and news travels fast, so it simply isn't possible for small creatures trapped in a tin can and adrift on a fast current to go unnoticed and unmentioned. Besides, the shiny, metal, underwater-boat was the talk of the River. So, when the trout and the eels and the tiny glittering fishes had peered in through the portholes and seen the strange and mysterious creatures trapped inside, and then seen the craft get caught in the wash and tumble about and finally drift off in, what seemed to them, a thoroughly aimless and irresponsible way, they all told their friends and neighbours and various shopkeepers, who, in turn, told all *their* friends and neighbours and shopkeepers. In this way, the news speedily got back to the ducks, who, of course, told the Otters and the Water Rat, who were sitting on the river bank.

The Rat immediately leapt to his feet and ran to his boat, shouting "The Weir!" and "Nets!" while he quickly untied the painter. The Otter, always good in a crisis, ran to and fro barking orders to his family, who filled the Rat's boat with fishing nets. All the Otters then leapt into the water and began swimming as fast as possible in the direction of the weir with the Rat sculling furiously after them.

For some minutes all was a blur of anxiety for the Rat, and he struggled to keep his attention on sculling, so filled was his mind with visions of his friends in a watery grave. He scanned the surface of the water closely and sniffed the air, searching for any clue to the submersible's whereabouts. He could see the sleek backs of the Otters moving swiftly ahead making for the weir. This was their first priority – there would be time to search the river's banks and beds later – for they were all certain that no animal could survive a tumble over the weir and, even if they did, the trip to the sea would then be swift. Once in the sea they would be lost to the river bank forever.

Just then, the weir came in sight and at the same moment a flurry of joyful barking went up. The Rat could see a sharp blade of sunlight bouncing off something in the water. His heart leapt with gladness and relief and he offered a deep-felt sob of thanks to the River. Minutes later he was alongside the little submersible, which was bouncing merrily on the current, seemingly enjoying freedom from propellers and rudders and captains. He clanged the roof with his oar and shouted, "Mole! Toad! Are you alright?" There was no reply but then the periscope creaked upwards, searched frantically in all directions and finally fixed its eye upon him. He waved and the sub seemed to bounce a little, as if from excitement.

"Ratty? O, Ratty!" he heard metallically from within.

"Mole! Stay where you are – don't move – you're...well... you're a bit close to the weir to be honest. Nothing to worry about – but – stay – where – you – are," called the Rat.

Meanwhile the Otters had been busy. They had scrambled into the boat and collected the nets and then swum towards the weir, downstream of the submersible. Taking one end each, they stretched the nets across the path of the submarine, while the Rat gave instructions from his boat. "Left a bit! Right a bit!" Finally the submarine veered straight towards them, at which point the Otters threw the nets over and under the craft, as if it were a giant fish, and then swam upstream with all their might, away from the weir and the strong current, to the shallows and to safety.

Ratty came alongside, clanged again on the sub with his scull and called with enormous relief, "Come on up, Mole," and after a moment the hatch rose and the Mole came up, trembling and weak with a large bump on his head.

Below The Waves

"Hullo Mole," said the Water Rat.

"Hullo Rat," said the Mole.

At that moment, Toad popped up next to the Mole, which was a squash as it wasn't a very big hatch. He was still very green, but more alert than he had been, and there was a wild look in his eyes.

"Weir?" he croaked, and looked frantically around. Then he hopped fully out and onto the roof, and yelled, "Every toad for himself!" and plopped gracelessly into the shallows and swam for his life. The Rat looked disgustedly after him, but Burly, ever the loyal servant and very fond of his employer, in spite of his eccentric demands for cycling skills in his under-butlers, went after him and helped him to the shore.

Later that evening, at home in Ratty's back parlour and full of supper, the Rat and the Mole discussed the day's events. The Rat didn't once say, "I told you so," or "You should have listened to me," or "This is what I would have done," but instead showed great interest in the Mole's experiences and his views of the River's underwater world. He wanted to know all that the Mole had seen and what his impressions had been. He spoke when it was needed and kept quiet and simply nodded when it wasn't. He sympathised at every point where sympathy was required. He tutted over the inconsiderateness of steamers and their masters and agreed with the Mole on the foolhardiness of storing tinned goods on high open shelves. In this way, he encouraged all the terror of the Mole's experiences out of him, so that, when the Mole finally went to bed he was feeling exhausted but calm and more like his usual self.

Lying in his little bed in the Rat's best guest room, the Mole looked back on the day and thought that, although it had certainly been eventful and at times very frightening, on the whole he was grateful for it, for he had come through it with one lump and many lessons learned. For one thing, although adventure and exploration were very proper for an animal with the right amount of spirit, they needed to be embarked upon sensibly. For another, the world around him was full of many strange and beautiful and mysterious things, so he didn't need to go to the Amazon after all. And, finally, he now knew his limitations, and it seemed they were not so limited as he'd always suspected. On that final thought the Mole drifted into sleep, just as the rain started once again to fall softly on the River, and he sailed away into pleasant dreams of ships and stars and isles where good animals rest.

The Naiads In Arcadia
by Professor Peter Hunt

The early morning sun was just lifting over the reed-beds, and sending its most delicate golden light onto the thin mist on the river, when the skiff pushed off from the landing-stage outside the Water Rat's house. The Mole, who had greatly enjoyed himself packing the hamper for the day's expedition, was at the oars, and scarcely a drop of water spilled from the blades or disturbed the oily-smooth surface of the river, as he pulled out into mid-stream. He had long since ceased even to think about the skills of rowing, and his mind was partly on the perils of the adventure ahead, and partly on the prospect of making breakfast on the new portable cooking stove that lay on the bottom-boards next to the hamper. The Water Rat, lounging in the stern, watched him with the satisfaction of a master whose lessons have been well-learned, and felt how well the Mole now fitted in with River Bank life. Two ducks, disturbed at their early-morning ablutions, flapped away up-river, and the perfectly straight wake of the skiff passed across the concentric circles where their webbed feet had splashed.

No-one on the mist-laden fields on either side of the river saw the skiff and its crew moving upstream, but one pair of sharp, intelligent eyes watched from the windows behind the landing-stage.

Mrs Vole, who had been the Water Rat's housekeeper since he had first moved to this bijou residence, sighed, closed the door onto the landing-stage, and went back into the kitchen. The Mole, enthusiastic as ever, had left an impressive detritus of empty tins, crusts of bread, lumps of butter, and a cheese that looked as though it had been run over by one of Mr Toad's motor-cars. There was watercress all over the red-brick floor. Mrs Vole, reflecting that life had been rather more orderly when Mr Rat had lived on his own, and she had only poetry and painting soirées to worry about, set to work to clear up.

She was tidying away the last of the empty beer-bottles from the previous night, when there came a knock on the back door. Mrs Vole smiled to herself: there was only one person it could be – it was too early for the field-mice to be delivering the daily supplies from the village, and the grocer's cart didn't come this far along the river bank until the sun was well clear of the coppice. She wiped her hands on her apron, and lifted the latch.

Outside, standing nervously on the doormat, was a young lady

The Wind In The Willows Short Stories

Mole, dressed most respectably in her Sunday-outing best.

"Miss Mole!" said the housekeeper. "How delightful that you could come." She ushered her into the kitchen.

Miss Mole looked around, approvingly, at the glowing floor and the gleaming copper pans. "I'm pleased to be able to help, if I can," she said. "How did you manage to find me so quickly?"

Mrs Vole smiled. "It's very easy, really. I know lots of the grandmother rabbits and word can be passed along the hedgerows very rapidly – although the Swallows aren't very reliable. Do sit down. We've got time for a cup of tea before we have to start."

"Let me put the kettle on," said Miss Mole, and soon they were sitting drinking nettle tea and eating golden-brown Garibaldi biscuits, still warm from the oven, studded with currants, and sprinkled with caster sugar.

Mrs Vole said, carefully, "At least you don't have to clear up this sort of mess at Mole End, now." She looked through into the scullery at the heap of wet towels and muddy boots.

Miss Mole sighed. "Well, me and Susan – she's one of the field-mice, you know – we keeps it all smart and clean and aired, and I dusts the statues and keeps the kitchen cupboards full." She looked very sad. "But it's very quiet and lonely."

"But Mr Mole does come back now and again, doesn't he?" said Mrs Vole.

"Hardly ever, now," said Miss Mole. "And he doesn't stay long. It's as if his heart's not in it. I wouldn't be surprised if he sold up." She hesitated. "And when he does visit, he always avoids me. You know..." she paused nervously. "You know, we did have a kind of ...understanding at one time ...and then he upped and offed to the river..." She finished her biscuit. "Still, I suppose it's a more exciting life here, with Mr Rat and the river and all."

"There's animals for you," Mrs Vole said. "Only thinking of themselves. But," she said, significantly, "I think it's time for a change, don't you? Now, have some more tea, and another Garibaldi, and I'll tell you all about it."

"You said it was something to do with that Mr Toad," Miss Mole said. "He's not in trouble again is he? Everyone says that he's a reformed character."

"It depends what you mean by trouble," Mrs Vole said. "The fact is, that he's gone and" – she paused dramatically – "fallen in love!"

"With someone unsuitable, I suppose," said Miss Mole.

"It depends what you mean by unsuitable," Mrs Vole said. "By all accounts she's a well-off, well-brought up Gentle-Toad, from a

The Naiads In Arcadia

good family with a big house up along the river. Mrs Bullfrog – that's Mr Toad's housekeeper at Toad Hall – says she's just lovely, and she – Mrs Bullfrog – couldn't be happier for them."

Miss Mole sighed, and then recovered herself. "But I don't understand the problem."

"The problem," Mrs Vole said, darkly, "is them animals." She poured more tea. "It's this way. Last night, Mr Mole and Mr Rat had a conference at Mr Badger's house in what used to be the Wild Wood. Of course, it's not so wild as it used to be, so they say."

"What was the conference about?"

"Ah," said Mrs Vole. "It was about What to Do About Mr Toad. Mrs Hedgehog – that's Mr Badger's housekeeper – she's been with him for years and years, you know – nobody else would put up with his temper – there's nobody to touch her when it comes to the store-cupboards, and her cured hams are just famous. Anyhow," she said, getting back to her story, "Mrs Hedgehog, she just happened to be passing Mr Badger's study door, and – she couldn't help herself – you know how it is – she just happened to overhear what they were saying."

Miss Mole looked at her with wide eyes. "And what *were* they saying?"

"Well, Mr Badger was saying it would all come to no good, this Messing Around with Females, and it would be the ruin of Toad Hall. And then Mr Rat said, for all Toady's faults, he was a free spirit, and all that women did for you was crush your free spirit – which I think is a bit of a cheek when you think what *they* did to Mr Toad over that motor-car business."

"And what did Mr Mole say?"

"Well, even Mr Mole said he thought it would be a pity to break up what he called the good fellowship, and that it would be an end to their jolly escapades." She laughed. "Mrs Hedgehog said she thought it was time they all grew up, and she included Mr Badger in that as well. So then Mr Badger said they would have to go and Lay the Law Down to Mr Toad, the way they had before, and Mr Mole said he thought it was probably just another passing craze, when there was a knock on the door – and who should it be but one of the weasels from Toad Hall. I don't know if you heard, but after that time when Mr Badger and the rest saved Toad Hall..."

"It was in the paper," Miss Mole said, dreamily. "How Mr Mole was the hero..."

Mrs Vole smiled at her benignly. "Of course, dear. Anyway, most of the stoats and weasels ran away, but Mr Toad kept some on to work in the kitchens – only this one had never forgiven Mr

Toad for whacking him, and he'd been prying and listening at doors!" She shook her head.

Miss Mole clicked her tongue. "Well, I never!"

Mrs Vole went on: "So this weasel told them that he'd overheard Mr Toad talking to Mrs Bullfrog. Apparently, Mr Toad had realised that his friends – his so-called friends, if you ask me – would try to spoil his romance, and so he'd decided to elope – to run away with his lovely Miss Toad – and drive to Gretna Green, and get married over the anvil! Mr Toad has bought a big new motor-car, all secretly, like, and at nine o'clock this very morning, he's planning to meet his love at the park gates – and they'll go off to Scotland!"

"Oooh, how romantic!" said Miss Mole.

"But it isn't going to be unless we do something!" Mrs Vole said, putting her teacup down and glancing at the mahogany grandfather clock in the hallway. "Mrs Hedgehog said that there and then at Mr Badger's the three animals hatched a plot! This morning, Mr Rat and Mr Mole would pack a hamper and scull up the river to Toad Hall, and call in to see Mr Toad. They would invite him to come on a picnic, and of course, Mr Toad would say "no", and so off they would go, leaving him thinking that the coast was clear. But the moment they got back to the river, they would hide the skiff, and meet Mr Badger by the entrance to the secret tunnel to Toad Hall. Then Mr Rat would sneak round the lawns and through the trees to Mr Toad's coach-house – that's where he keeps his new motor-car – and make sure that the car wouldn't work – just in case of accidents. And Mr Mole and Mr Badger – both being good at underground work – would go through the secret tunnel that comes up in the Butler's Pantry..."

"The squeaky board in the Butler's Pantry," said Miss Mole. "I remember reading about that from the paper..."

"And sneak up on Mr Toad, who wouldn't be on his guard, and grab him and lock him in his bedroom – but just in case he got away from them, Mr Rat would be waiting for him in the coach-house, and he would lock him in there!"

"But what about poor Miss Toad, waiting at the park gates?"

"Well, they thought that either she'd give up and go away, or perhaps she'd come down to the Hall to find out what had happened. So the plan was then for Mr Rat to stroll out to meet her, and he would tell her that Mr Toad had changed his mind, and gone away on a world cruise."

"But the poor lady," said Miss Mole. "She'd be broken-hearted!"

"Mr Badger said that Females were Always being Broken-Hearted, and that she'd get over it."

The Naiads In Arcadia

"And what about Mr Toad?"

"Mr Rat said that Toad would soon come to his senses – he always did – and then things would go back to being the way they'd always been, and they could go on having fun on the river and going on jaunts like they used to. Mrs Hedgehog said that she could have hit him with a ham. Mr Mole wondered whether it wasn't rather strong medicine, but Mr Rat said they'd got to be cruel to be kind. Anyway: that's what they're doing now! They were planning to meet at the tunnel at eight thirty."

Miss Mole looked at the clock. "But we've got to stop them!" she said. "Can't we go up the river and talk to them? It's eight o-clock now!"

There was a sharp rap at the back door, and Mrs Vole got to her feet with a satisfied smile. "I don't think you really understand the male animal, Miss Mole," she said. "There would be no chance at all of changing their minds if we confronted them when they are all together. They wouldn't hear us; they'd only hear each other! No, there's a much better way. Come along."

She took off her apron and opened the door. Miss Mole gasped. On the doorstep was the most elegant creature she had ever seen.

"Ah, good morning, Mrs Vole," the creature said, languidly. "Splendid day for the business, what?"

Mrs Vole bobbed very slightly. "Good morning, Mrs Otter," she said. "Have you met Miss Mole?"

Mrs Otter extended an immaculately groomed paw. "Absolutely top hole," she said. "Delighted. I must say you look like just the gel we need to kick some sense into that Mole. Sound enough chappie, but easily led! Come along! No time to lose." She turned and led them up the overgrown garden-path to the lane, where a smart carriage was waiting. Sitting inside was a short, formidable-looking person, who greeted them with a grave nod. They all got in.

"This is Mrs Hedgehog," Mrs Otter said. "Miss Mole." She nodded to the driver. "Toad Hall," she said. "As quickly as you can." The carriage pulled away along the deep lane, with the rich bronze of the beech leaves forming an archway overhead, and the ferns brushing the wheels.

"I take it you were able to get rid of Otter," Mrs Hedgehog said, dryly.

Mrs Otter laughed. "Oh, I didn't have to get rid of him," she said. "He's visiting Portly at prep school. There's a swimming gala or some such." She adjusted the scarf around her neck. "Not that it would have been a problem. Otter's not the chap to get himself mixed up in this sort of nonsense." She smiled at Mrs Hedgehog, showing her bright white teeth – a smile that Miss Mole thought would not necessarily always be friendly. "I would have expected you to have knocked some sense into that old Badger by now."

"It's not too late," said Mrs Hedgehog. Miss Mole looked at her.

"Excuse me," she said, feeling very much like an intruder. "I'm sorry, but no-one has explained to me what we are going to do."

"Ah, that's simple," said Mrs Vole. "Mrs Otter has kindly agreed to take us to Toad Hall: we should be there a good half-hour before Mr Rat and the others. She is then going to wait with the carriage at the park gates to reassure Miss Toad, when she arrives, in case of any mishap. Mrs Hedgehog will then go and lock both the doors of the Butler's Pantry – there are two – one goes into the kitchens, and the other into the banqueting hall. So, when Mr Mole and Mr Badger emerge from the tunnel into the Pantry, that will be as far as they'll get! Meanwhile, Mrs Bullfrog, Mr Toad's housekeeper, will ensure that Mr Toad makes good his escape."

"But why don't we just tell Mr Toad now?" Miss Mole said. "Then he can escape in plenty of time."

"Oh, no, no, no, my *dear*," Mrs Otter said. "That would just ruin it for poor Toad. He probably would refuse to go, if he knew we had anything to do with it. He'd want to think that he'd managed the thing on his own. Very proud chap, you know." She smiled that smile. "But he's not the fastest minnow in the pool. So he's got to do exactly what he thought he was going to do in the way he thought he was going to do it."

They were going smoothly along the high road now, between the tall summer hedgerows, and under the pure arc of a cloudless sky. They startled a flight of larks out of the broad meadows, and in the faint far distance they heard the whistle of a railway engine. A white smudge of smoke on the horizon. Miss Mole looked out at the morning and the Wide World, and admired it, but she was still thinking.

"And what are you and I going to be doing?"

"I," Mrs Vole said, "will be looking after Mr Rat in the coach-house."

"A most important job," Mrs Hedgehog said, and then, cryptically, "seeing as he has more to lose than anyone in this little affair."

"And me?" said Miss Mole, deciding to ignore this.

Mrs Otter smiled. "You, my dear, are our secret weapon."

They pulled up at the park gates, and looked down the long sweep of pale, cow-cropped parkland, with the occasional chestnut trees spreading pools of shade on the grass. The yellow gravel

The Naiads In Arcadia

drive ran down through the park, and curved around the side of the Hall, towards the river-front, while a left-hand branch ran to the broad stone archway into the stable-yard. The Toad may have been a boastful creature, but he spoke the truth about Toad Hall: even seen from the back, it was a residence any animal would be proud of.

"You know," Mrs Otter said, thoughtfully, "the last time Toad Hall was attacked, it took pistols and cutlasses and clubs to do the job. And what do we have?"

Mrs Vole grinned. "Brains," she said. "After all, we're females."

"If you keep in the lee of the wood," Mrs Otter said, "there won't be any chance of Toad spotting you."

"But don't his rooms overlook the river?" said Mrs Hedgehog. "He won't be looking this way."

"You can't be too careful with Toad," said Mrs Otter. "Remember when he had that craze for astronomy. I wouldn't be surprised if that telescope isn't still on the roof, and I wouldn't put it past Toad to be up there, surveying the horizon. After all, if there isn't any drama, he'll have to make some up!"

And so, while Mrs Otter waited in the carriage on the side of the high road, Mrs Vole, Mrs Hedgehog, and Miss Mole slipped along the edge of the beech wood, keeping close to the white-painted metal railings. They worked their way across the backs of the outbuildings until they came to the stable-yard arch – at which point everything very nearly went wrong.

The stable-yard and the coach-house had long-ago been cleared of the debris of the Toad's cars, but the old canary-coloured cart still stood in one corner. It had been repaired, but Toad's interest in it had never rekindled – although Rat and Mole had once caught him sitting on the driver's bench, whipping up a pair of invisible horses. Mrs Vole was half-way across the yard to the double doors of the coach-house, when there was a sudden crash as the house door was flung open, and the Toad himself, burdened with two huge new leather portmanteaus staggered into the yard. Mrs Vole, moving more quickly than Miss Mole (who had flattened herself back against the side of the archway) could have imagined, flung herself into the back of the cart. Toad, hefting the portmanteaus, rolled across to the coach-house, singing:

The world's the place for husbands,
    And bachelorhood be blowed!
And I'll have a wife for the rest of my life
    The magnificent *Mrs* Toad!

He pulled open one of the doors of the coach-house and swaggered inside. Behind him, Mrs Hedgehog shot across the yard and disappeared into the house; Mrs Vole jumped lightly out of the cart, paused at the half-open door of the coach-house, and then slipped in like a shadow; Miss Mole, her heart thumping, ran quietly along the side of the yard to where an alleyway, dank and perpetually in the shade, ran around the back of the house, and was swallowed up into the dim light.

Toad, in the coach-house, was strapping the portmanteaus onto the luggage carrier of his Silver Ghost, and muttering strange incantations, such as 'seven litre, straight six,' and 'three-quarter elliptic springs', and 'AX-201', and patting the sweeping silver mudguards, and so he didn't notice Mrs Vole, moving softy and silently to a hiding-place behind a stack of oil drums. With the portmanteaus secured, Toad climbed into the driver's seat, arranged a pile of thick blankets neatly on the passenger-seat, and stroked the wooden-rimmed steering wheel with one hand. He rested his other hand on the big black bulb of the horn, but he didn't squeeze it: he only murmured, 'poop poop' to himself, bounced slightly on the seat, and then got down and let himself out of the coach-house.

He came back into Toad Hall through the back door, and was halfway up the grand staircase when it dawned on him that something was not quite normal.

Mrs Bullfrog appeared from the doorway that led to the kitchens and the servants' wing, at the bottom of the stairs.

"Ah, Mrs B," said the Toad. "What's that infernal row? Sounds as though somebody's trying to break a door down."

Mrs Bullfrog cocked her head. "It does, rather," she said. "Actually, it's only the builders. They're making a few improvements to the kitchen."

"Ah," the Toad said. "Improvements to the kitchen. Excellent idea. Excellent idea."

Mrs Bullfrog lowered her voice. "It will all be done by the time... Well, by the time the new mistress gets here."

The Toad simpered slightly, and then drew himself up. "Well, Mrs B." he said, shooting his cuffs. "How do I look?"

Mrs Bullfrog took in the yellow check suit and the Union Flag spats. "Loud," she said.

"Yes, it is, isn't it," said Toad, as the door-battering became more frenzied. "Well, I'll just pop upstairs and get my driving cape. Thought I might go for a little drive, you know." He winked, roguishly.

The Naiads In Arcadia

"A very nice day for it," Mrs Bullfrog said. Behind her, the hammering stopped, and the Toad, laughing happily, proceeded lightly up to his apartments.

Mrs Bullfrog looked back along the corridor to the door of the Butler's Pantry, which was still vibrating slightly, and with a thoughtful look on her face, followed Mr Toad up the staircase.

In the Butler's Pantry, Mr Badger was coming close to losing his temper. It was a fine temper, and he was very proud of keeping it so well, but finding both the doors of the Butler's Pantry locked was testing his ability to keep it at all. The doors had never been locked! Even when he was a cub and had played with Toad's grandfather in the kitchens, they had never been locked! It was an outrage! By this time they should have had Toad locked up in his bedroom! The Badger became aware of something tugging at his ancient poaching-jacket. He stopped belabouring the door with his club and looked down.

"Mr Badger," the Mole said; "do excuse me, but I have a suggestion."

"Ah," said the Badger. "I might have known it. The good and deserving Mole comes to our rescue once again. And what is your suggestion, my young friend?"

The Mole was looking at the Badger rather more warily than usual, because he'd been rather taken aback by this display of violence. Bashing stoats and weasels and ferrets was one thing, because they could bash back, and would bash you anyway if you didn't bash them first, but doors were a different matter. Mole had been brought up to respect doors as being useful and generally good-tempered things, and he didn't like to see one taken advantage of – although he had to admit to himself that this one was putting up a very respectable resistance.

"I just thought," the Mole said, "that if you could lift me up, I could probably get out of that window." He pointed to a small square window in the wall above one of the big mahogany cupboards. "And then I could come round and unlock the door."

"I have always said it," the Badger said. "Mole is an animal one can rely on. It comes from living underground," he went on, picking the Mole up with one paw, and lifting him up to the window. "It sharpens the intelligence."

The Mole, rather torn between feeling pleased with himself and wondering whether this had been such a clever idea after all, found himself opening the window and scrabbling his way through it. There was an interesting moment when he realised that there was no outside sill to hang onto, and then he fell briefly, landing on the top of some rubbish bins and ending up half-buried by their contents.

But this was no time for niceties, Mole thought, scrambling to his feet and shaking potato peelings from his fur. There was a dark doorway, and the Mole turned the handle, and let himself in. Thanks to his experience of chivvying the Wild-Wooders around Toad Hall, he knew where he was: the door at the end of the corridor opened into the kitchen, opposite the Butler's Pantry. The narrow stairs on the right – one of several sets of back stairs – came out on the landing next door to Toad's apartments. He crept along the corridor and pushed the door open slightly.

Between him and the door of the Butler's Pantry sat, with her back to him, the formidable figure of Mrs Hedgehog: spiky by name and spiky by nature, the Mole thought. If the Badger could be frightening, he was nothing to his housekeeper; the Mole had always treated her with immense respect, and this did not seem the time to revise his practice. He let the door close silently, on its damper, and weighed up the situation. Suddenly, he had an inspiration! He could still save the day! If he went up the back stairs, perhaps he could slip into Toad's bedroom, grab the key, and lock him in! His kind heart hesitated – poor Toady – it would be a terrible disappointment to him. But he pulled himself together. He couldn't let the others down: this was all for Toad's own good – or, at least, that was what the Rat and the Badger said, and they were older and wiser than he. He turned and ran up the stairs, puffing as he got to the top, and as quietly as he could, opened the door onto the landing.

Down in the stable-yard, another door was being opened, and the Water Rat, whose whiskers were still recovering from being singed by the Mole's cooking-stove at breakfast, slid into the coach-house. He stopped and looked around, his ears twitching for the faintest sound, and the first thing he saw was the Silver Ghost, the Best Motor-Car in the World. For a moment, he was overcome. He was a Rat who valued tradition, the old ways, the quiet lanes and the tranquil highways. Things as they Used To Be. Cart-horses were fast enough for him. And here he was in the presence of the very enemy itself! He didn't see an elegant silver-painted work of art, or a masterpiece of engineering and craftsmanship: he didn't even see what the Toad saw – freedom and excitement. He saw something that must be stopped: a large silver monster that spelled "change". The railway was the same: it was not something that took you to new places, it was a thing that destroyed the old places, and whose noise, he had once thought, drowned out the song of all the birds of Oxfordshire and Berkshire.

The Naiads In Arcadia

Over his shoulder, the Water Rat carried his old leather sketching satchel, and he reached into it and took out a large bag of sand. He didn't know much about motor-cars, but he had a very good idea that they didn't go very far if the petrol tank had a lot of sand at the bottom of it.

He began to work his way around the car, wondering just where you put the petrol, and there it was! A tube, with a cap on it. He began to unscrew it, when there was a very delicate cough, and he looked up into the driving seat, and the eyes of Mrs Vole.

"Don't you think," Mrs Vole said, "that you should examine your conscience in this matter?"

The Water Rat hesitated, thinking first of all that he should have heard her moving about, and then that the questions that a Female might ask were not terribly important. But one has to be polite.

"Ah, Mrs Vole," he said. "What a pleasant surprise."

"Don't you think," said Mrs Vole, "that you should let people find their happiness in whatever way makes them happy?"

The Water Rat quietly put his paw into the bag of sand. "I think they should think of what's best for everyone," he said. "I mean, can you imagine the river bank without Toady? Or the river bank with Toad as a family man?"

"What difference would that make?"

The Rat seemed anguished. "Just think of those long walks we used to go on, and coming home after a long day, to...to..." (here his poetic feelings got the better of him) "to great chunks of cheese, new bread, great swills of beer, pipes, bed, and heavenly sleep!"

There was a pause. "I'm sure you could still have them," Mrs Vole said, persuasively. "Marriage doesn't mean that you'd never see Mr Toad again. Or Mr Mole," she added.

The Water Rat, with a strange light in his eye, said, "It means change, and things are very well as they are." He took his paw out of the sack.

"Well, if that's how you feel," Mrs Vole said, very quietly and very clearly, "just think of the change if you got home and found that all the poetry you had written over the past few years, and all the paintings you had painted over the past few years, and all the music you had composed...had all mysteriously disappeared!"

The Toad, radiant with life and ambition, flung open his bedroom door, and strode onto the landing in his driving-cape, his helmet, and his goggles. Mrs Bullfrog, who was standing on the landing, swept him an enthusiastic curtsey, and as she swung her right arm out to complete the gesture, it happened to hit the Mole (who had just opened the door from the back stairs) neatly in the midriff. He stepped backwards, missed the top step, and discovered that the world was suddenly upside-down and very bouncy. Mrs Bullfrog closed the door behind his descending form, and said:

"We all hope you have a pleasant trip, sir."

The Toad smiled broadly at her and set off down the staircase. There was a crash from somewhere in the servants' quarters.

The Badger, whose temper had got very tired of waiting for the Mole to arrive and turn the key, had, with very a determined blow, smashed the lock off the door of the Butler's Pantry, and now strode out, club in hand. Across the kitchen, the door stood open to the stable-yard, and the Toad was striding by, giving voice:

Now who was in the Silver Ghost
   As it came down the road?
It's the happiest two you ever knew!
   That's Mr and Mrs Toad!

The Badger took one belligerent step across the kitchen flagstones, and saw, out of the corner of his eye, a slight movement. He stopped.

"If you go out of that door," said Mrs Hedgehog. "You will have eaten the very last slice of my home-cured ham, and sat in front of the very last roaring fire. Do I make myself clear?"

The Mole lay upside-down and very bruised, in the corridor at the bottom of the back stairs, wondering, as he had throughout, whether the game was worth the candle. Still, if he ran around to the stable-yard, perhaps he and the Rat could subdue the Toad in the coach-house and save him from himself. He staggered to his feet, pulled open the door, and stopped dead. Outside was a small figure, smiling at him.

"Hello, Mole, my dear," it said.

The Mole took a step back. "Oh, hello," he said. "Miss Mole. How nice to meet you again."

"And it's at a very happy moment, isn't it," said Miss Mole, taking a step forward. "Just when Mr Toad is going off to be very, very happy."

"Ah," said the Mole. Around the corner of the house he could

The Naiads In Arcadia

hear the coach-house doors creaking open, and fragments of Toad's cheerful singing.

"And in a few years," Miss Mole said, "there will be a *family* in Toad Hall, and children playing on the river." She took another step forward, and Mole took a step back.

"Well, yes," he said, "but..."

"And there *could* be a family at Mole End, as well," Miss Mole went on. "Don't you think you should make a choice? Really it's between that nice Mr Rat and trips on the river, or Mole End with mole babies on your knee?"

Around the corner of the house came the sound of a car starting.

"May I come out now?" said the Water Rat.

Mrs Vole looked over the top of the oil-drum and watched the Silver Ghost, with Toad at the wheel, purring away up the gravel drive.

"Let's wait until he's at the park gates." She waited a moment. "Yes: it's alright now."

"Well," said the Rat. "That's excellent. Now, if you would be so good as to take your foot off my ear..."

Mrs Otter's carriage pulled up in front of the group standing by the gates of the stable yard.

"We told you there was a better way," she said to Miss Mole. "Pick them off one by one." She smiled that smile again, and turned to where the Water Rat and the Badger were standing. "Now, chaps," she went on cheerfully. "No need to be so gloomy. It's all for the best, you know. Not everyone's the same."

"Have they gone off alright?" said Mrs Bullfrog.

"Oh, yes," Mrs Otter said. "And Miss Toad has also gone with the benefit of my advice, so when they return, he may *well* be an altered Toad." Her carriage turned and moved smoothly away up the drive.

Then the three housekeepers, who had a lot to talk about, nodded to Miss Mole, and retired to the Butler's Pantry to take tea. The Badger and the Water Rat watched them go, with thoughtful expressions.

Then the Badger shook himself. "Very well! What's done is done! No use crying over spilled ale." He looked at the Rat. "I don't suppose you'd care to come and stay at my place for a few days?" He coughed. "Times of change, y'know. Might be good to get away to let things settle."

"That's very good of you, Badger," the Rat said. "I'd be pleased to." He paused. "I'll stroll along with you now – but there's one thing I have to do first."

And the thing he had to do was to walk down to the river with the Mole and Miss Mole, and to help her into the stern of the skiff, and to shake hands with his friend.

"We'll come to see you very soon," the Mole said, and the Rat nodded, and pushed the skiff off. The Mole pulled skilfully out into the middle of the river, and glanced up at Toad Hall, where the Badger waved a friendly hand in farewell. After all, the Mole thought, the Badger was said to be really quite fond of children.

He rowed quietly downstream, with Miss Mole watching him with admiring eyes. There were high cloudlets in the sky, now, and a soft wind that moved the reed-beds and the leaves of the willows that overhung the river, and the Mole thought what a beautiful place the World was, and how much more beautiful it was going to be.

Welcome To Toad Hall
by Marilyn Fountain

The plans to open Toad Hall to the public were beginning to take shape. In addition to the guided tours of the grand house, there was to be a tea room, a gift shop and sales of garden produce. Toad, naturally, was going to take charge of the tour parties. "It's my ancestral home, after all, and I'm the only one who knows its history," said Toad. "Just take this staircase, for instance. Now did I tell you about the time my great-great-grandfather–?"

"Stop!" said Rat, holding up a paw. "We haven't got time to hear another one of your stories right now, Toad. Do you realise we're opening this Sunday...?"

"Sunday?" gasped Mole. "Gosh, really, this Sunday? So soon...?"

"Yes, really, Mole," said Rat. "And there is a lot to be organised yet. How is the tea room coming on?"

"Come and see," Mole replied. "Just come and see." He ran through the Hall, stopping every few minutes to turn round and make sure Toad, Rat and Otter were following. "Do hurry up," he urged, beckoning furiously with both paws. "Do come and see what I've done." When he reached the old banqueting hall Mole flung open the doors. "Ta-ra!" he announced theatrically. The room was set out with a dozen or so circular tables, each dressed with a red gingham-checked tablecloth. There were china bowls for two types of sugar lumps, brown and white, and slender vases to hold a stem or two of seasonal flowers. Along one wood-panelled wall where, in the old days, hunting trophies and ancestral portraits had hung, a counter had been set up. On it were dishes of all sorts of jams – glossy raspberry, creamy rhubarb, viscous loganberry – made with fruit from the kitchen garden; a large copper of boiling water; and a glass cabinet to keep the cakes and pastries and scones fresh and safe from curious flies and overly inquisitive customers. On two long shelves sat piles of saucers, and from hooks hung matching teacups, all in a blue and white willow pattern.

"Well?" Mole looked intently at his friend's faces. "What do you think?"

Toad tapped one of the shelves and nodded approvingly. "Very fair workmanship, these shelves. I had my doubts about that Hedgehog when he said he was good with wood, but give him his dues, yes, he's a fair carpenter. I'll give him that –"

"Yes, but, Toad...?" interrupted Mole. He could hardly breathe for longing to know what everyone thought about *his* efforts.

As usual, Rat understood. "Never mind about the shelves, Toad," he said. "Look at everything else. Isn't it all beautiful? Hasn't Mole created a masterpiece of a tea room from your old tumbledown dining hall? Look at the attention to detail; the little paper napkin dispensers, the rack of pegs for visitors' hats and coats."

"A place for umbrellas to drip on wet days," added Otter.

Once everything had been pointed out, the Toad was quick to praise. "Mole, it's a triumph," he said. "You're a triumph."

"You have been very busy, Mole," said Otter.

"I have, haven't I?" replied Mole. He liked sitting and relaxing as much as the next animal, but he was never happier than when he was being busy. He loved straightening the piles of crockery and adjusting the tablecloths so that the same amount of cloth hung down all the way round.

"It would have taken me weeks and weeks to do all this," said Toad. "My dear Mole, I can't believe you've brought about such a transformation in such a short time."

"You know what they say?" remarked Rat.

"What do they say?" asked Otter.

Rat smiled at Mole. "If you want something done, ask a busy person."

A spring of happiness coiled ever more tightly somewhere deep inside Mole. "Shall I make us all some cups of coffee on the new machine? Sit down, sit down everyone. It won't take me a moment." He scampered round to the serving side of the counter and disappeared through a door into a little kitchen beyond that, in the old days, had been the butler's pantry.

The coffee maker had been Toad's idea. It was a gleaming, snuffling, snorting, steaming silver dragon of a machine, and Mole was scared of it. Rolling up his sleeves along with his courage, he bravely flicked a couple of switches and busied himself with twisting knobs and shifting levers. "It's a bit tricky," he called through to the others, trying to hold one cup under two spouts of gushing hot coffee, "but I'll soon get the hang of it."

"You'll need to," Otter called back. "If you're having this much trouble making four cups of coffee, what are you going to do when a coach party of twenty or thirty people turn up all at once?"

"Oh, dear," muttered Mole, who hadn't thought of that at all.

"And they'll want cakes, and probably sandwiches too," said Otter.

"Oh, dear, oh, dear," said Mole. He was so alarmed by the prospect that he forgot the jug of milk he'd been warming until

Welcome To Toad Hall

the froth bubbled over and ran everywhere. "Ouch!" he yelled.

Rat went through to the old pantry to help him, while Otter and Toad chose a table and sat down.

Toad slapped a paw down on the tablecloth, causing sugar cubes to leap from their bowl. Otter picked one up and popped it into his mouth.

"Staff," Toad exclaimed. "That's the answer. I'll need to hire some extra help. I'll put up some notices in Bluebell Wood. There are bound to be a few young squirrels and rabbits looking for work."

"I might need some more people to help me patrol the grounds," said Otter, who had been appointed Head of Security. "Unless you get that Hedgehog back to fence everywhere in."

"Oh, that won't be necessary," said Toad. "I'm sure you'll be able to cope, Otter. Now Rat," he called out, leaning back in his chair until it wobbled dangerously. "I wanted to talk to you about another idea I've had."

"Another idea, Toad?" Rat called back, who thought that Toad had probably had quite enough ideas for one year as it was. Opening Toad Hall to the public for the summer had seemed a wonderful idea in the depths of winter, when they'd all felt dreary and dozy and thoroughly fed up with short days, grey skies and steely east winds. But now, with the late spring days drawing ever longer, and places to explore, and picnics to take and the summer visitors starting to arrive, Rat could think of a hundred and one better things to do with his time than help Toad with his latest scheme. But there, he'd given his word and there was nothing he could do about it except make the best of it.

"Boat trips," said Toad. "How about that for an idea! When the visitors have been amazed and entertained by my splendid stories of Toad Hall and its splendid occupants through the years, and tasted a cup of Mole's splendid coffee..."

"We've not had any of it yet," interrupted the Otter.

"But when we do, it's bound to be splendid," Rat called from behind the counter, where he was setting out cups and saucers on a tray.

"And then," continued Toad, "when the visitors have visited the gift shop and bought a splendid memento of their visit, what better way to round off a perfect day than with a splendid punt down the river?"

"Y-e-s-s-s," Otter said slowly. Personally, his preference to round off a splendid day would be a swim in the river, but he could quite see that the mice and the hares and the deer and other daytripping landlubbers might prefer to keep their paws dry.

"And who would make a perfectly splendid boatman?" said Toad, with a twinkle in his eyes.

"Rat," murmured Mole, his tongue peeping from between his lips. He had finally managed to persuade the machine to produce a large jug full of coffee, which he was now pouring carefully into the cups that Rat had set out, but he had caught enough of the conversation to know who would be ideal for the job.

"Rat, of course," agreed Otter.

Rat was delighted. "Well, if you insist," he said modestly. And, of course, everyone did.

On Sunday afternoon, at two o'clock sharp, everything was as ready as it was going to be. Rat broke off from giving the paintwork on his boat a final polish and shielded his eyes as he raised his face to the sun. In the distance came the breezy three-note peep of a motor horn. It was the first coach, pulling up at the main gate to Toad Hall.

Otter, impressive and important in a navy blue uniform with silver epaulettes, jumped down from his security kiosk and motioned for the coach driver to wind down his window.

"Yes?" asked the driver.

Otter was stumped. He hadn't thought of what he should say. "Er, um, er, who goes there?" was all he could think of at short notice.

"Well, um, er, it's us," replied the crow at the steering wheel. "Me and – er," he gestured over his shoulder to a party of giggling sparrows and gossiping starlings and jabbering pigeons, "that lot."

"Righto," said Otter, feeling enormously relieved that it had turned out to be so simple. He dashed back and pushed down on the short end of the lever that raised the long arm of the barrier. The coach sailed through and picked up speed along the drive, leaving a cloud of dust in its wake.

"Have a nice day," Otter called after it, thinking he should say something and that was the only thing that came to him. He went back to his little kiosk to practise something more original before the next party came. Then he tried some experimental signalling and pointing before he was finally satisfied. "Before you lies Toad Hall," he announced to the tranquil afternoon, "and you're welcome to it."

In the old butler's pantry, Mole was hot and getting hotter by the minute. It was so hot the icing for the cupcakes wouldn't set. The coffee maker was steaming up his spectacles, and every little while he had to stop buttering bread or mixing sardine sandwich

Welcome To Toad Hall

paste to take them off and wipe them clean with the hem of his apron. Everything was such a bother and a worry. What if he ran out of teabags or caramel shortbreads, or sausage rolls? What if he ran out of clean cups and saucers? What if the coffee-maker ran out of steam? What if he, Mole, ran out of steam...?

Every inch the Master of the Estate, Toad positioned himself in front of the enormous front doors of Toad Hall, making sure the panel with the peeling paintwork was well hidden. He was having a pleasant daydream where he'd just been dubbed Sir Toad of Toad Hall by the Queen, having been made a Knight of the Realm for Services to Culture, History, Conservation and Sunday Afternoon Activities. "It was nothing, Your Majesty," he murmured modestly. When he looked up, a coach had stopped in the drive and the very first party of visitors were tumbling out and looking around with a mixture of curiosity and bewilderment.

"Is this it then?" asked a sparrow. One pigeon broke away from the group and began heading for the vegetable garden. The others followed.

"No, no, this way for the Grand Tour," Toad waved his arms wildly and beckoned towards the Hall. No one took any notice. He ran down the steps and chased after them into the garden. The birds had already spread out. For a couple of pigeons, the temptation to let rip and eat the spring lettuces was too great. A starling surreptitiously nipped off a cutting from a chrysanthemum and slipped it into her bag.

"Where's my head of security?" called Toad. "Where's Otter when I need him?"

But even if Otter had been able to hear Toad, he would have been too busy to leave the gate. He was having trouble with the barrier, which seemed to have stuck fast. A line of coaches had backed up the lane as far as the eye could see, which in Otter's case was the slip road leading from the motorway. In the distance came the sound of a police siren, which Otter hoped had nothing to do with him. Unfortunately it had. A police car squeezed along the gap between the traffic and the lush hedgerow, and parked by the kiosk. An officer lumbered out. The coach drivers stopped tooting their horns and one or two passengers gave a few cheers. Then there was silence. The sun, in a fierce mood, glared down on the proceedings.

"Now, now," said Badger, lifting his helmet to give his white stripe a thorough scratch. "What seems to be occurring, Otter?"

"It's not my fault," Otter said quickly. "It's nothing to do with me. It's the barrier thingy-me-jig. It's only gone and got stuck."

"So it has," said Badger, solemnly inspecting the apparatus. "I think I know what the trouble is. I'd better see your licence first."

"Licence?" gulped Otter. "Toad never said anything about a licence."

"It's a very new piece of legislation," said Badger. "It's a Sunday Afternoon Hall Opening Security Barrier Arm Licence. And luckily for you, I am one of the very few officers authorised to grant such a licence." Very slowly, very officiously, Badger unbuttoned his breast pocket and removed a little blue notebook. From behind his left ear, he plucked a stub of pencil and carefully licked the point. "Name?" he said.

Inside the coaches, tempers were reaching boiling point. Eventually coach doors began opening with wheezy gasps and the passengers rushed out. "If we wait for him and his stupid licence," muttered a hare, "by the time we get to the Hall, it'll be time to leave."

So, while Otter answered Badger's long list of questions, people began pouring up Toad's driveway on foot. They began at a leisurely trickle, until a party of Scottish wildcats put on a bit of a spurt and rushed to the front of the procession.

"Just a minute," called an extended family of pine martens, running to catch up and overtake. "We were here first."

"Actually we were before you," a Sunday school outing of shrews remarked, although their voices were so high-pitched not everybody actually heard them. Nevertheless, they too rushed forward to reclaim their queue place, and suddenly everyone was bumping, bustling, streaming, and ultimately stampeding at Olympic Games standard towards Toad Hall.

Half a mile and a whole world away, with his hat tipped over his face, Rat reclined in his boat and dreamed of the celebratory cream tea Toad was bound to offer once the visitors had departed and the whole Hall-opening thing was declared a success.

In the banqueting hall, Mole watched the water in the tea urn evaporating into steam, steam and more steam, and wondered what could be keeping the first party of visitors. The sandwiches were already turning up at the edges and the wings of the butterfly buns were disappearing into the melting butter cream. And probably most worrying of all was Toad's absence. Mole hoped he hadn't suddenly taken it into his head to pop into town for a new jacket or something.

"Now you've seen the gardens, ladies and gentlemen," Toad said, rounding up the birds and shooing them through a kissing gate, "we might as well continue through the Bluebell Woods which, in olden times, was known as the Wild Wood. And over to the river bank, from where, ladies and gentlemen..." – Toad

Welcome To Toad Hall

lowered his voice so that the birds had to press closer to hear him properly – "...from where we will enter the secret tunnel that runs to the Hall, and I'll tell you all about the night my grandfather's grandfather fought the greatest battle of his life to save his beloved home from invaders..."

"Hello? Excuse me?" called out a voice. The tea room door opened and a narrow face peeped round. "Is there anyone there?"

At last, thought Mole, dashing through to the counter to begin serving. "One at a time, please," he said. But there was only one; a stoat wearing the type of peaked cap popular with Sunday afternoon coach drivers.

"Where does the tour start from?" asked the stoat. "We've been waiting in the hall for ages, but there doesn't seem to be anyone around."

"But where's Toad?" Mole said, hoping he didn't sound as cross as he was feeling.

"We've not seen any Toad," replied the stoat, sounding precisely as cross as he felt. "We've not seen a soul. We've come all this way to see the Hall, and we've not even seen as much as a ghost."

"Ghost?" said Mole. "I don't think we've got one of those." Toad and Rat had thought of a lot of things that might attract visitors, but he was pretty sure they hadn't thought of a ghost. Mole wondered whether he dare mention it to Toad, but decided a wiser course might be to run it past Rat first. You never could tell how Toad would take ideas. Besides which, there was obviously no Toad around at the moment to tell anything to.

"Mr Toad has been unavoidably detained," Mole told the driver. "But if you wouldn't mind waiting–?"

"Yes, we would mind waiting," interrupted the stoat. "We've been waiting for twenty minutes already, and some of us are getting a bit fed up – a bit disruptive, if you know what I mean."

"Oh, dear," said Mole, wondering how disruptive a party of stoats could be. He hoped they weren't sprawling over the antique chairs. Toad was a hospitable fellow, but he was very particular where his soft furnishings were concerned.

"Wheeeeeeee!" came the distant whoop of merry voices.

"That's them," said the coach driver. "Sliding down the stair-rail banisters. There were organising races when I left them."

"Oh, dear, you'd better go and get them and bring them in here," said Mole in desperation. He was thinking if he could fill them up with teas and cakes and sandwiches, the boisterous stoats might be too stuffed to do much damage. By the time he'd served them all, Toad was bound to have turned up.

But it didn't happen in that order at all. The stampede had arrived, breathless but determinedly eager, at the front steps. Some people stopped so abruptly that other people ran into the back of them and fell over. Some complained loudly, and some muttered under their breath, and rows and scuffles broke out. After grievances had been aired, and tempers and lost hats restored, deer and mice and a large party of free-range hens from Hampshire stood about wondering where they should go first and what they should see first. Eventually they followed their ears and noses to the sounds and smells of Mole's splendid tea room. The queue for light refreshments ran twice round the Hall and the people in it started to get restless. And when people on a day's outing begin to get restless, and then begin to feel right at home with restlessness, they get peculiar ideas about what is right and proper to occupy their time. The stoats instructed a family of beavers in the intricacies of banister-rail racing. While other people were selecting and cheering on their team of choice, a pair of magpies took the opportunity to pick up a few of Toad's shiniest objects d'art, slip them under their wing-pits, and saunter nonchalantly back up the drive. But as they neared the security barrier they caught the sight of Badger's police helmet, panicked, and threw the gewgaws into the hedge.

"Date?" Badger was asking Otter, waving his notepad and repeatedly licking his pencil.

"Sorry, no idea," replied Otter, yawning.

The magpies realised they could have walked through security wearing the crown jewels without being noticed, and argued about their hastiness all the way back up the drive.

Mole was rushed off his feet. He'd never imagined such small feet could hurt so much. He reckoned he had made enough sandwiches to stretch to the moon and back, not that there had been time for an accurate calculation. He had served food, wiped tables, collected dirty crockery and washed up. No one had asked where souvenirs could be purchased, but the teaspoons had all gone missing. Mole was in the old butler's pantry, buttering more slices of bread, when his legs started to quiver and wobble. Gradually he became aware of the sounds of faint whispering and murmuring. He wondered if the stoat had been right; perhaps there really was a ghost of Toad Hall. Mole was too busy to be frightened. If a ghost could butter scones and make tea, any ghost would be more than welcome. But then suddenly the ground beneath his feet began to rumble and shake and Mole was convinced that he wasn't experiencing a haunting, but an earthquake. With a violent involuntary jump, Mole found himself tipped

Welcome To Toad Hall

over backwards. He stared in amazement as a trapdoor in the floor flipped up, and Toad's smiling face appeared. "And here we are – Oh, hello, Mole!" He frowned with surprise at the sight of his Tea Room Manager flat on his back on the pantry floor. "Well, if all you've got to do is laze about, Mole, you could give me a hand with some of the tours. I've been rushed off my feet – oh!"

Toad pressed himself to the wall as starlings, sparrows, and pigeons – plus two bewildered water voles, who five minutes earlier had been in the tunnel minding their own business before being swept along with the party – streamed up and out, through Mole's kitchen, into the tea room, where they all clamoured for glasses of strawberry milk and custard creams.

Mole was so exasperated he was unable to speak. He stared at Toad for ages, opened and closed his mouth several times like an organ bellows, fighting for breath, until he finally had enough air to puff, "I resign!"

Waking up with a start and finding a distinct lack of enquiries regarding boat rides, Rat decided to take a stroll up to the Hall. On the way he discovered Badger and Otter still stuck on the finer points of Security Barrier Arm Licences.

"Poor Toad," said Rat. "He'll be so disappointed that no one came to visit the Hall."

"Oh, I think one or two people might have gone up," said Otter. "I'm not sure how many exactly, because I've been very busy with Badger here."

"I wouldn't mind having a look round Toad Hall," said Badger. "I've never been inside, but I remember my old grandfather telling me about all the times his grandfather had been entertained up there. And a nice cup of tea would be very welcome."

So Rat, Otter and Badger strolled on up to the Hall, completely unprepared for the scene of devastation that confronted them. Tourists were spilling out of every door and every window, running up and down the stairs and swinging from the chandeliers. Toad was waving his arms about like a windmill, trying to gain attention and restore order. Rat ran to the old banqueting hall to see how Mole was getting on. The tea room looked as if a tornado had blown through it – two tornadoes; Rat revised his estimate on closer inspection. Poor Mole.

"Mole?" he called. "Moly, where are you?"

Mole had run out of the Hall and into the grounds. He was more exhausted, more confounded and more upset than he had ever imagined it was possible to be. Collapsing onto a clay rhubarb forcer, he kicked off his plimsolls and plunged his aching feet into deep, cooling clover. Then he closed his eyes and practised some deep breathing. After the passing of time, he opened his eyes again and took stock. His long distance eyesight wasn't perfect, but sufficient to take in the soothing view across the parkland towards Bluebell Woods. Mole found it difficult to believe, on a deliciously bright, glad-to-be-alive and all's-right-with-the-world sort of springtime afternoon that it had once been a fearful, jumpy, scary place. Just squinting at it now, with the spiky pines and poplars sticking up through the velvety mounds of oaks, chestnuts and sycamores, it reminded Mole of a pincushion. It gave him a warm, domestic sort of feeling that he associated with comfort and home and all familiar things like that. Somewhere a pigeon cooed; not a stray visitor, but a dweller of Bluebell woods, for Mole recognised the local dialect in his tone. Closer to hand – or, more accurately, closer to nose – the warm and peppery Maytime aromas of newly unfurled bramble leaves, hogweed and cow parsley acted like smelling salts on Mole's jaded senses. At first, when Toad had not seemed to understand or appreciate all that Mole had done to hold the fort in Toad's absence, Mole had wanted to run and run and run until he was far, far, far away. But now, resting calmly, he recalled something important, something his mother had told him when he had been very young. *Never forget this is where you belong. See that carpet of forest leaves, that track of soil, that verge of grass? Scratch the surface, my dear, look under that carpet, that soil, that grass, and you'll see our footprints go down for miles.*

And that was how Rat found him, lost in childhood reverie. Rat lightly squeezed his arm. "Oh, my dear Mole, what an absolutely dreadful afternoon of it you must have had."

"Oh, dear Ratty." That was all Mole could say without his voice cracking. Trust Rat to sum up things in an instant and understand everything. And with that, on top of being back outdoors and the restoration of his strength and senses, Mole felt so much better.

"I must find Toad," Mole said eventually. "I'm afraid he'll think I left him in the lurch." He struggled to his feet. "There are teas to serve, and mess to clear up, and more washing up, and teaspoons to find..." Mole started to feel the panic inside him bubble to the surface again.

"Now sit back down," said Rat. "We've done all that – well, after a fashion. Badger and Otter escorted the visitors back to where the coaches had gone off to park. Toad has washed up, and I've tried to tidy up the Hall. Oh, look, here they come now."

Into view came Otter, bearing a tea tray. Behind him was Badger, carrying what looked suspiciously like a picnic hamper, which is exactly what it turned out to be. Toad was carrying nothing, but then he needed his arms free so that he was able

Welcome To Toad Hall

wrap them round Mole. "I'm so sorry, my friend. I had no idea what you'd had to cope with. I'm such a stupid, insensitive fellow sometimes..."

"No, you're not," said Mole, comforting Toad. "How could you be expected to know what had happened? Please don't take it to heart," he begged, his whiskers quivering, "you'll make me feel bad too."

"Yes, come on, you two," said Otter, pouring the tea.

"Yes, food, that's what we all need now," said Rat. "Mole, I bet you've been so busy feeding everyone else, you never thought to stop and have something yourself."

"Well, no, actually I didn't," Mole said.

"Everything seems better with a full stomach," said Badger, munching on a cheese and onion sandwich.

After they'd eaten and rested, Toad, Otter, Badger, Rat and Mole made their way back inside Toad Hall. It was a depressing sight. There was an awful lot of work still to be done to restore the Hall to its usual comfortable standard. Curtains were hanging off poles, there were muddy prints all over the floor due to a party of roe deer who had refused to use the door but jumped in and out through the windows instead. Rat found long-handled brushes and dustpans, and set to work sweeping up the pieces of broken plaster of the Toad family statues that had been knocked from their pedestals. Otter went round with a basket, collecting lolly sticks and fruit pastille wrappers, while Badger set to with a duster and polish on the woodwork. Mole was straightening pictures when he suddenly heard a rumbling sound. For a minute he wondered if it was another earthquake, until he remembered there hadn't been an earthquake to begin with.

The others, too, stopped their labours and cocked their heads upwards, listening to footsteps, and singing, and the sounds of furniture being dragged across floorboards.

"It's the ghost!" whispered Mole.

"Toad?" said Rat, "I didn't know you had a ghost."

"I haven't," replied Toad, "not to my knowledge. But it's an idea..."

"Hush, listen," said Otter, holding up a paw.

A door opened and the singing voice grew louder. Tiny footsteps scratching on bare wood passed overhead, drew near the top of the stairs, and descended towards them. Mole clutched Rat's arm. Otter puffed up his chest in a show of bravado. Badger tried to look officious. Toad leaned a few inches towards the nearest exterior door. They focussed on the stairs until the owner of the footsteps and the voice came into view.

"It's one of the sparrows from the coach party," announced Otter, recognising her headscarf decorated with ladybirds.

Toad was very taken with the distinctive garment, and wondered whether he might obtain something similar in the cravat line, perhaps with a sausage motif. "You've been left behind," he told the sparrow. "Your companions have gone back home."

The sparrow shuffled her feet. "I've been hiding in the attic. I didn't expect to like the quiet life, but once I got here I found myself right at home."

"I think you'll find it's far from quiet in the country," remarked Mole.

"It's a lot quieter than the city," replied the sparrow. "And this place," she added, spreading her arms to indicate Toad Hall, "is not that much different from the place where I live and work. I hope you don't mind," the sparrow looked at Toad and blushed, "but I've been rearranging a few things upstairs. If you please, and if you don't mind me saying so, you really ought not to let the visitors go wherever they please. That's not how we do it in London. Her Majesty doesn't let the visitors have the run of the place."

Toad suddenly had a good idea of where the sparrow lived and worked in London, but he asked her anyway. She confirmed she did, indeed, come from a royal palace: "Only in a very minor and lowly capacity," she was quick to admit, "but long enough to have picked up the general principles of how to run really successful opening days. Signage," she added, "that's the key."

Toad thumped his forehead with his paw. "Signage! Of course! Why didn't any of us think of that? Still," added Toad, with his usual generosity, "let's not dwell on the oversight." He could see how a triumph might be achieved from what had been – however cheerful a gloss was put on it – a disastrous first day. "Is everyone thinking what I'm thinking?" he said. They all were.

The sparrow was formally offered, and accepted, the post of Visitor Manager. First thing Monday morning she set everyone to work making signs. Signs with pointing fingers showing the way to proceed round the house. Signs giving directions to the tea room, the gift shop, the ornamental gardens. And polite signs with instructions regarding behaviour: "Visitors are respectfully reminded that windows are for the looking out of, not the jumping through of. Please use the doors." and "Please do not make off with Mr Toad's nice things." and "No snacking of the vegetable garden, if you please. Lettuces can be tasted in the tea room, by ordering Salmon Salad sandwiches. Thanking You."

Welcome To Toad Hall

Mole wondered if they were rather too wordy in places, and whether some visitors might lose interest, and the gist, half way through, but Rat assured him otherwise. After the rooms were prepared and the tour route roped off to the sparrow's satisfaction, she reorganised staff duties. Mole, who always did his best whatever the task, was first and only too glad to admit he was more of an outdoors person, and was delighted to be given the job of Head Gardener. Toad was the new Head of Hospitality. He was a little dubious to begin with, but once he realised he could regale the visitors with his stories while they ate, he thought it was a really splendid idea. He insisted on engaging a couple of school-age hedgehogs to wash up and sweep underneath the tables, so he didn't have to do too much of the hard work himself. Because of his brisk manner and efficiency of movement, the job of leading the tour parties round the Hall was given to Otter. And Badger decided to leave the police force and accept the post of Head of Security. Curiously enough after that, the necessity of having a Security Barrier Arm Licence never came up. After the coaches had gone through, Badger would trot briskly up to the Hall, where he would patrol the rooms, armed with a stern countenance that banished all thoughts of visitor mischief. And what about the Rat? Well, Ratty stuck to river-trip duties, because there was nothing in life he liked so much as messing around in boats. The sparrow took to the country life like a kingfisher to the river bank willows. The opening of Toad Hall on Sunday afternoons was a splendid success. As far as the friends were concerned, what was even more splendid was that it left six days over at the end of each and every week to enjoy the new summer as she cast her ancient magic over their world.

Afterword

(The Plausibility Of *Willows* Sequels.)

The Kenneth Grahame Society short-story competition had nearly one hundred entries, representing the work of over ninety different authors. It was a unique privilege to read such a range of individual approaches to writing a short story that captured and extended aspects of *The Wind in the Willows*; some stories, where the approach corresponded with Grahame's original and the body of academic critical analysis, produced many echoes, while other stories, where the approach or details seemed to conflict implausibly with Grahame's original or the body of academic critical analysis, raised thought-provoking questions. Ultimately, it seemed a worthwhile exercise to record these observations and share them with *Willows* sequel writers of the future. This Afterword, presented principally as food for thought, is a discussion of the main observations on the plausibility of such sequels.

A few acknowledgements are necessary to give a clear sense of context to the subsequent discussion and its limitations, so, somewhat like Shakespeare's weaver, who "rid his prologue like a rough colt", let us dash off these acknowledgements in a short, unembellished list. Firstly, writing a *Willows* sequel cannot be reduced to a formula about plausibility; this discussion really only presents one of several essential perspectives on the subject, and the sequel writer will need strong creative-writing abilities too. Secondly, the discussion is largely a reaction to the short stories which were submitted as entries to the competition, and, derived in this way, it cannot be regarded as a comprehensive or academic survey. Thirdly, there are wide-sweeping generalisations in the discussion, and exceptions will surely be found, but there is enough core truth in it to justify the claim that the topics merit consideration by the sequel writer.

In attempting to attach some structure to the numerous, discrete observations, it proved helpful at times to explore the analogy of a counterfeiter's work being like that of a sequel writer. The two processes which the counterfeiter uses – analysis and production – could lend many concepts to the sequel writer. For example, the banknotes which a counterfeiter produces are, in many respects, similar to the short story or full-length sequel which the writer hopes to produce, and the counterfeiter's meticulousness is similar to the attention to detail which the sequel writer must exercise.

Afterword

The analogy of the counterfeiter will be revisited a few more times in the course of this discussion, but one significant aspect which should be considered at the outset is the audience. The counterfeiter consciously decides who the recipients will be. Will they be the general public, who have neither the information nor equipment to spot any flaws in a poorly produced counterfeit banknote? Will the group also include informed people, like astute shopkeepers, and even bankers, who would spot flaws in such a banknote? In that case the counterfeit banknote must be of a higher standard. Or will the group include experts, like the police, who can be deceived only by a flawless banknote? In that case the counterfeit banknote must be of the highest standard.

The sequel writer must make similar decisions about the audience of the sequel and the level of plausibility he or she wishes the sequel to achieve. The sequel writer's general readers correspond to the counterfeiter's general public, the reviewers and literature enthusiasts to the counterfeiter's informed people, and the academic critics to the counterfeiter's experts. Decisions about the target audience will determine the standard the sequel must reach. Even if the sequel writer decides, for whatever reasons, not to aim at the most plausible sequel, it is probably still useful for him or her to know what works, what does not, where the flaws and cracks appear, and so forth, in order to avoid producing a novel or short story which is dismissed by the majority of readers.

Let us look at some of the specific details relating to the competition entries.

The vast majority were sequels, but a significant number of prequels and counter texts were submitted as well. The final publication contains all three. Interestingly, each category has different challenges for the writer. A sequel must show a clear awareness of the original and remain consistent with the characters and world the original created, and with the original author's style. A prequel must also remain consistent with all these things, but must also avoid relationships and knowledge which cannot exist before the original. For example, any prequel which features Mole can hardly include Ratty, Badger or Toad, because the original leaves virtually no doubt that Mole had not met them before the period detailed in the first chapters of *The Wind in the Willows*. The counter text has the advantage that it can use a different voice and style, as clearly demonstrated by Jan Needle's *Wild Wood*, but it has the disadvantage that the range of plots is restricted by the need to interleave plausibly with events narrated in the original.

Afterword

Outside these main three categories, two distinct subcategories worth a brief mention at this point are the immediate prequel and the immediate sequel. These are, as the terms suggest, prequels which end immediately before *The Wind in the Willows* begins and sequels which begin immediately after it ends. Such stories have a few additional complications, necessitating something very similar to the careful interleaving of a counter text with the original. A prime example is the whereabouts of Ratty's boat. An immediate sequel which tells of him paddling back in his boat to Toad Hall, a day or two after the Toad Hall banquet, is virtually unbelievable, because Ratty's boat sank under the bridge when Toad rowed up to Toad Hall, and the Weasels and Stoats stopped his reconnaissance by dropping a stone through the bottom of it from the bridge. Consequently, that immediate sequel virtually must, however briefly, account for the raising and repair of Ratty's boat, or tell of him acquiring or building a new one. A later sequel does not have this obligation; the repairs, or whatever alternative, could be regarded as an undocumented activity carried out in the intervening period.

A key aspect of any sequel, and one to which most writers will devote some detailed study, is the creation of characters very similar to those in *The Wind in the Willows*. Coming to the right conclusions in such character studies and then recreating similar characters are not simple tasks. There are numerous pitfalls. Of the four friends, Badger is commonly the least understood. Many draw him flat, focussing on his being gruff and hating society. Grahame gives us a much more rounded character, and there is more than enough detail in *The Wind in the Willows* to identify the richer aspects of his character. Mole is a different challenge to represent. It is important to remember that the novel is, among other things, a *bildungsroman*, focusing on Mole's development. At the beginning of the novel he appears to be weak, naïve and childish, but he grows to be much more mature, a loyal friend and a courageous combatant, earning even the respect of Badger in the end. This means that a prequel will need to portray a very different Mole to the Mole a sequel would portray. Toad and Ratty present fewer pitfalls of that type. While some impression is given that Toad is a changed character by the end of the novel, many critics hold the opinion that he never changes, and Ratty, although described at one point as a "wiser and a sadder Rat", is probably, in the course of the novel, the least changed character of the four friends.

Studies of characterisation generally examine a character from four perspectives – what the character does, what the character says, especially what he says about himself, what others say about him and what the narrator says about him. Aside from the

Afterword

obvious recommendation that the characters in *The Wind in the Willows* receive an in-depth study along these lines, it must be added that the last three of these perspectives leave scope, as in almost any novel, for that narrator to be unreliable. Toad is clearly an unreliable narrator when it comes to what he says about himself, and most sequel writers will absorb that detail, but Ratty may also be, unintentionally, an unreliable narrator in what he says about Badger, especially in chapter four, "Mr. Badger".

References to voice in literature can mean simply what a specific character or the (omniscient) narrator says or what the tone is, especially the narrator's tone. Reproducing the voices of the main characters, Mole, Ratty, Toad and Badger, as stated above, requires careful study. Plausible results can be achieved. However, although Ratty and his friends may speak and describe things in simple terms, sometimes even using colloquial expressions, the narrator's voice in *The Wind in the Willows* is on a different level entirely. The reproduction of an authentic-sounding, omniscient-narrator's voice, emulating that of Kenneth Grahame himself, who wrote with immense sophistication, insight, wit and style, is one of the most difficult challenges for anyone who attempts to write a *Willows* sequel. Consider the almost poetic prose in the following excerpt from chapter three, "The Wild Wood":

> "It was a cold still afternoon with a hard steely sky overhead, when he slipped out of the warm parlour into the open air. The country lay bare and entirely leafless around him, and he thought that he had never seen so far and so intimately into the insides of things as on that winter day when Nature was deep in her annual slumber and seemed to have kicked the clothes off. Copses, dells, quarries and all hidden places, which had been mysterious mines for exploration in leafy summer, now exposed themselves and their secrets pathetically, and seemed to ask him to overlook their shabby poverty for a while, till they could riot in rich masquerade as before, and trick and entice him with the old deceptions. It was pitiful in a way, and yet cheering—even exhilarating. He was glad that he liked the country undecorated, hard, and stripped of its finery. He had got down to the bare bones of it, and they were fine and strong and simple. He did not want the warm clover and the play of seeding grasses; the screens of quickset, the billowy drapery of beech and elm seemed best away; and with great cheerfulness of spirit he pushed on towards the Wild Wood, which lay before him low and threatening, like a black reef in some still southern sea.
>
> There was nothing to alarm him at first entry. Twigs crackled under his feet, logs tripped him, funguses on stumps resembled caricatures, and startled him for the moment by their likeness to something familiar and far away; but that was all fun, and exciting. It led him on, and he penetrated to where the light was less, and trees crouched nearer and nearer, and holes

Afterword

made ugly mouths at him on either side.

Everything was very still now. The dusk advanced on him steadily, rapidly, gathering in behind and before; and the light seemed to be draining away like flood-water.

Then the faces began.

It was over his shoulder, and indistinctly, that he first thought he saw a face; a little evil wedge-shaped face, looking out at him from a hole. When he turned and confronted it, the thing had vanished.

He quickened his pace, telling himself cheerfully not to begin imagining things, or there would be simply no end to it. He passed another hole, and another, and another; and then—yes!—no!—yes! certainly a little narrow face, with hard eyes, had flashed up for an instant from a hole, and was gone. He hesitated—braced himself up for an effort and strode on. Then suddenly, and as if it had been so all the time, every hole, far and near, and there were hundreds of them, seemed to possess its face, coming and going rapidly, all fixing on him glances of malice and hatred: all hard-eyed and evil and sharp.

If he could only get away from the holes in the banks, he thought, there would be no more faces. He swung off the path and plunged into the untrodden places of the wood.

Then the whistling began.

Very faint and shrill it was, and far behind him, when first he heard it; but somehow it made him hurry forward. Then, still very faint and shrill, it sounded far ahead of him, and made him hesitate and want to go back. As he halted in indecision it broke out on either side, and seemed to be caught up and passed on throughout the whole length of the wood to its farthest limit. They were up and alert and ready, evidently, whoever they were! And he—he was alone, and unarmed, and far from any help; and the night was closing in.

Then the pattering began.

He thought it was only falling leaves at first, so slight and delicate was the sound of it. Then as it grew it took a regular rhythm, and he knew it for nothing else but the pat-pat-pat of little feet still a very long way off. Was it in front or behind? It seemed to be first one, and then the other, then both. It grew and it multiplied, till from every quarter as he listened anxiously, leaning this way and that, it seemed to be closing in on him. As he stood still to hearken, a rabbit came running hard towards him through the trees. He waited, expecting it to slacken pace, or to swerve from him into a different course. Instead, the animal almost brushed him as it dashed past, his face set and hard, his eyes staring. 'Get out of this, you fool, get out!' the Mole heard him mutter as he swung round a stump and disappeared down a friendly burrow.

The pattering increased till it sounded like sudden hail on the dry leaf-carpet spread around him. The whole wood seemed running now, running

173

Afterword

hard, hunting, chasing, closing in round something or—somebody? In panic, he began to run too, aimlessly, he knew not whither. He ran up against things, he fell over things and into things, he darted under things and dodged round things. At last he took refuge in the deep dark hollow of an old beech tree, which offered shelter, concealment—perhaps even safety, but who could tell? Anyhow, he was too tired to run any further, and could only snuggle down into the dry leaves which had drifted into the hollow and hope he was safe for a time. And as he lay there panting and trembling, and listened to the whistlings and the patterings outside, he knew it at last, in all its fullness, that dread thing which other little dwellers in field and hedgerow had encountered here, and known as their darkest moment—that thing which the Rat had vainly tried to shield him from—the Terror of the Wild Wood!"

Style is a vast subject, but, other than the general suggestions that the writer replicate some of Grahame's rich use of metaphor and avoid the use of colloquialisms and contractions in the narrator's voice, little more can be added here to the emphasis that the narrator's voice and Grahame's style merit the most extensive study of all aspects of writing a *Willows* sequel.

Some of the entries had material for a novella or three or four chapters of a full-length sequel. A few others were very slow-paced. It seems to be a challenge to get the pace right. If we consider the pace of many of the chapters in *The Wind in the Willows*, which are approximately the same length as the specified length of the short stories, we see that a chapter covers a lot of action. For example, chapter six, "Mr Toad", begins with Badger calling on Ratty and Mole to recruit them for the admonishing of Toad, continues with the new car arriving at Toad Hall, Toad coming under house arrest, his escape through the window, his meal at the Red Lion, his theft of the car, his farcical trial and his imprisonment. Other chapters, with only one or two exceptions, have a similar pace. Some factors which make this pace possible relate to the fundamental structure of each chapter's building on previous chapters and being continued in subsequent chapters. A short story of similar length cannot cover as much material, because it needs to be self contained and allow some space for an introductory exposition and a conclusive ending. This is not an unmanageable challenge, and some leverage of the background that Grahame's original provides can be exploited, but the difficulties of pace and word limit can multiply into something more challenging if the author introduces too many new characters and new locations, and then tries to accommodate an elaborate plot. A slower pace is not necessarily a problem, unless it appears to the reader that the author is taking too long to say something lightweight which could be expressed in fewer words. Interestingly, of

Afterword

the two main criticisms levelled by one academic at Dixon Scott's *A Fresh Wind in the Willows*, one was that the pace was too slow and the descriptions too detailed in several places. (The other was that it was episodic.)

Since *The Wind in the Willows* is an animal fantasy, or even simply a fantasy, there is a danger of thinking that the unreal nature of fantasy provides a flexibility in which almost any plot or topic will sound plausible. That is a fallacy. The plot or topic of a sequel may push the boundaries, and even overstep them carefully, but a sequel demands an element of "relative reality", especially when its forerunner has established a distinct precedent and framework for its canon. In *The Wind in the Willows* Grahame created a very unusual world – the River Bank and Wild Wood – and populated it with unusual characters. Some of those boundaries, such as the crossovers of the human and animal worlds, and the almost total absence of servants and women, may seem undefined, but care must be given to plots and themes so that they fit reasonably well into this established world. And sometimes very trivial details can do a disproportionate amount of harm. In some of the short stories there were minor details, such as brief references to modern inventions or the inclusion of non-British animals and pets as new characters, which seemed to proclaim themselves surprisingly loudly to be outside the world of *The Wind in the Willows*.

Returning to the counterfeiter analogy, one of the first things which will raise people's suspicions, when they are passed a counterfeit note, is an incorrect general tone. Indeed, their suspicions are raised by, for example, a very dark banknote, even before they begin to examine the banknote's details. The analogy does not completely carry over to literature, but some of the main aspects of it do. Some short stories had plots where some of the main characters were captured, misused, or in real peril; effectively they were "seriously distressed" over long periods. One of the main reasons why William Horwood's sequels, especially *The Willows and Beyond*, sound unlike Grahame's original is the tone. It is much too dark. There are a few darker elements in *The Wind in the Willows*, but, on the whole, Kenneth Grahame gave the story a positive tone. Of course, Grahame adheres to that Victorian novelists' tradition of rewarding good and tying everything up with a happy ending. But it is not that only good things happen in the plot or that the characters are all supremely virtuous. Such is not the case. Cars get stolen, Toad is jailed, Portly goes missing, the weasels and stoats ambush Badger and Mole rather viciously, they shoot at Toad, and much more. But the tone of the novel remains upbeat. Grahame uses several techniques to achieve this.

Afterword

Most of the negative incidents in the novel are overlaid with humour, particularly in the form of farce, so that the reader does not take any of these incidents too seriously. And the main characters, Ratty, Mole, Toad and Badger, are not always sweet and mild. At times they are snappy and gruff. But, in it all, Grahame achieves a balance that comes across as a realistic account of healthy friendships. It is also to be noted, conversely, that Grahame rarely included instances where the main characters made glowing professions of friendship. Their statements of friendship were generally restrained, and much of the image of friendship was portrayed by the omniscient narrator.

"Feelgood literature" is a term which is almost always used in a derogatory sense now. This is largely justified, because there are too many stories which try too hard to have a feelgood effect on the reader, and only finish up sounding sickeningly sweet, unrealistic or, in the worst cases, downright irritating. It is also most unfortunate for literary analysis, because it may deter students from proper academic study of reader-response theory in this area. Perhaps, in view of the growing interest in positive psychology elsewhere in academia, the tides may turn, and this may be explored in the not-too-distant future. *The Wind in the Willows* is a wonderful example of feelgood literature well constructed. It is positive, but well balanced, so that it does not fall to the slushy depths where most other feelgood literature resides.

Of similar importance to tone is the human/animal balance in *The Wind in the Willows* and its sequels. Again Grahame creates a fine balance that contributes to the success of *The Wind in the Willows*. But in the wrong hands a sequel can veer too far towards the human or towards the animal extremes, with far-reaching effects on the story and the reader. If the tale becomes too human, the story can sound very much like a tale of middle-aged men indulging in their hobbies and comforts. This is likely to retain buoyant appeal for the reader who is middle-aged, male and enjoys his hobbies and comforts, but its appeal is likely to plummet among women and young readers. *The Wind in the Willows* is predominantly a human tale, but Grahame always kept a backing chorus of animal aspects alive in the story – animal names, exclusively animal activities and sentiments, like migration, hibernation and living underground, and even inclusion of the animal-demigod, Pan. Equally, if the tale acquires too much of an animal tone, it may appeal more to the younger reader, but may risk displaying dissimilarity to *The Wind in the Willows* and also risk becoming a single-level children's story, somewhat akin to fairy stories, with limited appeal for adult readers.

Incidentally, the general view that the four friends, Ratty, Mole,

Afterword

Toad and Badger, were all middle-aged men, is not entirely consistent with a variety of references in *The Wind in the Willows*; it would appear, rather, that Ratty and Mole were relatively young, Toad somewhat older, and Badger older still – perhaps collectively spanning almost two generations.

Giving first names to any of the characters needs particular care. All the main characters are named after the animal which represents them, with that name being used and capitalised as if the animal name were a surname. Only Billy the hedgehog and Portly the young otter are given first names. It is probably best to avoid first names for any of the main characters or their close relatives. Using one numerous times throughout the story can unravel the effect of the story if the reader doubts the writer's choice of something like "Freddie Toad" for a name. "Toad's grandfather", "Mole's nephew" and suchlike, although bland terms, sound much more appropriate. Cosgrove Hall created a wonderful, dim-witted Aloysius Weasel in their TV series, and carefully selected names might work better for the weasels, stoats and other Wild Wooders, especially if the character is not named too frequently in the story, but descriptive terms are likely to work better than first names in virtually every case.

Titles are a similar consideration. Academic critics seem to be in agreement that Toad was not titled and that, if he was, he would surely have used that title rather than referred to himself as "Mr. Toad". It is thought that he was probably just a squire, one of the landed gentry who had no noble title, and some support for this is found in the last chapter of the book where Toad proposes an evening of events which includes and address "Back to the Land – A Typical English Squire". In a recent discussion, one of the short-story authors, Ruth Sheppard, put forward the possibility that Toad's father had a title, but one which was not hereditary and, hence, did not pass to his son. The local squirearchy often obtained titles; the titles were earned for occupations such as building railways or inventing new machinery or for service in the colonies. In such cases, Toad's title would, at most, have been The Honourable Mr. Toad, a diluted title which passed to the sons of a nobleman. It is certainly not beyond the bounds of possibility. Somewhat surprisingly, academics reckon that the only character who may have been a member of the aristocracy is Badger. There is no very strong case for this, however. In general, the introduction of titles is probably best avoided, unless in some obviously farcical sense, where they are applied to Toad, the weasels, the stoats or some other Wild Wooders.

The relevance and applicability of genre is sometimes overemphasised, but genre has its uses for the writer even more than for the reader or critic. If, for example, a writer writes within a specific genre, he or she can leverage various expectations and familiarities which the reader holds for that genre. *The Wind in the Willows* is commonly classified as an animal fantasy, a genre within its own right, but the novel has several significant secondary genres – adventure, particularly in relation to Toad's adventures, *bildungsroman*, in tracing the development of Mole, autobiography, since Grahame includes numerous autobiographical details and allusions, and even classic myth, in the chapter referring to Pan. Actually Grahame, like many other Victorian authors, wrote a multi-genre novel. There are, however, genres which he did not use, and the sequel writer should consider carefully whether these genres were omitted simply because one novel cannot contain every genre or because they are genres which do not lend themselves to *The Wind in the Willows*. The omitted genres include romance, horror, crime and detection, and several others. The important question, which several short stories triggered, is whether some genres, which work in a short story of a length equivalent to that of one or two chapters, may crack if spread over a whole novel.

It is outside the purpose of this discussion to explore many general aspects of punctuation or grammar, except where one or two of them may have specific relevance to *The Wind in the Willows* or Victorian literature. One issue, which may sound a little negative, is so common, however, that it does need to be mentioned. More than fifty percent of the entries for the short-story competition had weak punctuation and grammar, and this was not just a missing comma or two, mistakes which anyone could make, but numerous errors on every page. Often the basic story was fairly good, in that it was no drudgery to read it, but it needed a complete rewrite to produce something which could be published. Organisers of other short-story competitions have confirmed that this is something that they regularly encounter, and in similar proportions too. Studying grammar and punctuation, to improve the standard of writing, may strike many authors as taking all the fun out of creative writing. Be that as it may, these are the areas where many writers need to concentrate first, and time spent on these technical aspects of writing will pay great dividends when it comes to getting work published.

Another relevant area of punctuation worth mentioning may be the stylistic levels of punctuation referred to as overpunctuation and underpunctuation (or heavy and light punctuation). These levels are, debatably, all within the overall range of correct punctuation; neither level is more correct than the other. The most

Afterword

visible identifier for them in text is commas – commas around virtually every clause where they could be applied generally indicating overpunctuation and the omission of many of these optional commas indicating underpunctuation. Victorian authors and, more relevantly, Kenneth Grahame tended towards overpunctuation; or, at least, their editors did. Consider the punctuation in the following passage from *The Wind in the Willows*:

> "Now, with a rush of old memories, how clearly it stood up before him, in the darkness! Shabby indeed, and small and poorly furnished, and yet his, the home he had made for himself, the home he had been so happy to get back to after his day's work. And the home had been happy with him, too, evidently, and was missing him, and wanted him back, and was telling him so, through his nose, sorrowfully, reproachfully, but with no bitterness or anger; only with plaintive reminder that it was there, and wanted him."

This is a level of punctuation that was seen in very few competition entries.

(As an aside, for anyone wondering what Mole's day's work, mentioned in the above passage, may have been, one plausible possibility is that he was a lift operator in a mine. Grahame's short story, *Bertie's Escapade*, while not attempting to mirror or embrace any aspects of *The Wind in the Willows*, does have a Mole which operated a lift at a mine or quarry face. Mole's occupation may be relevant to some *Willows* prequels.)

While the focus of this discussion is sequel plausibility rather than creative writing, it may be worth mentioning two or three elements of general writing style which are relevant to *The Wind in the Willows* and its sequels.

The partitioning of a novel or short story into paragraphs is not often addressed. Apart from standard guidelines about starting a new paragraph when there is a change of subject or to denote a new speaker, the structure of the paragraphs have implications on style and pace. Long paragraphs, assuming they are long for correct reasons, tend to slow down the pace of the section where they appear, while a series of short paragraphs will speed up the pace of the section. If such paragraphs are coupled with long and short sentences respectively it emphasises the effect even further.

It is true that Grahame sometimes wrote a block of several paragraphs describing the location and scenery, before moving on to the action, but, more often, he wove such exposition and action together. Especially in the limited space of a short story, but also in a longer novel, skilled exposition interwoven with the action

Afterword

has many advantages: increased interest for the reader who struggles with too much scenery description, efficient use of the short-story word limit, richer writing style, and much more.

Stream of consciousness and, to a lesser extent, interior monologue appeared in several of the short stories. (While stream of consciousness and interior monologue are not synonymous, they are discussed here as if they were interchangeable terms, since the differences are not particularly relevant to the points being made.) Examples of stream of consciousness can be found in Victorian literature, although it is true that such inner perspectives are much more common in contemporary literature. To some extent the characters in novels have progressed from being flat, through rounded to this further, inner dimension, and many of these multi-dimensional portrayals of characters are very sophisticated. But stream of consciousness does not always succeed, and badly written stream of consciousness, where the reader can hardly discern whether the comments are being made by the character or the narrator, does little for the story. Moreover, there are some readers who do not find stream of consciousness or interior monologue at all interesting; they prefer reading the tidied-up version of the story, as told from an external perspective. One group of readers likely to dismiss stream of consciousness is younger children. Hence, if the story is to be enjoyed by younger children, stream of consciousness and interior monologue are probably best kept to a minimum or omitted altogether. Grahame had numerous opportunities to use these devices, such as times when Mole or Toad were alone, but he used it very rarely – only an isolated sentence here and there.

Another element of general writing style which has changed over the years is the inclusion or omission of dialogue tags, e.g. "said the Mole", "retorted Toad", "scoffed the Weasel" and suchlike. Several entries to the competition made very sparse use of these dialogue tags and, as a result, the dialogues seemed more challenging to read. Authors are very familiar with their own text, and sometimes they are not aware that the reader, coming fresh to the book, is not always as able to trace fluently who is saying what in the dialogue. For the creative writer, dialogue tags are an opportunity rather than a tedious labelling chore because, if they are used creatively, they can add inflections to the tone, attitude and reactions of the speaker, and to the relative balance of the characters – nuances which the speech alone cannot always be made to convey. Grahame rarely dropped dialogue tags (and rarely had lengthy dialogues consisting of single-sentence exchanges). Moreover, Victorian novels, especially children's novels, were often read aloud to the family. Dialogue with minimal

Afterword

dialogue tags, which just about works for the solo reader who can see clues like new paragraphs for new speakers, often fails when read aloud. The original competition announcement stated that the winning entry would be read aloud at the Society AGM in Fowey. Admittedly, that target proved elusive in the end, but the idea of sequels which can be read aloud is a cause worth promoting.

There is one famous phrase, used by Grahame's old friend, Arthur Quiller-Couch, which applies to virtually all creative writing including writing sequels to *The Wind in the Willows*. In one of his lectures at Cambridge, later published in *The Art Of Writing*, he advised the writer "Murder your darlings". Frequently there are themes, phrases and passages that the writer has an irrational love for, to the extent that he or she has shoehorned them into the story and continues to ignore any inner voice which suggests that the "darling" does not really fit or work to the advantage of the story. The advice is to murder such darlings by cutting them out of the story. Several entries for the competition had ill-fitting elements which had many of the characteristics of a writer's "darling". A spot of murder, or at least some grievous bodily harm, would have improved the writing.

There are a few pieces of key background information which many sequel writers may not stumble across, unless they have done a considerable amount of background reading, so an overview of some of the main ones may be useful.

It is generally agreed that *The Wind in the Willows* is a multi-layered, or multi-level, novel. It has a layer which appeals to children and a layer which appeals to adults (and perhaps other intermediate levels and other dimensions as well). This is not the same as a children's novel which appeals to adults, and many classic children's stories do appeal to adults without being multi-layer novels. A small example may be seen in comparing the farce, and even the occasional elements of slapstick, in Toad's adventures with the nostalgia in many parts of the novel. Farce, when it reaches slapstick proportions, generally appeals to children but has limited lasting appeal for adults, whereas nostalgia is a concept with virtually no meaning for children but has great appeal for adults reflecting back on their past childhood and on bygone eras. Few sequels to date have succeeded in reproducing such multiple layers and, instead, tend to be either children's novels or adult's novels but do not appeal equally to both groups in the way which *The Wind in the Willows* does. Potential sequel writers having to confront this aspect of *The Wind in the Willows* is possibly like the counterfeiter having to cope with watermarking and, as with the

Afterword

counterfeiter, this effect is unlikely to occur by coincidence; the layers must be understood and their reproduction planned carefully.

When asked to pen a description of the book, Kenneth Grahame wrote:

> "A book of Youth – and so perhaps chiefly for Youth, and those who still keep the spirit of youth alive in them: of life, sunshine, running water, woodlands, dusty roads, winter firesides; free of problems, clean of the clash of sex; of life as it might fairly be supposed to be regarded by some of the wise small things 'That glide in grasses and rubble of woody wreck.'"

Several critics have contested some aspects of this statement and have written at length on peripheral issues, related to feminist theory, in the novel. Their points are not entirely incorrect, but most of them fail to note that there is a large element of truth in Grahame's statement. The novel has no aspect of romance, and no marriages among the major characters, except Otter. It also has little or no parental references, and particularly no maternal references, among the major characters, except Otter. Very few women are mentioned at all, and they have relatively minor roles in those instances where they do appear. Grahame was alluding to portraying, in *The Wind in the Willows*, a River Bank and Wild Wood world that was not concerned with any of the main human relationships, other than friendship. It may help, too, to remember that the novel has its roots, no matter how distant and small, in bedtime stories told to his young son Alastair; as epitomised, just over a decade later, by Richmal Compton's fictional character William, a Victorian boy of that age could be expected to have had no interest in romantic themes and, conceivably, no interest in any female characters in a story. Many sequel writers have tried to include romantic themes in their stories, and sometimes they read very well – two of the best stories in this collection of short stories deal with Toad's marriage – but, ultimately, it is probably correct to say that romantic themes would be outside Grahame's ideas for the novel, and the sequel writer needs to handle such themes carefully.

Grahame omitted to mention many details which logic would suggest were in existence in the River Bank and Wild Wood. It is not always that Grahame denies the existence of these characters, beings or things. Rather, they complicate the story or introduce a theme which he does not wish to emphasise, and so he almost totally omits any mention of them, or consigns them to minor references. This is true of women, as discussed already, and it is also true of servants. Toad Hall could not have existed without

Afterword

servants, but only the briefest allusions are made to them. For example, in chapter two, "The Open Road", we read:

> "Eventually, a slow train having landed them at a station not very far from Toad Hall, they escorted the spell-bound, sleep-walking Toad to his door, put him inside it, and instructed his housekeeper to feed him, undress him, and put him to bed."

Ratty probably had a cook or housekeeper, but the reference to her in chapter eleven, "Like Summer Tempests Came His Tears", is even more obscure:

> "The Toad was simply wild with jealousy, more especially as he couldn't make out for the life of him what the Mole had done that was so particularly clever; but, fortunately for him, before he could show temper or expose himself to the Badger's sarcasm, the bell rang for luncheon."

When questioned about servants, some years after the publication of *The Wind in the Willows*, Grahame even added that Mole probably had a charmouse. Badger may have been the only one of the main characters who actually led a totally independent existence. The self-catering breakfast which Mole and the hedgehogs prepared at Badger's house in chapter four, "Mr Badger", would seem to confirm that. Sequel writers need to be aware that these servants existed, and either follow Grahame's example in barely mentioning them or incorporate them into the story with care. The main pitfall to avoid is writing details which clearly contradict the existence of such servants.

Some academic critics correctly point out that the framework of *The Wind in the Willows* delicately hangs together. There are several aspects where it comes close to falling apart, and would do so with less-skilful handling than Grahame's. One of the main fragilities is the meeting of the animal and human worlds. It should be noted that Toad is the only character who meets real humans to any great extent. Mole and Ratty had a few barely-mentioned, barely-representative encounters in "The Open Road" and "Dulce Domum", and it is not implied that they could not have met humans, but the fact remains that all the main incidents with real humans are experienced by Toad. And there is quite a list of them – the Red Lion restaurateur and couple whose car he stole, the courtroom judge, jury and policeman, the jail staff, including the jailer, his daughter and the washerwoman, the railway official, the train driver and the pursuing police, the bargewoman, the gypsy, and the couple who gave him a lift in the car. A closer examination of Toad's adventures leads to the question of whether Toad regularly mixed with real humans or whether this was a bounded foray into the

Afterword

human world for him. Possibly it is also worth asking whether this is even a bounded foray into the human world for the novel itself, in other words, a necessary departure from the norm. In any case, the sequel writer who indiscriminately mixes the River Bank and Wild Wood animals with real humans may struggle to keep the fragile framework standing.

Let us look, finally, at a few pointers for those who want to leave no stone unturned.

The counterfeiter has a box of tools for analysing, measuring and identifying the details of a genuine banknote. The sequel writer has an equivalent box of literary analysis tools. It would be a mammoth task to describe how they might all be used. Instead, a mere recommendation is made that the more useful ones to consider are probably historical context, reader-response, close reading and intertextuality. Whichever tools the author uses for the analysis, one thing, conflicting to some extent with contemporary literary theory, should be remembered: useful literary analysis can be done with imperfect tools. Much traditional literary theory has been discredited in recent years. This includes, for example, the author's intent, aspects of the author's autobiographical perspectives, and others, which have been collectively described as "the death of the author". Be that as it may, the sequel writer is still likely to find some of those imperfect tools of great use in a serious literary analysis of *The Wind in the Willows* and Grahame's other writings.

Many academics have written books and papers on *The Wind in the Willows*, most of them being quite accessible. It is debatable how much study of literary criticism is beneficial to the sequel writer; probably the Pareto rule applies – eighty percent of the benefit comes from twenty percent of the effort – meaning, in this context, that a small selection of literary criticism could provide much of the relevant knowledge. Reading even one or two of the key works would be invaluable, and the following bibliography section includes books which are recommended as an introduction to the wider area and are considered to be an ideal starting point.

In case any potential sequel writer would begin to think that the amount of reading presents an insurmountable obstacle, a last word on the counterfeiter may offer some sense of proportion. It would seem that a counterfeiter spends far more time studying the minute details of a valid banknote than he or she spends studying forged notes and other documents. The best preparation anyone can make for writing a sequel to *The Wind in the Willows* is to study the novel itself in greater depth, in order to acquire

Afterword

that more complete understanding of what it is, why it works, what does not work and all of its many perspectives.

Nigel McMorris

Bibliography

To provide a reference section, mapping to all the sources which were mentioned in the preceding discussion, would include many books and papers which are difficult to obtain and/or of questionable general relevance. (A comprehensive listing of academic papers and books can be found in the bibliography section of the Kenneth Grahame Society website, should anyone wish to do extensive research.) Instead, in the same vein as the observations offered above as food for thought, a list of recommended books, which might be useful to a *Willows* sequel writer, is included here.

Kenneth Grahame: A Biography by Peter Green (World Publishing Company 1959)
Beyond the Wild Wood: The World of Kenneth Grahame by Peter Green (Grange Books 1982)
A biography which presents extensive literary analysis and background to *The Wind in the Willows*. The 1959 edition contains valuable notes which are omitted from the 1982 edition, but the later edition has a much larger number of photos and illustrations.

The Wind in the Willows: A Fragmented Arcadia by Peter Hunt (Twayne 1994)
A very comprehensive and accessible literary analysis of *The Wind in the Willows*, which also summarises a broad range of previous analyses of the novel.

Kenneth Grahame by Lois Kuznets (Twayne 1987)
This book, while older than Peter Hunt's *Fragmented Arcadia,* is similar in style to it. It covers all of Kenneth Grahame's works, however, rather than just *The Wind in the Willows.*

Fairy Tales and After: From Snow White to E. B. White by Roger Sale (Havard 1978)
A broad analysis of children's literature, but with an excellent section on *The Wind in the Willows,* which is cited in many other critical writings.

Afterword

Complete Works of Kenneth Grahame (Kenneth Grahame Society 2009)
Full collection of Kenneth Grahame's published writings, which is very useful for a wider appreciation of the author's style and recurring themes.

Paths To The River Bank by Peter Haining (Souvenir Press 1983)
An insightful examination of some of Grahame's early writings which contained themes that he revisited in *The Wind in the Willows*.

Wild Wood by Jan Needle (Andre Deutsch 1981)
A fascinating counter text to *The Wind in the Willows*, which retells Grahame's original classic from the perspective of the weasels and stoats.

A Fresh Wind in the Willows by Dixon Scott (Heinemann/Quixote Press 1983)
A charming sequel to *The Wind in the Willows* with some fine touches of humour.

The Authors

Jessie Anderson.

Born and brought up in New Zealand, Jessie was introduced at an early age to the company of Mr. Toad and his friends. Later she rediscovered the enchantment of *The Wind in the Willows* through the eyes of her children and, later still, her grandchildren. The voyage of rediscovery was enhanced by new insights achieved through reading accounts of Kenneth Grahame's extraordinary life, particularly in Alison Prince's meticulously researched book, *An Innocent in the Wild Wood*. Jessie has worked in Britain as a journalist for many years, initially on the staff of Aberdeen Journals and later *The Scotsman*. Following marriage and family commitments, she became a freelance writer for various local and national publications including *Times Educational Supplement*, *The Teacher*, *In Britain*, *Cumbria Life*, *Period House* and *The Countryman*. More recently she has begun to write children's fiction and has had one book published.

Robin Bailes.

Robin viewed writing Moonglade as a good excuse to reread a book which enthralled him as a child and which got him interested in writing in the first place. Robin lives in Cambridge, is the author of two pantomimes and has written for BBC Radio, Newsrevue at the Canal Cafe Theatre and the magazine *My Weekly*.

Belinda Beasley

Belinda has been reading and writing stories since the age of five, finally reading *The Wind in the Willows* when she was in her twenties and living in Oxford. She now lives in Sheffield, where she divides her time between working with disabled students and organising classes and lectures on theatre. In her spare time, she writes children's stories and is studying the works of Jules Verne. Below The Waves is her first published story.

Wendy Bradley.

Wendy was born and brought up in Belfast, Northern Ireland, but now lives in Tynemouth, North East England. There have been storytellers in every generation of Wendy's family as far back as the early 1900's. She has been fascinated by *The Wind in the Willows*, ever since she first heard it, sitting on her father's knee in 1950. Thirty years later she passed on her love for Mole, Ratty and their riverside friends to her three sons. Turnip Soup is dedicated to the next generation. She still has a 1970's edition of

The Wind in the Willows, beautifully illustrated by E.H. Shepard, and she used Shepard's frontispiece map to envisage the path taken (in Turnip Soup) by Mole from the farm to Toad Hall. Wendy has been writing with children in mind for nearly 10 years. She believes her work is perhaps best appreciated when read aloud. Turnip Soup is her first publication.

Margaret Bulleyment.
Margaret began writing fiction after a long career in comparative education. This encompassed an international school in Stockholm, an American High School on a N.A.T.O. base and teaching Music, English and Expressive Arts, with inter-cultural diversions to the former Czechoslovakia and a children's opera workshop in Canada. In 2007, she won first prize in the Swanwick Writers' Summer School Competition for the first 1,000 words of her children's book *Chime Child*, which she has almost completed. Recently, she won third prize in the Society of Civil and Public Service Writers' Annual Competition. She was born beside the Thames at Twickenham and now lives in an Oxfordshire village, through which the same river flows. Understandably, she would pack *The Wind in the Willows* for desert island reading. She enjoys lunching, singing and researching family history. The latter is centred on the river Dart, but that's another watery story...

Marilyn Fountain.
Born and brought up in the city of Norwich, Marilyn's earliest and lasting impressions of wild animals have come from Kenneth Grahame's characters. Now living happily in the Norfolk countryside, she is reminded of *The Wind in the Willows* on every woodland and riverside walk. A writer of articles and short stories for adults and children, her work has appeared in the *Mail on Sunday's You* magazine, *BBC Homes & Antiques*, *Woman's Weekly*, *Take A Break* and *The People's Friend*.

Professor Peter Hunt.
Peter is Professor Emeritus in Children's Literature at Cardiff University. He has lectured worldwide on children's literature and has published widely on the subject. His works include *An Introduction to Children's Literature*, *The Wind in the Willows: A Fragmented Arcadia* and, more recently, the foreword to *Complete Works of Kenneth Grahame*. He has also published several works of fiction for children.

Jennifer Moore.
Jennifer was first introduced to *The Wind in the Willows* as a

bedtime story in a Norfolk cottage formerly known as Frog Hall (a far less grand affair than Toad Hall). It was also one of the first books she read to her own daughter. She now lives in Devon with her husband and two children. Her short fiction and poetry have appeared in a number of publications on both sides of the Atlantic, including *The Guardian, Mslexia, South, The First Line, Pulp Net* and *Short Fiction.*

Elizabeth Parkhurst.
On her 10th birthday, Elizabeth received a Rackham edition of *The Wind in the Willows* signed "To Elizabeth, with love from Mummy & Daddy", and dated 1st January 1957, in her father's neat copperplate. She was fascinated by the book, and has reread it many times since. She heard of the Kenneth Grahame Society competition from other local writers, and decided to enter; At The House Called Beautiful is her first publication. Elizabeth recently took the Diploma course at Northern College, near Barnsley.

Ruth Sheppard.
Ruth spent her childhood in close proximity to *The Wind in the Willows* country; she has memories of days in her youth spent "messing about in boats". The school she attended taught *The Wind in the Willows* from an early age; it was considered part of the local culture. Ruth always loved it. She emigrated to Australia forty years ago. Both she and her husband Bryan are retired; they have two children and two grandchildren. Her articles have appeared in the *Perth Sunday Times* and the *British Czech and Slovak Review*. Ruth and other Albany Seniors have recently published an anecdotal, photographic history of the City of Albany, as part of the Dinosaur Project.

Janet Lesley Smith.
Janet was born in Cambridge in 1940. Her early childhood was spent "messing about in boats" on the River Cam, before the family's removal to Liverpool. She was educated there, with the advantages of having a schoolteacher mother and an attic full of books (including *The Wind in the Willows*). After marriage and motherhood, and with a continuing career in the Civil Service, she moved to Frome 25 years ago. On retirement she took a creative writing course at Frome library and, in 2002, began to write short stories and poetry for competitions, some of which have been published in anthologies and magazines. Janet is presently a member of Frome Writers Group and Frome Society for Local Studies. Apart from literary and domestic pursuits, she enjoys walks along the River Frome observing the creatures of the riverbank.

Authors

Martin J. Smith.
On Martin's first day at Secondary School, Mr Johnson, his English teacher, started to read *The Wind in the Willows*. Martin was captivated. He went on to study English at the University of East Anglia where he was taught by Malcolm Bradbury, Lorna Sage and A.E. Dyson, amongst others. Martin has written two novels, a number of stories, plays and a collection of children's stories, one of which was broadcast on radio. He is currently writing a novel which is set in the turbulent times following the Norman conquest of England. Entering the Kenneth Grahame Society competition has been an inspiration to him, and he is now completing a novel which follows on from the events of Mr Toad's Wedding. Martin lives with his wife in Somerset, England where he runs his own training company. He has two grand-children, and he is looking forward to introducing them to the delights of *The Wind in the Willows*.

Dr E. J. Yeaman.
As a teacher of Chemistry, Eric seemed to spend most of his working life writing - worksheets, revision notes and examinations, not to mention plans, reports and minutes. When he escaped ("took early retirement"), he revelled in the freedom to write fiction. Having heard his short stories, other members of Dundee College Writers' Circle suggested that he should write for children. Taking that as a compliment, he adopted the suggestion, and continues to enjoy doing so; he currently has a novel under consideration by a major publishing house. He welcomed the challenge of writing in the spirit and style of *The Wind in the Willows*.